"I need

"Come to my office." The stranger followed her. She was convinced he was checking out her butt. Or maybe it was just wishful thinking. Either way, she needed to keep her mind on business and not how good he looked in *his* jeans.

He settled into a chair before her desk. He had a strong jaw, a semi-straight nose, and a small scar that dissected his right brow.

"What can I do for you, Mr.—"

"Silva. Rick Silva."

"Yes, ah, Mr. Silva. What brings you to Brash & Brazen, Inc.?" It proved difficult to concentrate on anything but his gorgeous gray eyes.

The man was all alpha male. Add the tattoos peeking out from beneath his t-shirt sleeves and she wondered if he'd done time.

"I'm searching for someone. His name is Teddy Brinkman."

His voice had gone hard. There was danger in his expression. She forced herself not to show fear. "Are you going to kill him?"

Silva's eyes widened at her bluntness. "And if I was?"

Damn. She'd hoped for a new client, not a murderer looking for an accomplice. "Then I can't help you."

And she'd have to call the cops ASAP.

The Sweetheart Racket

Cheryl Ann Smith

LYRICAL SHINE
Kensington Publishing Corp.
www.kensingtonbook.com

LYRICAL SHINE BOOKS are published by

Kensington Publishing Corp.
119 West 40th Street
New York, NY 10018

First Electronic Edition: September 2016
eISBN-13: 978-1-60183-737-0
eISBN-10: 1-60183-737-2

First Print Edition: September 2016
ISBN-13: 978-1-60183-740-0
ISBN-10: 1-60183-740-2

Printed in the United States of America

There are many people to thank when dedicating a book and not enough space to add all the names. So I'll keep it simple. First, I'd like to thank my agent, Kevan Lyon, for sharing this ride with me since my first manuscript appeared in her inbox in 2009. For my new editor, Tara Gavin, who enjoys my humorous voice and doesn't think over the top is too much. Thanks! And to the outstanding ladies in my family: Joyce, Genevieve, Michelle, Steffanie, Joan, and Pam. I'm very lucky to have you in my life. You are the best!

Finally, I couldn't do this without the support of my husband, Duane, and my three awesome kids, who are collectively convinced that I love the cat more than them. Truthfully, it really depends on the day. After all, you are teenagers! Thanks for taking this ride with me and for all the love and adventure that comes with being a wife and mother. I love you all!

Prologue

Taryn Hall was tired, sweaty, and fit to kill—right after she emasculated her boss with the spiked stripper heels she'd been coerced into wearing last night. It was because of that rat bastard that she was homeless, jobless, and seconds away from committing her first felony.

"I hate Willard," she grumbled, and tugged her skintight uniform away from her damp skin. The effort didn't help the cooling process, as the sun continued to beat down with unusual ferocity given the early hour.

"Me too," Summer said, as she wobbled on loose gravel on high heels. She righted herself with outstretched arms to keep from pitching sideways into the shallow, weedy ditch that paralleled the desolate country road. Summer had an unnatural fear of snakes and was convinced that they were waiting just out of sight for her to make one wrong step.

"I think I just inhaled a bug," Jess said, and coughed to expel it. When that failed, she made a face and gave up. "Yum. Breakfast."

"You could have shared," Taryn said. "I'm starving."

"I think I have a gnat stuck in my mascara." Summer blinked and touched her lashes. "Would that help?"

Taryn sighed. "Give me another hour without food and I'll take you up on your offer."

Despite the fact that Michigan summers normally hovered at temperatures around a humid eighty degrees at midday, it had to be that already, and it was only six a.m. Add this to the misery of skintight, sweat- and grit-damp red-white-and-blue polyester, matching sequins, and heels that defied any explanation—other than that a man must have invented them—the normally cool-headed Taryn Hall was near her breaking point.

"What are the chances of rain?" Summer said, examining the blue sky and fanning herself with her hand. "I could use a shower."

Taryn looked over to see Summer's damp blond locks escaping her ponytail, and Jess's once carefully tamped-down brown curls losing the fight against what felt like nearly one hundred percent humidity. Her heart filled with guilt. Her two friends were a bedraggled mess and there was nothing she could do.

They were all miserable and it was her fault. "I'm really sorry, you guys. This isn't the way I expected the night would end. I thought we'd be ogled a bit and that's all. I should have known Willard was up to something when he coerced me into wearing these stupid shoes."

"Don't apologize," Jess said with a fierce stare. "You didn't cause this mess. You were the victim of that letch."

"She's right," Summer chimed in. "Willard is a jerk."

Leave it to Jess to be the voice of reason and for Summer to agree. The three of them were friends to the end. If Taryn had to be fired and dumped in the middle of nowhere, to limp her way to civilization on screaming feet, she was glad it was with her two best friends.

"I wish I was back in Texas." Summer sighed. She swiped her hair out of her bright blue eyes. "At least it's dry heat."

Jess snorted. "Great. We'd be in an oven rather than a sauna. Which is worse?"

They began a debate about dry heat versus humid heat.

Taryn ignored them and looked up, expecting to see buzzards circling, just waiting for one of them to drop over. If she was the first to fall, she wasn't entirely sure she'd fight off the beaked scavengers. It was that kind of day.

"As soon as we get to a phone, I'm renting a car, hunting down Willard, and finishing him off," Taryn snapped. "Then I'm having him stuffed."

"You can't do that," Jess interjected before Taryn got off on a tangent. "Lawyers first. By the time you're done suing his sorry butt, you'll own the Muskrats."

Her friend had a point. Willard had a ton of money, but he was an obsessed coupon-clipper and cheapskate. His children wore garage sale clothing, and not the good stuff, and his wife cut her own hair, much to the horror of professional beauticians everywhere.

The idea of prying a huge settlement check from his pudgy, groping fingers lightened her mood. Just a little. "The image of thinning his accounts does sound fun."

Summer grinned. "See, something to look forward to. Well, if we ever get back to civilization." She looked into the weeds and shuddered. "I hate Willard, too."

Willard J. Covington III was the owner of the newly minted upstart pro football team, the Lansing Mighty Muskrats and their cheerleading squad, which Taryn, Summer, and Jess were on. Willard was the trio's former employer. He was the kind of guy who, had it not been for his wealth, would be just another perv on the street.

Willard liked to brag that it was his superior negotiating skills that led to the approval of a new team, but Taryn wasn't convinced. There were whispers of a wild night in Vegas five years past involving Willard, several strippers, a famous football player, and a billionaire team owner. Within weeks of that night of debauchery, Willard was pre-approved for a new team and the stadium had been completed late last year.

Coincidence? Maybe. Maybe not.

However, that had nothing to do with the current circumstances. During a small private party last night with Willard and his icky friends, aboard their traveling bus, he'd finally stepped over the line with Taryn. After consuming a copious number of whiskey sours, he'd gleefully trapped her against the bathroom door, shoved his hand down her uniform top, and groped her.

Taryn, always prepared for the worst when Willard was around, carried a small pink can of Mace in her bodice for any eventuality. As he fumbled for a grip on her left breast, he'd dislodged the can, enabling her to miraculously retrieve it with quick reflexes before it was able to fall to the floor.

Armed and ticked off, she'd quickly aimed and squirted him dead-on in his beady little eyes.

He'd gasped from the burn and pitched sideways, squawking and gagging under the onslaught of noxious chemicals. They both bounced off the back bench seat and fell into the aisle in a tangle of arms and legs, she landing on top of his doughy body, his hand still hooked in her bodice.

Despite not being able to see or breathe, he still managed to squeeze her left buttock with his free hand as she struggled to push off his porcine frame, which earned him an elbow to the face and a broken nose.

His yelp and her outraged screams alerted Summer and Jess, and they jumped into the fray.

Unfortunately, Willard had a bodyguard on board: Alvin the Ape, they called him, as the man was obscenely hairy. After a flurry of fists and nails, and arterial spray from Willard's hairy nostrils, the three women were ejected from the bus by the huge primate, sans luggage and cell phones, and left to whatever fate awaited.

Worse, she still had Willard's blood on her uniform, compliments of his crumpled nose.

Thinking about his yucky DNA on her made her itch. "I've got to wash this blood off before I get cooties," Taryn said and shuddered. Dark red stains marked the white sequins. "Where is a dry cleaner when you need one?"

"Oh, no, you don't. It's evidence of a crime," Summer said. "When we get back home, we're going to take pictures, bag your uniform, and give it to the lawyer. Then it won't be your word against his."

Taryn shot her a sidelong glance. Most (men) dismissed Summer as a ditzy blonde, but Taryn and Jess knew better. She was crazy smart and a killer with anything techy.

"You're right," Taryn said and stopped walking. "Thanks. But still, yuck."

Summer hugged her. Jess jumped in. Taryn was the first to pull away. She wrinkled her nose. "One of you smells funky. Like cheap cologne and sweaty gravel dust."

"It's me," Summer said. "Saul Fleischman pulled me into a bear hug after he proposed. His cologne comes in big spray bottles, and is also used as a bear repellent."

"Really?" Jess said.

"He told me so."

Taryn skipped over the cologne comment. "Isn't he married with six kids and something like forty grandkids?"

"Yup. He's been married for fifty years," Summer said, and waved away a second gnat looking to join the first in her lashes. She blinked again. "Creep."

They tottered along for a couple of minutes in silence. Taryn felt a bit light-headed and wondered how many gnats she'd need for a decent breakfast. Summer did wear a lot of mascara.

She glanced back up at the vultures and thought about lying down as bait. If one landed on her, the three of them could catch it and eat it. But the plan faded with the absurdity of the idea. She made a face and prayed for a quick end. Surely hallucinating was a sign of impending death.

"We never should have agreed to that party without the guys for backup," Jess said. She kicked her shoes off into the ditch and kept walking. "We were set up as Willard's personal harem."

"True. And by the time I realized the rest of our squad wasn't coming, the bus was already rolling," Taryn agreed. "We were lambs being led to slaughter."

"Baa." Sweet Summer's face turned red. Her hands curled into fists. "Did he really think he could pimp us out and we'd go along with it? Do I look like a hooker?"

Okay, the skimpy cheerleader uniform and the stripper heels they'd been asked to wear instead of their usual sneakers didn't scream librarian. But she was right, Taryn thought. Every man on the bus probably had some sort of cheerleader fantasy. And a deluded Willard had expected them to perform.

"Clearly, he did." Jess yanked up her low-cut bodice and grimaced. "We're cheerleaders, not hookers."

"Yeah, cheerleaders," Summer said and they fist-bumped.

None of the trio saw their job as a lifelong career. It was all about travel and having fun while they were young. They each had other plans, but had never thought they'd have to make a career change this soon. The money wasn't great, but it was enough for a twenty-something to live on if she was frugal.

Food, clothing, and saving for her future were why Taryn had ignored Willard's creepy innuendos. Big mistake.

Cheerleading was for kicks and cash. They'd all done it in high school and college. Now they'd been fired because she wouldn't do Willard.

Taryn scratched her grimy arm and looked around. They really were in the middle of nowhere. There were overgrown fields of weeds, scattered clumps of trees, and an occasional wildflower thrown in for fun. Fifteen minutes back, they'd stumbled upon the dump site of an old white refrigerator with a missing door and a computer monitor from a previous decade.

After an hour of walking down this empty road and not one car passing by, Taryn was losing hope of rescue.

A ramshackle red barn from another century was the only sign that people once lived in the area.

"Willard is so done. Unless we get murdered by some freak out here in the sticks," Jess, the city girl, said. "Then Willard's home free to debauch for another day."

The trio glanced nervously around. Fields, fields, and more fields, as far as the eye could see.

Then, "Wait, there's something," Taryn said. "Look. Cows." Hope welled inside her sweaty breast. "They usually don't roam around feral. There must be a farm nearby."

"Good," Summer said. "I'm tired of walking."

Taryn slipped an arm around her. "Me too. But if we can't find the farmhouse, then we're taking our chances and hitching a ride with the first axe murderer that comes along. Deal?"

"Deal," Summer said with a shaky laugh.

As if on cue, a car engine rumbled from behind them, cutting the silence. Surprised, they spun around to see a sparkling black limo speeding up the road, trailing a cloud of dust in its wake. The three women darted to the narrow shoulder as the car skidded to a halt a few feet away.

"Is it Willard?" Summer whispered.

"I'm not sure." Taryn waved dust out of her eyes and strained to see through the smoked glass windows of the vehicle. All she saw was her own reflection. Her hazel eyes were wide and worried and her hair was sweat-plastered around her face. It wasn't pretty. "I don't recognize the car."

The three grouped together for protection.

For a moment, the car idled with no obvious signs of human habitation. For a second, Taryn imagined a black-and-white bovine behind the wheel. She was seriously losing it.

"The car is sizing us up for death like creepy Christine from an old scary Stephen King movie," Jess offered in an ominous tone. Despite the jest, her expression was concerned.

"Not funny," Summer snapped.

The car inched forward until it was parallel to them. Taryn wished she still had her Mace. Then the back window slid down and an innocuous face appeared behind an oversized pair of reflective sunglasses. Fifty or eighty, it was impossible to determine the man's age at first glance. But despite his bland appearance, she couldn't rule out danger.

Taryn, as unofficial leader of their group, held out her arms in front of her friends in a protective gesture. "Be ready to run," she said softly.

Bracing for flight proved unneeded when the stranger's mouth split into a wide, crooked, and disarming grin. He slid his sunglasses off to reveal a face well past the age requirements for a senior-discounted McDonald's coffee.

"Good morning, Angels," he said. "My name is Irving."

Chapter 1

Over the course of the last two years, Taryn had often reflected upon the day, stuck on that deserted dusty road, when she, Summer, and Jess took a chance. They had climbed into Irving's limo and changed their destiny.

It was hot then, too.

At times like this, when she was sitting in a steamy car, camera in hand, waiting for a money shot, she wished Irving had just driven on and left them to follow those cows to civilization. Being a private investigator meant long hours, boredom, and gallons of coffee. And she wasn't a fan of coffee.

"I should have stuck with cheerleading," she said and waved a celebrity gossip magazine in front of her face. "At least the stadiums were shaded."

But she loved this gig and wouldn't—couldn't—trade it for anything else. She had something to prove.

A year ago, when she'd faced off with Willard in their first court appearance, he'd found out she was a PI and he'd scoffed, saying, "Girl, you're only good for shaking your ass and waving your pom-poms. Nothing else." It was then that she vowed to be the best damn PI in the business.

Okay, current circumstance aside, there were exciting moments to her job, too. Interesting cases, working with her friends, and her monetary piece of Brash & Brazen, Inc. made the tedious stuff all worthwhile.

Mostly. "Why won't it rain?" she groused and grabbed a fresh water bottle from her small cooler. Ann Arbor, Michigan, was a large city, a melting pot of people and cultures that circled the University of Michigan and the U of M hospital. It was a fun place to live and work, but summers could be a bear during dry, hot days. Even now with August coming to a close, they were experiencing a heat wave. Taryn was looking forward to fall.

Hoping for some relief from the cloying simmer inside the beat-up old Oldsmobile, she rubbed the water bottle across her chest. The chilly condensation trickled down into her cleavage and took up residence in her lacy lavender bra. She sighed happily.

A polished-up, nerdy man in chinos and boat shoes walking a rodent-sized pooch past the car stopped, stared in at her, and waggled his brows as if her sigh had been some sort of sexual invitation.

Right. Like she'd ever have sex with a man who dressed his wimpy rodent in a pink wifebeater t-shirt and spiked collar. Who did he think he was impressing? Not her.

"Move along, buddy. I have a gun." She glanced evilly at the furry lump as if sizing it up for termination.

He gasped and yanked the mutt up by the leash. The dog gacked against the tightened collar and swung back and forth like a yipping pendulum. The owner tucked the mutt in a football hold under his arm, glared, and scurried away.

"That was just mean," Taryn said and sucked on the bottle. The heat made her surly. Truthfully, she wouldn't shoot a dog. The owner, maybe, but not the dog, if one could call it that.

She wondered if she should fire up the ancient car for a few minutes of questionable air conditioning. Then she decided no. The idling car with its turbo-charged engine could give her away. Besides, the air usually came out lukewarm anyway. So hot it was. In another hour or two, she'd call it a day.

"I should have stayed in bed. Darn you, Gregory Peach."

Forty-eight-year-old Gregory Peach was the owner of an auto parts manufacturing company and a cheater. He knew it, his wife knew it, and Taryn knew it. She'd followed him to this hotel, texted Penny with a smiley face emoji, and watched him vanish inside. Whoever he was meeting had obviously already arrived and pulled the drapes. Darn.

A tryst was the only reason for a hotel visit at two in the afternoon. Mrs. Peach wasn't about to put up with his behavior, not when she'd already kicked her first philandering husband to the curb.

"Gregory was supposed to be different," Penny had tearfully explained on Tuesday when she'd hired Taryn. "A good guy. At least that's what the online service, Match-Mate, said when they dumped his profile into my in box. He got a four-star rating!"

Taryn wanted to point out that there was something sketchy about finding love on a dating site that offered coupon discounts in the Sunday paper.

Instead, she'd choked back the comment and let it go. Penny hadn't yet hit rock bottom. She still believed in true love. Who was Taryn to yank her back to reality?

Taryn was once wide-eyed and delusional about love, too. But it only took one husband to smack that innocence out of her: in the form of their overly endowed maid, Gloria, riding him in their marital bed like a cowgirl on a county fair pony, cowboy hat and all.

The ensuing cat fight—which, looking back, Taryn was not exactly proud of—had somehow deflated one of Gloria's oversize silicone implants. How was still in dispute. But Tim and Gloria were still together, Gloria's cup size had gone up another two sizes during the repair, and Taryn was free of that nonsense.

That made her pursuit of cheating spouses personal. She couldn't help herself. And Gregory Peach was in her sights.

In the last week, Taryn had managed to take only a couple of grainy photos of Peach hugging his mistress in a grocery parking lot and splitting a tuna on rye at a local diner. However, those weren't the shots Penny needed to nail him in the pocketbook.

So Taryn drank sips of water, fought the urge to pour the whole content down her back, and waited outside the pay-by-the-hour hotel for Peach to do something divorce-worthy. She'd happily settle for a naked embrace in front of the window or even an amorous clutch in the backseat of his brand-spanking-new Ferrari. Otherwise the previous pics could be argued down by a good divorce lawyer to meetings with a friend.

Ultimately, though, it was Mrs. Peach whom Taryn should've been watching. Taryn was about to open the second bottle of water, her bladder be damned, when a silver Town Car flashed past her, did a hard left muffler-drag over the curb into the hotel parking lot, sideswiped Gregory's car, and crashed full on into the door of Gregory's room, causing that block wall to crumple inward.

Then, with a scream that rivaled a choking howler monkey, Penny Peach, resplendent in teased-up salt-and-pepper hair and enough makeup to drown a hippo, climbed out of the driver's window of the

Town Car, carrying a golf club, as both Mr. Peach and a woman dressed up like June Cleaver, wearing an apron and all, appeared in the damaged doorway with wide-eyed expressions.

"What in the hell?" Taryn said as she clicked a quick photo, then launched herself from the Oldsmobile.

"Penny?" Gregory shouted.

June Cleaver wasn't waiting around to get her butt kicked. She quickly assessed her chances against an outraged wife in a pink jogging suit, then scrambled over the damaged bumper of the Town Car and took off shrieking for someone to call the police.

Gregory, dressed only in tighty-whities and what looked like chocolate syrup and whipped cream, ducked right to avoid the swinging club to the temple. Without waiting for a second swing, he launched through an opening between the car and the broken block wall, rolled, and came to his feet.

All while his hands were handcuffed behind his back.

Impressive.

He took off running.

His wife was right on his flabby tail.

"Penny, no!" Taryn yelled. Feeling partially responsible for having sent the text leading Penny directly to her cheating husband, she took up the chase. If nothing else, she was sure that if Penny was imprisoned for murdering her husband, Brash would not get paid.

"I'm going to kill you!" Penny screamed.

Mr. Peach darted right into Taryn's path. Her appearance didn't elicit more than a brief glance. Penny yelled something about Taryn getting the hell out of the way and almost knocked her over with a shoulder-to-shoulder bump.

Taryn kept to her feet and ran.

Peach, despite being barefoot, cuffed, and covered with goo, kept a good distance between himself and his murderous wife. Taryn, as any good PI would do, clicked off a few rushed photos of the action, hoping at least one or two would be clear enough for the divorce case.

With a final sprint, Taryn closed the gap with Penny. She couldn't grab her without risk of getting hit by the swinging club, so she stayed back slightly and waited for the two Peaches to tire out. How far could a forty-eight- and forty-three-year-old run anyway?

It was Gregory who ended the race when he tripped on a curb and pitched forward with a yelp. He grunted, did a half twist, and hit the grass at an odd angle. His body contorted into the protective shape of a taco shell to keep his man-parts protected from the lethal golf club.

Giddy, Taryn aimed and got the money shot. "Yes!"

"I hate you!" Penny cried, lifting the club overhead and aiming for his bald spot. Taryn swung her camera around to her back for its protection and managed to catch Penny's arm before the club did any damage to her or the supine male.

Gregory rolled onto his back and pleaded, "Honey, I can explain!"

"Explain through broken teeth!" Penny shrieked.

"Penny, stop!" Taryn grabbed Penny's arm and twisted the club out of her hand. "Remember your children! Think about little Daisy, and . . . and the other one." The mention of the kids froze her client. She finally had the outraged wife's attention. Penny turned to her and the fight left her.

"Eddie Junior," Penny said and hiccupped.

"Right. Eddie Junior." Taryn stared into a pair of wounded eyes. She lowered her voice for calm reasoning. "Penny. You can't raise them from prison."

She kept her eyes on Penny but retrieved and turned her camera in the general direction of Peach and clicked off a few more shots.

Hey, why waste the opportunity?

Penny slumped against Taryn and broke into tears. "He ruined our marriage. He was supposed to be my knight in shining armor. Not like my ex, Eddie Senior. Greggie was older and stable."

"I know." Taryn frowned down at the whimpering Peach, who was anything but knightly, and turned his wife back toward the hotel. "With my help, you'll get your divorce and a huge settlement. Then you'll find yourself a revenge boy-toy half his age that lives an un-complicated life on a surfboard . . . and loves cougars."

"Do you think so?" Penny sniffed and rubbed her eyes.

"I know so.

After making a police report, and persuading the officer that he'd gain nothing by arresting her client on the spot, she'd settled Penny at the office of her lawyer, with the photo card from the camera to use as evidence, and returned to her office.

Normally, she would have gone home first to shower and change, but they had a mandatory staff meeting. Irving loved his mandatory meetings. It was the only time he had his staff all in one place.

Aside from his "girls," he had accountants and assistants and even a full time lawyer on staff. It took a lot of people to run Brash and most never missed a meeting.

She laid a box of semi-stale doughnut holes in the center of the table and dropped into the nearest chair. A dozen pairs of eyes widened. Then, within thirty seconds, like a hyena fight over a wildebeest carcass, the doughnut bites were gone.

Jess snorted and shook her head at the carnage. Summer stopped midbite, shrugged, and popped the remaining bit into her mouth. Taryn just shrugged.

Irving stood and rapped the tabletop with a gavel. "Attention, everyone. Before I get started with the boring stuff, I've passed a resolution to allow Fridays to be casual day. Tube tops and short shorts for everyone!"

Irving started each meeting as he usually did, with some sort of teasing sexual-harassment-worthy opening. He'd heard all about Willard and played Taryn's woes up like a comedy show.

Any other person would get tossed out the tenth floor window, but Taryn only sent him an eye roll. He was a harmless oldster and the father figure she'd never had. He'd willingly hobble in front of a bullet for her and for everyone who worked for him. And they'd return the favor.

"Irving," Taryn interjected before he suggested pastie Wednesdays or naked Mondays. "We've already covered this. No one wants to see you in a tube top."

The boss chuckled, flashing a new set of perfect artificial choppers. "What about bikinis?"

One hidden microphone and a really good lawyer, and she, Summer, and Jess would own the firm.

The rest of the staff was either related to him or long-time employees from his cement pipe days. They all accepted his eccentricities with good humor.

Besides, Taryn was chin-deep in depositions with Willard and weary of the legal system. The court clerk told her just yesterday that the case should be resolved soon. Of course "soon" had already dragged on for two years since she'd first filed the case, and it seemed unending. But her lawyer was confident enough in a successful outcome to have ordered a forty-foot sailboat with his cut of her future winnings. He'd be thrilled if she called him with another harassment suit.

She watched her boss, now seated back in his scuffed, yet comfy, wheelchair, grinning at something Summer said, and she smiled. His comb-over was already escaping a generous slathering of industrial-grade Brylcreem and he resembled a happy parrot in a yellow shirt and matching yellow-and-lime-green plaid pants.

He was something to see.

Jess, who'd followed Taryn's attention to Irving, leaned to whisper, "We should pass a resolution to ban plaid pants."

Taryn smiled. "He only owns plaid. Think of the alternative."

Jess made a face. No one wanted to see their boss without pants.

Fortunately for Irving, the three women adored the crusty senior citizen. He'd saved them and trained them and loved them like a father-mentor. They'd do anything for him, even letting him call them the "girls." Well, almost anything. They drew the line at wearing tube tops.

Although he tried to pass for sixty-nine, Taryn suspected he was heading toward ninety at a rapid clip. Not even a yearly facelift and jaw tuck could hide the telltale signs of a birthdate somewhere pre–World War II.

"As I've already told you a thousand times, Irving, no short shorts, no braless Tuesdays, and no feathered hair," Taryn said. "And your unfortunate choice of name for the business aside, this is a professional PI firm. Jiggle is not allowed."

"Drat." His eyes twinkled. "I guess I'll have to live with my disappointment. Let's get to business."

For most of his later years, Irving had wanted to close up his industrial cement pipe business and open his own PI firm. Unfortunately for him, his late wife liked making zillions of dollars a year in pipes and his dream was put off until widowerhood had come knocking four years ago. Then he opened his business and waited for his ideal Brash & Brazen women to appear.

And waited. And waited. Then his miracle happened.

Taryn, Summer, and Jess's bad luck turned into a happy day for Irving. He'd been visiting a sick friend in the boonies when his driver spotted them tottering down the road.

That they weren't strippers or hookers was a welcome relief to

Irving. Despite his not-secret hope that one day they'd wear tube tops to work, he wanted his ladies to have class.

The meeting covered the usual dry topics involving business goals, clients, and profit margins. The three women each had a three percent stake in the company thanks to an unexpected Christmas present last year, so they had an interest in the company's success. When they broke up an hour later, Taryn was ready for a shower and dinner. She left Jess and Summer with a promise to go clubbing soon, and headed out.

Alas, her escape was foiled by a six-foot-two-ish of tattooed male, intimidating yet intriguing at the same time, who walked into the reception area wearing a black t-shirt and holding a motorcycle helmet in one hand. His short brown hair was mussed and his face covered with shadow that went way past five o'clock.

Taryn felt a tug of feminine appreciation.

When his intense gray eyes landed on her, she was eternally grateful she wasn't a giggler, because he was the kind of guy who could elicit that kind of response from women.

Maybe some swooning, too. He was dangerously sexy to look at, a hard-edged man who was the entire list of all things mothers warned their daughters away from. She didn't have to know anything about him to sense trouble. She felt it from her head to her toes, and in all her good parts in between.

So she squelched a longing sigh and glanced around for Gretchen to make him an appointment. The receptionist was MIA.

Resigned that her hot bath had to wait, she stepped forward. "Hi. I'm Taryn Hall. How may I help you?"

His eyes beat a path up and down her body, taking her measure. She may have shivered a little, and she wasn't a shiverer, either. She chalked it up to being exhausted and brain-fried. The Peaches had wiped her out with their antics.

"I need a PI."

She was just tired enough to make a sassy comment about his good fortune of stumbling into a PI firm, but profit margins danced fresh in her mind. Why chase off a perfectly good client with a smart comment?

"Come to my office." The stranger followed her. She was convinced he was checking out her butt. Or maybe it was just wishful thinking. She hadn't had a date in ages, and was beginning to feel a bit withered. Either way, she needed to keep her mind on business and not how good he looked in *his* jeans.

He settled into a chair before her desk and looked around the space. He had a strong jaw, a semi-straight nose, and a small scar that dissected his right brow.

"What can I do for you, Mr.—?"

"Silva. Rick Silva."

"Yes, ah, Mr. Silva. What brings you to Brash ?" Despite a professional outward demeanor, it proved difficult to concentrate on anything but his gorgeous gray eyes. They were a stark contrast to his dark brown hair and tanned face.

The man was all alpha male. She'd be shocked if he'd ever eaten a bean sprout on purpose or ordered a vanilla mocha latte with lite whip and cinnamon sprinkles.

Add the tattoos peeking out from beneath his t-shirt sleeves and she wondered if he'd done time.

"I'm searching for someone. His name is Teddy Brinkman."

His voice had gone hard. There was danger in his expression. A chill trilled through her. She leaned forward and knitted her fingers, forcing herself not to show fear. "Are you going to kill him?"

Silva's eyes widened at her bluntness. "And if I did?"

Damn. She'd hoped for a new client, not a murderer looking for an accomplice. "Then I can't help you." She stood. "We are not in the business of playing intermediaries to murder. You'll have to find him on your own."

And she'd have to call the cops ASAP.

Unmoving, he stared. She fought not to fidget. He was intense, unreadable, and very intimidating. As something of a control freak at her job, she didn't like feeling off kilter.

Usually she could tell the inner workings of someone within a few minutes of a first meeting. Of course, she hadn't known Penny Peach intended to bash her husband's head in. Maybe she was getting rusty.

No, this guy was different from the Peach duo and her usual clients. She sensed something off about him. But what?

"Please sit, Ms. Hall."

Taryn paused. Then sat. Her curiosity overcame her desire to call 911. She wanted to know more about him and the case, even if she might have to call the cops to intervene.

He stretched both hands over his head and took a deep breath. His knuckles were scarred—likely from fighting—and his eyes held a weariness that was not obvious before, as if he carried the weight of something big in those hands and in his heart.

She waited. Reading him.

Finally he broke the silence. "Brinkman is a lonely hearts con man who married my mother and took her for almost everything she had. Although I'd like to wring his chicken neck, I want to do this legally. Then maybe I can get her money back."

Huh. This turn was interesting and quite unexpected. She'd never worked a sweetheart con. Her curiosity notched up. Perhaps she could help him after all. "I assume you know he's somewhere in Michigan?"

"I do. Last week he married a woman from Ann Arbor, Honey Comstock, under one of his other known aliases and vanished again. He now has six wives that I know of. Could be more."

"Seriously?" she asked. "Wow."

Silva arched the scarred brow. "I guess you could say that." He paused and pulled out his phone. "I tracked her to an apartment in Ypsilanti. She hadn't been there long, but one of her neighbors said she was quiet and her only visitors were her two adult sons. She did start going out at night all dressed up over the last few weeks, but they never saw Brinkman."

"And you checked the apartment?"

"I did. It was cleared out and cleaned out. She vanished."

Poor woman. Having suffered through her own miserable divorce, she felt sympathy for the victims of this man. She pulled a note pad and pen out of her desk drawer. Irving liked hard copies. She'd enter everything into her computer once she got the information down. "Where did he and your mother meet?"

"Online. Match-Mate."

Figures, Taryn thought. The Peaches had met on the same sketchy site. "How long ago?"

"Last year. They married after four weeks."

"That isn't very much time to date and marry," Taryn agreed. This Brinkman sounded like a skilled player. Lock a woman in before she sees his true nature. "He works fast."

"He was the first man she dated since my dad died." His tone was defensive, as if daring Taryn to judge his mother.

"Everyone has fallen for at least one jerk in their past," she said truthfully. This seemed to relax him. "Why don't you show me what you have on Brinkman?"

He pulled a folded printout from his jeans pocket and pushed it over the desk. The man in the picture was in his early sixties and bland looking, with graying hair and pale blue eyes. He'd worn a gray suit with a blue bow tie for his picture and had a charming smile.

"He'd not raise red flags for women looking for love online," she said. "He doesn't look felonious. He'd blend in anywhere. No wonder he's been hard for you to find."

Silva slumped back. "The guy's a ghost. I haven't been able to track him back more than a couple of years. This leads me to believe that Brinkman is an alias. His real identity is a mystery."

"You're probably right. Con men are good at hiding anything personal from their victims," Taryn said. The more Silva talked, the more intriguing the case became. She really could use a break from spying on the Gregory Peaches of the city. She wanted a big case. "His entire backstory will be lies."

Silva nodded. "I've already contacted one of his exes, who lives in Arizona, online. She started a web page devoted to catching him. He took her for ten grand and told her he was a retired spy."

"People often ignore their intuition when looking for love." Taryn wondered how the guy got past Silva. He didn't appear to be the type who would be easily duped. "Didn't you have suspicions about his character when he married your mother after four weeks?"

"I wasn't around." Guilt filled his eyes. "I've had minimal contact with my mom for several years."

"Estranged?"

"Nope. I was in prison."

Chapter 2

Rick watched the expression freeze on her pretty face. He almost smiled. After one hell of a bad week, he'd felt the need to shake her up. Mess with her. Knock out some of her calm professionalism. After all, she'd taken one look at him with those amazing hazel eyes and assumed he was capable of murder. Just because of a few tattoos and a scuffed black bomber jacket.

He'd dealt with snap judgments since his first tattoo and it never bothered him. With her, it did. Why?

"What were you in for?" she said, her tone guarded.

"Drugs, murder, racketeering, and dognapping." This time he did grin when her face went white and one hand clamped around her pen as if it were a shiv. "Is that a problem?"

The pretty PI sat silent, reading him. She was dressed as he was, in a black tee and skintight black jeans that covered a very nice ass, and low-heeled black boots. Her brown-blond hair was pulled back into a high, sleek ponytail. She wore very little makeup, as if she had better things to do in the morning than worry about lipstick. She was dressed like a tough girl, but would she balk at this bit of bullshit and flee?

The clock behind him ticked. He waited.

Right when he thought she'd refuse the case, her body language changed, her eyes darkened, and she released the pen. Then she dropped back in the chair with a touch of casual arrogance. Tough girl was back.

"Why don't you cut the crap and tell me what's really going on here, Mr. Silva."

The corner of his mouth twitched. "Damn. You're good."

"I've been a PI for two years and a student of life for many years before that. I seldom get conned. And if I do, I discover it quickly and make corrections." Her eyes skimmed over the tattoo on his bicep. "You talk like a felon, you dress like a felon, but you don't have the look of a felon."

"And what look is that?"

"A hard hopelessness in your eyes." She rolled the pen on the desk. "Besides, five years in prison barely covers dognapping. Unless you escaped over the wall, this is BS."

Following her lead, he rocked back in the chair and locked onto her stare. She didn't twitch. Taryn Hall was one sexy piece of work. Suddenly, he couldn't wait to dig into this investigation with her. She was smart and confident and would look damn good on the back of his bike.

"I'm a special agent with the DEA." This got her attention. He retrieved his wallet and flipped it open to his ID. "I spent the last five years working a drug case that spanned several countries."

He waited for her to absorb the information and continued. "I did spend time in prison, as part of my cover as drug thug Richard DaSilva, but only during the day and just enough to be seen by the other inmates to establish my cover. The rest was spent in 'solitary confinement.' I was snuck in and out of the prison at night."

"That's why you didn't know about your mother."

He nodded. "That, and I worked in Los Angeles, while she's in Indiana. Our phone calls were brief and months apart. I knew she'd been online dating, and warned her about cyber safety, but Teddy Brinkman duped her anyway." He reached for the note pad and pen. "My brother is in the Marines overseas and my sister lives out of state, so Mom was lonely. She was a perfect mark."

As he took the pen from her, their fingers touched. Heat washed up his arm. Her breath caught. She extracted her hand.

Damn. She had soft hands. The rest of her was likely just as soft. Her full mouth looked intriguing, the kind of mouth that would make men beg for a kiss, and she had the kind of body he'd never tire of exploring.

Rick felt a stir in his boxer briefs. Shit. He hadn't been this attracted to a woman in years. If he didn't get control, she'd be a distraction he didn't need.

He'd already failed his mother. It was time to make her a priority.

Still, he didn't have the time or energy to find someone else to work the case. And for a new company, Brash & Brazen, Inc. had a reputation for being the best. No, he'd just have to deal with Taryn and keep things professional. It couldn't be that tough.

Focusing, he wrote down the information she'd need to get the case going. Although he'd told her that he wouldn't harm Brinkman, he wasn't sure there wouldn't be any neck wringing once they found the bastard. Maybe not enough to kill him; just enough to leave permanent fingerprints that he'd see every morning when he shaved. Mom deserved her pound of flesh.

"Here's the link to my online file. Everything I know about the man and the case is there," he said. "But don't expect much. Brinkman has more aliases than wives."

Taryn crossed her arms and fell silent. She rocked back and forth in her wheeled office chair as if running everything through her mind.

"Don't you have the full weight of government resources at your disposal? Why do you need me?"

Silva shrugged. "Two reasons. One, the agency frowns on using their 'resources' for personal investigations. And since Brinkman doesn't fit under DEA guidelines, I can't officially investigate him through them."

"Makes sense. And two?"

"My mom is embarrassed that she was conned. She wants to keep the investigation quiet."

"That also makes sense." After a minute, she stopped rocking and nodded. "I'll take the case." She rattled off the fees. Then, "Tonight, I'll poke around Match-Mate and read your file. Our computer tech, Summer, can run facial recognition to see if Brinkman has a new profile. I'll text you daily with updates. Deal?"

He said nothing for a beat. Then, "No deal. We're working together."

She frowned. "We have a team of investigators here."

"Then consider me transportation, or a bodyguard. Whatever. You're not working this case without me."

For a moment, he thought she'd refuse. Instead, she sighed and nodded.

"Fine. Meet me here tomorrow at eight a.m. I like to start early." With that, she ushered him out. It wasn't until he was standing next to his bike that he realized she'd conceded too fast for comfort. She was up to something.

Tomorrow, he'd find out what.

Of course, he hadn't been entirely up front with her either. Part of the reason he'd missed the marrying the con man thing had been because of selfishness and neglect. Over the last couple of years when he'd had a long weekend off, instead of flying to Indiana for visits with his mother, he'd usually take some woman he barely knew to Vegas, or surfing along the coast, or to Mexico. Aside from Christmas, he'd let his sex life rule over his responsibilities as a son.

Not anymore. No women and no distractions until after the case was solved. His mom deserved nothing less.

He fired up his James Dean–era vintage Triumph motorcycle and made it to the far end of the parking lot before his mother's most recent scolding rose up in his head. So he pulled over, put his helmet on, and headed off again with the rumble of the engine in his ears and the power of the bike between his legs.

Joyce Silva had enough to worry about without the trauma of burying her son.

For the first twenty-two of his twenty-nine years, he'd grown up a clean-cut middle class kid. Well, outside of some normal boyhood mischief. Joining the DEA after college had turned him to the dark side. His first tattoo led to the next and that was enough to give his mother fits. If not for his undercover work, he might not have gotten inked. But he liked them and the tough persona he portrayed to the world.

Another checkmark in the plus column was that women loved the look. The griffin across his back and shoulders was a particular favorite.

His mind flashed back to Taryn. What would she think if she saw it? Would she like it?

Why did he care?

Sun beat down on his back as he slid into traffic. Beneath his jeans, his stomach rumbled.

However, it was another part of him that had all of Taryn on its mind. She was sexy, in the way of a woman who was confident in herself and her abilities. She wasn't hard-edged despite her black clothes, but she still gave off an attitude that attracted him. The way her tee and jeans fit her like a second skin left him wondering what she looked like beneath. And that troubled him most.

"Damn," he said, cursing himself for losing perspective. He was so used to playing the part of a selfish and entitled drug lord that sometime over the last five years he'd kind of lost himself in that life. Partying, women, fast cars; the only thing he didn't indulge in was drugs. Now he was free and wanted the real Rick Silva back.

Thinking of Taryn as anything other than an employee would be a mistake.

Taryn hit heavy traffic while driving through the university, having forgotten that it was move-in week for the upcoming fall semester. Weary, she arrived home in time for the news and clicked on the living room TV. The shabby two-story blue Victorian belonged to her parents, purchased as an investment property, or so they said. But she was convinced they'd done it entirely for her benefit after her marriage left her dazed and broke. After all, why would die-hard Iowans need a house in Ann Arbor, Michigan?

She tugged her t-shirt over her head and wandered through the house and up the creaky stairs. The old place had gone through years of college students and the smell of beer and cigars still clung to tattered old wallpaper and worn carpet.

"If only these walls could talk." She unsnapped her jeans and longed for her comfy PJs.

"Bath first." She loved the old claw-footed tub. She could sink up to her chin in bath oil and bubbles.

Her bedroom was in the far back corner of the house and she passed four other rooms to get there. A dying air conditioner in the backyard spit out just enough cool air to keep the house a couple of degrees cooler than the temperature outside and her room from becoming a sauna. Only slightly.

"I need to move to Alaska," she groused. It wasn't that she didn't like summer. It was just that she liked it in small doses.

Thankfully, the leaves were already changing color. Cooler temps were ahead.

She'd considered taking in students to help pay the bills and pay for updates to the AC and the furnace. However, she liked the quiet that came with living alone.

So no boarders. Yet.

The bedroom was the largest in the house, with a private bathroom. The faded pink floral wallpaper was picked out, she assumed, somewhere in the mid–nineteen hundreds and never replaced. With college students moving in and out during the changing school years, only negligible maintenance from the previous owners kept the roof and walls from falling in. After all, why bother with any new decorations when busy college students didn't care what the house looked like?

Weathered hardwood floors ran throughout the house, including her room, and slanted slightly to one side. The builders hadn't had the fancy leveling tools of today. An old orange hard-water stain marked the ceiling above her bed, like a dried-up river with finger-like tributaries spread out from the main stain. The leak had been long fixed but evidence of it remained to mock her for not doing something about the ugly eyesore.

"I really need to pull down the paper and repaint this room. Heck, the whole house." A good plan, if she had the money to make an overhaul. Maybe once her case with Willard was settled she'd splurge on some updates.

Tossing the shirt into the hamper in the corner, she dug around in her dresser for her favorite old PJs, a long-ago Christmas gift from her nana. Tonight was Thursday, so it was Investigation Discovery and frozen dinner night.

Her cell rang. She checked the screen. Tim? That was odd. He hadn't contacted her since the conclusion of their divorce three years ago.

What could he want? Nothing she cared about. She was done with him. So she hit ignore and reached back into the drawer.

She pulled out gray PJ pants covered in a daisy pattern with holes in the knees and the matching top, turned, and screamed.

Outside her window, a man—or, rather, a boy—froze. A pair of owllike eyes stared, wide open in shock and enlarged by thick glasses. In his white-knuckled hand were several pairs of what looked like women's panties.

Taryn dropped the clothes, raced to the window, lacy lavender bra and all, and pushed up the pane. "Who in the hell are you! How did you get there!"

They were two stories up!

Her yell startled the Peeping Tom and he lurched back on an ancient wooden ladder. Before he could right himself and find a handhold, the ladder tipped away from the window and knocked him off balance.

"Whoaaaaaa!" One arm whipped out and tried to catch the sill, but it was too late. He pitched backward like someone in a scene from a teen comedy movie and vanished from view. "Ahhhhhhhh!"

Thump.

She leaned out the window to peer through the leafy tree branches of the ancient oak and down over the gutter, expecting to see a dead body broken on the rocks below. The space of mostly dead grass and packed dirt between the two houses wouldn't offer any cushion for the kid's fall.

Thankfully, the little peeper and panty bandit was still breathing, as confirmed by a rustle in dried leaves. Excellent. The cops would have something to cart off to jail.

First, she had to catch him before he roused himself and fled. She leaned farther out and quickly assessed the situation. The guy had landed among a pile of empty beer cans. He whimpered pitifully. Good, he wasn't up for a foot chase.

Taryn retrieved and slipped on her black shirt as she ran downstairs and out the front door.

Muted moaning led her onward and she found him still lying as he fell, rubbing his forehead with a pink thong still wrapped around his index finger. The rest of his cache was scattered around him like shards of a shattered thong rainbow.

Creep.

Her boot heel in the center of his chest roused him quicker than a slap and he opened his eyes. Blinking, he appeared dazed and on the verge of tears. She bent to point a finger in his face. He whimpered.

"Would you like to explain why you were peeping in my window, little freak, while clutching panties?" Only his pained expression kept her from kicking his ass.

Well, that, and he could have broken bones. It wouldn't be a fair fight.

"I wasn't p-peeping." He took a breath, groaned, and tried again. "I was doing clean-up." He pointed upward. Several more panties hung from the branches of the crooked oak tree between their houses. "From our first coed party last night."

Her mind flashed back to her wild college years of not that long ago. The explanation, and the clues, made sense. Too much sense. Still, she wasn't about to let him off the hook.

Grumbling under her breath, she removed her heel. "I swear to God. Boys never grow up." She reached down, unhooked the thong strap from his finger, then helped him up with her fists twisted in his polo shirt. He wobbled a bit but remained standing. "Are you hurt?"

"I don't think so." He inhaled deeply and winced. The fact that he was upright was a sure sign he'd survive. His face turned contrite. "I'm sorry for scaring you."

It was hard to stay mad when he peered up at her from behind ridiculously thick glasses. He was pitiful. He couldn't be more than eighteen, short and skinny; a dark-haired nerd through and through.

"I could have shot you. I still might shoot you. I haven't decided yet." She brushed leaves out of his hair. Although she was only six or seven years older than her panty-peeper, she felt decades more mature. "I do have a gun. A big one. Lots of bullets." She stressed that last fact, in case he ever got any ideas about using the ladder again.

He gulped and his lower lip trembled. "Please don't shoot me. I'm my parents' only child."

With panties in her tree, his story of innocence held water. Still, there was no excuse for trespassing outside her bedroom window. Worse, she'd looked forward to capturing a peeper and possible future serial killer. That would show Willard he was wrong about her only skill being pom-pom waving for football fans. Instead, she'd caught a goofy college kid with none of the sense God gave him. Not exactly a big-time criminal.

Hell. She sighed. There was only one thing to do.

"Come on. Let's get this mess cleaned up." Taryn went inside, grabbed a box of trash bags, and rejoined him. While she was gone, he'd scooped the panties into a small pile and was using the handle of a rake to collect more from the tree. She wondered how many he'd shoved into his pockets while she wasn't looking. "What's your name?"

"Andrew."

"I'm Taryn." She held open a bag. How had she not heard the party or the panty toss? She used to be a coed and had lived for parties. U of M cheerleaders were always invited. Was she getting old?

"Cans first, Andrew." He tossed a few in the bag. "At ten cents per returnable, there's almost enough here to pay for a week of groceries." She looked around. "Please tell me you didn't drink all these yourself?"

He grinned. "Nope. Fifteen of us live here."

Fifteen? Ugh. The house was almost a mirror of hers and not huge. She'd seen guys come and go at all hours over the last few days, but fifteen?

"How?"

At her puzzled expression he chuckled. "Bunk beds."

Sigh.

They filled two bags with cans, and part of a third with panties. She laughed when Andrew found a pair of men's black boxers in the mix. "Oh, the joys of living smack in the center of a college town," she said. So much for living quietly.

"Campus is a crazy place and the term hasn't even started yet," Andrew agreed with a grin. "I'm from a small town in Ohio. Two traffic lights. This place is so cool."

"That is a small hometown." She opened the bag for the briefs. "It must have been some party." He opened his mouth as if to explain, but she held up a hand. "I really don't want to know."

She glanced up into the branches and puffed out a breath. Two thongs and a pair of white granny panties were well out of reach. It would take a tree climbing pro to reach them. "We'll leave those last few up there. We shouldn't risk death on that ladder."

"Good idea." He took the bags from her. "Thanks, Taryn. I apologize again. And thanks for not shooting me."

"You're welcome."

She watched him place the can bags next to his house, in a wide wooden crate designated by red paint for returnables. At least the drunken students were environmentally conscious.

Then he took a few steps toward the front of his house, paused, and turned back to her.

Just when she thought she had him pegged as just a misguided but harmless nerd, he sent her a mischievous grin and held up the panty bag. "Next time we have a party, you're invited. And remember to wear your best thong."

With a naughty grin he vanished around the corner clutching the treasured bag of panties and whistling a happy tune.

Taryn rolled her eyes and laughed. "Harmless nerd? Right."

Chapter 3

One thing about Michigan weather was that one day you could be percolating in your own sweat, and the next, shivering like Jell-O on a crack high. A misty morning rain had lowered the temps to a pleasing degree and Taryn had her car window down, as she stuffed the last of a rubbery deluxe breakfast sandwich past her teeth, chewed, and washed it down with a latte loaded with an extra shot of light cream.

She sent a quick text to her mother and was about to head out when the surprising and sexy scent of spice and male wafted in through the open car window with the morning breeze to dance happily in Taryn's senses. She enjoyed the moment for a second before a familiar voice came out of nowhere, startling her and almost causing a coffee cup mishap on her lap.

"Where do you think you're going?"

Taryn righted the cup and looked over to see a tattooed arm leaning on the open window frame. That arm led up to a perfectly muscled bicep to a broad shoulder and farther up to a scruffy and handsome face she recognized.

Silva.

"Um. To breakfast?" Drat. She'd hoped to get on the road before he showed up; the whole lone wolf working by herself thing and all. But Irving had purchased a new set of faux crocodile golf shoes he'd wanted to show off. The appropriate time spent admiring the bright green-and-black shoes had pushed her back a half hour, while Irving explained in mind-numbing detail the benefits of this type of shoe on the fairway.

"Is that so? Then what is that?" He pointed to the greasy breakfast sandwich wrapper draped across the console, held down by a small red box that once held a deep-fried hash brown patty.

Shoot. Caught. What could she say?

Taking a quick second, she fumbled around in her mind for an appropriate excuse and came up empty.

"That's what I thought." Rick crossed his arms and leaned back on his heels. "It's only seven-twenty. I thought we were meeting at eight?"

"Was it eight?" Her eyes widened. She took a second to admire the solid wall of muscled male before answering, "I must have accidently typed in seven on my calendar." She feigned irritation. "And here I was mad that you were late. I was getting ready to call and lecture you about being punctual."

Rick frowned. "Right."

The man was really cute when he was annoyed.

"Then you won't mind if I join you." He bent to retrieve something by his feet and walked around the front of the car, keeping her from speeding off. He placed a small black duffel bag on the car floor and was inside before she could come up with an alternate strategy for escape that didn't involve turning him into a speed bump.

While he settled in, she covertly admired the view.

Agent Silva wore an old black Metallica t-shirt, jeans faded at the knees, and low black boots. He had a silver ring with a wolf head on his right hand and dark sunglasses that made her wonder if he was looking at parts of her he shouldn't.

There was a touch of danger about the guy that worried her good-girl side, yet intrigued bad Taryn. Had he come upon her in a dark alley, dressed like an outlaw biker, she'd be convinced she was about to be robbed of her pocket change.

Since she knew him to be on the side of the law, she just found the whole biker get-up hot.

No, no, and no to thinking inappropriate thoughts about her client! She scolded herself.

Although he looked ready to work the case, it didn't keep her from trying one last time to extricate him from the investigation. If she was to get anything done, she didn't need him slowing her down.

"Look, Silva. I appreciate that you want to spend the day together in the search of justice, but I should warn you that I don't play well with others."

"How so?"

"I like to follow my own rules. I don't share my toys. And if I get angry, I've been known to bite."

A nice set of teeth flashed. "I like women who bite."

Mmmmm.

"I'll bet you do." She ignored the innuendo and the tingle beneath the pink satin and lace covering her girly parts. The scent of him wafted around the car and didn't help. There was nothing yummier than the smell of a freshly showered male, with a splash of some guy product to top it all off.

"Look, I'm here to do what you hired me for and nothing else. No personal space invasion whatsoever is allowed. Got it?"

"Got it." The smile didn't waver but went from amused to something darker. He locked onto her eyes. "Then let me reiterate something that you clearly didn't process yesterday during our previous conversation. This case is about my mother. Her losses. My guilt. Period. I failed her once and won't fail her again." He took a breath and seemed to calm a little. "Where you go, I go. Or I'm taking my case elsewhere."

The blunt words did their job. She gave up the fight.

"I hear you, loud and clear." Although she hated to work the field accompanied, for this one case, she'd make an exception. The whole sweetheart con thing was an exciting new challenge. She'd do anything to keep the case. "We'll work together but I'm in charge. And you won't be covered on the Brash insurance plan. You eat your own hospital bills."

Rick stared blankly for a couple of seconds. "Insurance? Why would I need insurance?" As he waited for her answer, suspicion took over his face, then finally, understanding. "How often do you get injured on the job, Taryn?"

"Not that often, really."

"How often is not often?"

Clearly he wasn't giving up without an answer.

Taking a page from the guys comparing scars in the famous scene in *Jaws*, she rolled up her sleeve. There were two small puncture scars on her forearm. "Dog bite." She slid up her right pant leg to expose healing damaged skin on her knee. "Concrete rash from slipping on wet pavement while chasing a car thief."

"You chased a car thief?"

"Wait. This is the worst one." She pulled down the neckline of her shirt to show fingermark bruises on her collarbone. "Two days ago a neighbor's abusive boyfriend assaulted me. He pushed me against a wall. I damaged both his testicles. He'll need surgery." She paused. "Although technically that wasn't a Brash case, so it doesn't count. I jumped in when he tried to beat Angie with a claw hammer."

"She'll take him back," he said without missing a beat.

"Not this time," Taryn assured him. "If she does, the state will take her son. There isn't anyone she loves more. Little Jacob will save them both."

They sat for a moment while Rick rubbed his jaw. Finally he asked, "Is that it for scars?"

"Nope. I have a few more. But I'd have to take off my pants to show you and we haven't known each other long enough."

His eyes narrowed and heated. "Tomorrow then?"

"Maybe."

A deep chuckle followed. It had been so long since she'd flirted that she was rusty. Thankfully, Rick didn't notice.

As his hired PI, she shouldn't flirt at all. She'd never crossed the line with a client and didn't intend to now, just because she was sitting next to the most attractive guy she'd ever met. If she'd learned anything from her ex, Tim, it was that her judgment was skewed when it came to men. This tattooed bad boy was just the sort of man she should flee from.

Too bad he was so darn appealing.

That was all the more reason to stay away. She wasn't looking for an emotionless hook-up and she wasn't ready for a serious relationship. Rick didn't fit either scenario. He was a client. Period.

With that thought in mind, she mentally shook herself and turned on the engine. Thankfully, she was a consummate professional. She'd get through this case and on to the next without stepping over any boundaries with Special Agent Rick Silva.

"Let's get to work." She fired up the Oldsmobile and pulled out of the lot. The bottom of the wreck scraped the pavement on the short incline to the street. "Oops."

With him distracting her, she'd forgotten to take the exit at an angle. The old vehicle rode lower than her dearly departed SUV.

The beast's black ragtop and medium blue façade were a scuffed and dented mess, so she couldn't hurt it with an occasional rock chip or curb scrape. The Olds had once been an undercover cop car and had all the bells and whistles inside, including a top-rate radio. The outside could use body work and new paint, but the car had one hell of an engine.

Good old Detroit ingenuity. If she had to drive a wreck for a couple of weeks, it might as well have power beneath its crusty old exterior.

Rick smirked. "Maybe we should take my bike."

Annoyance bubbled up. Twenty seconds on the road with her and he was already complaining about her driving. Her ex used to complain about her driving, too. All. The. Time.

Fire burned in her chest. "So you think because you're a guy, you're a better driver than me?" she snapped.

A brow cocked up. "I never said that."

"But you think so. All guys do." His silence irked her and confirmed her assumption. Insulted by the "men are better drivers" myth—proved untrue by several studies, by the way—a wicked mischief welled in her. She'd show him. "I'll prove you wrong. You'll want to wear your seat belt."

Without warning, she spun the steering wheel hard right and the car tires squawked as they entered the empty metal stamping factory parking lot next door.

"Okay, not the best way to prove me wrong," he said.

"Zip it and hold on," she warned.

Rick had only a second to click on his seat belt when she hit the gas and spun the wheels left, sending the car into a slide. Next, she weaved in and out of the empty parking rows at a high speed and took satisfaction that Rick grabbed the roof strap over the window.

"Shit!" he said.

As she turned the car in a figure eight, Rick rocked back and forth on the seat, still clutching the strap. Taryn had his attention now. For the finale, she tore from one end of the massive lot to the other and hit the brakes so hard that the tires screamed as they stopped a foot in front of a chain-link fence.

"Yes!" she yelled. "That's the way a girl drives!" She turned to her companion and fist-bumped the steering wheel. His tanned face was a shade lighter than before. "Convinced I'm a better driver, Agent?"

He blew out a shaky breath. "Nope. I'm convinced you're crazy." He peeled his fingers off the roof strap. To her surprise, there was reluctant admiration in his eyes.

Ha.

Unfortunately, smug could only last so long. All good things had to end. Hers came with her cell chiming the James Bond theme. Uh-oh. "Hello?" Her bravado faded when Irving gave her a brief lecture about her antics and hung up.

"Bad news?" he asked.

"My boss," she said, sheepishly. She should have proved her point in a parking lot that wasn't overlooked by Irving's third-floor office. "He told me if I ruin another set of new tires and burn out the engine again, replacements are coming out of my yearly profit sharing check."

Rick Silva threw back his head and laughed.

Deep in his chest, Rick was sure that his heart had been one more doughnut spin away from complete failure. The woman knew how to drive. Like a monkey on LSD. Still, she'd managed to not kill them in her death lap around the lot, so he gave her props for that.

And she'd been sexy as hell while scaring the shit out of him. He had a serious hard-on beneath his jeans.

Now what would scare the hell out of her.

When he finally stopped laughing, he whistled and shifted to a more comfortable position, if he could find one in his condition. Hopefully, she wouldn't notice. "Where in the hell did you learn to drive like that?"

Taryn smiled smugly and drove out of the lot. "Irving sent us to a defensive driving school when he hired us. It was run by a former NASCAR driver. I kind of dated Dave that week and he taught me everything he knew about stunt-type driving at night, when everyone else was sleeping. I learned maneuvers they don't teach during business hours."

That certainly explained her crazy mad skills.

A tug of envy filled him. Her blush convinced him that driving wasn't the only lesson she'd learned from Dave at driving school.

Taryn was wearing relaxed jeans and a tight dark blue V-neck tee in deference to the cool morning. She'd tossed a black leather jacket onto the backseat; he bit his tongue to keep from asking her to model it for him. He normally liked women who dressed flashily and drew attention to themselves, but for some reason her casual clothes hit him hard in the groin.

The high ponytail that held back her silky-looking hair left her soft neck exposed for nipping. But it was her perfect mouth that led him to thoughts of that mouth on parts of him. This did nothing to ease the strain in his jeans.

Reality raced in on the ding of a good-morning text from his mom and broke up one hell of a fantasy. This partnership was not about getting naked with his PI.

They'd barely spent an hour together since last night and already he was losing control. Then again, thinking wasn't acting. As long as he kept his hands off her, he was still moving toward his goal.

So he dragged his eyes away from Taryn's mouth and remembered that despite that teen boy myth, lack of sexual release did not cause permanent damage to the testicles. He was an adult and should be able to control himself.

Setting his mind to Brinkman was like a cold shower. "Now that you've proved yourself to be unhinged, what's first on today's agenda?" he said.

"I'd like to do another sweep of Honey's neighbors. I know you said you spoke to one, but I'd like to follow up with a couple more." She pulled out her phone and typed. "I can't believe no one saw Brinkman or gossiped with Honey around the mailboxes. Someone has to know something about the mysterious Honey Comstock."

They headed for the apartment. The two-story brick building sat between a lawyer's office and a proctologist's practice. Rick made some sort of under-his-breath comment about the connection between the two and received an eye roll in response.

They spent the next half hour speaking to the residents who were home on the first floor. Most worked at either the university or one of the hospitals and thankfully didn't work straight nine-to-five shifts. No one knew anything about Honey. The one woman who had talked to her a couple of times had exchanged pleasantries about the weather and little else.

"I already spoke to the woman across the hallway from her. She rarely saw Honey but admitted to flirting with one of her sons a couple of times," Rick said, as they headed up carpeted stairs to the second floor. "The unit on her left is empty. There was no sign of the couple on the right. According to the landlord, they travel a lot."

Taryn rapped on several doors. No answers. They headed to the last unit past Honey's and lucked out. The traveling couple was home. The woman who answered was deeply tanned with a slightly burnt and freckled nose. It was hard to gauge her age by the leathery look of her skin, but Rick guessed low to mid thirties. With a few more years of sun baking behind her, she'd look seventy.

"Yes?"

While Taryn introduced herself and was led inside, Rick examined the woman's outfit. She was wearing a pink crop top to showcase her belly ring and a pair of cutoff jeans shorts that barely covered her ass. Not that he noticed.

"I'm Cindi with an *I* and that's my boyfriend, Chad." She indicated the guy sprawled on the couch. He was in his late twenties, shirtless and wearing board shorts in a bright red-and-black floral pattern. Several surfboards leaned against one wall and framed photos of a surfer riding waves covered one wall.

"Wassup?" Chad said.

"They're here about the lady that lived next door," Cindi-with-an-I explained. "The one with the little white dog."

"Cool." Chad laughed and added in a stereotypical surfer-dude-stoner voice, "Hey, dudes, that dog was gnarly. He liked to hump my leg." He made the motion with his arms and a full-body pump. Cindi giggled.

Great. They'd fallen into the middle of *Bill and Ted's Excellent Adventure*.

Chapter 4

While Rick squelched a grin, Taryn pushed aside the image of Chad and the dog doing a mating dance and refocused. She opened her phone to Brinkman's old Match-Mate profile. "What we want to know is if you ever talked to her, or her sons, and if she ever had this man around her apartment?"

She showed both the grainy photo.

Cindi shrugged. Chad nodded. "I saw him a few times. He made late-night booty calls." He winked at Taryn. "Spread a little Honey on his bread, if you know what I mean?"

Yet another unwanted image. Why hadn't she become an accountant like her father wanted?

"Did you ever talk to him?" she asked.

Chad scratched his neck. "Yup. Once in the parking lot. He said he surfed Baja back in the day. Baja is rad. But, like, I think he was messing with me. He didn't, like, know my dad or Issie. Everyone who surfed back then knew those dudes on the coast. They're, like, legends, man."

Despite the heavy stoner accent, she got the gist of what he was saying. Having spent four years in college, she understood stoner-speak. "You think he was lying?"

Shrugging, he picked at a toenail, as Cindi dropped on the couch beside him. "Maybe. Maybe not. He was old. Old guys lose their memories, right?" He paused, grinned, and added, "And their boners, too."

Cindi giggled again and slapped his leg. Taryn frowned.

Rick wandered off to look at the photos.

"What about Honey?" Taryn said patiently, when the giggling faded off. She reminded herself that working as a burger flipper or road kill collector had their disadvantages, too. Grease burns and a gagging stench were two. "Can you tell me anything personal about her? Did she have a job? Did she donate time to a charity?"

Chad grinned. "She was hot. So hot." Cindi pinched him on the arm. "Ouch! Dude, what was that for?"

"She's, like, your mother's age!" Cindi said, miffed.

"So? She's still hot."

Another pinch. He yelped and rubbed his arm. "That is so not cool!" They began a heated exchange. Good grief.

Rick snorted and shot Taryn a pitying glance that was laden with humor. Some help he was.

"Hey. Hey!" Taryn yelled over the noise. They stopped and looked at her. She lifted her hands palms out, took a breath, and remembered it was never too late to take up accounting. "Other than hotness, what do you know about Honey?"

The pair exchanged a glare. "She liked to bake cookies," Cindi said. "Honey brought us some when we moved in."

"She also drove a white Mustang convertible," Chad said.

"Oh, and she read celebrity gossip magazines," Cindi said. "I saw her get them out of her mailbox."

Chad nodded with another wink at Taryn. "And she liked to wear tight tank tops."

Cindi exploded. "Seriously?" The shouting began again. Taryn rubbed her fingertips on her temples. This was leading nowhere.

She glanced at her client for assistance. Instead of coming to her aid, Rick leaned forward and closely examined a photo of what she assumed was Chad on a huge wave. His eyes went wide. He leaned closer, frowned, and turned to the arguing couple.

Pointing at the photo, he asked, "Are those sharks under your board?"

The pair fell silent. Chad grinned and nodded. "Yeah, dude. Totally rad, right?"

After confirming that a cameraman had indeed captured the image of a pair of great white sharks almost having Chad as a snack off the coast of Australia—a cool picture, by the way—Taryn and Rick left the apartment having learned zero useful information to advance the case.

"Remind me why I do this for a living," Taryn grumbled, as they walked back to the car. "I've heard hooking for cash has its rewards. You make your own hours and I think they offer dental if you get in with the union."

"There's a union?"

She shot him a quelling look. "Sometimes it's better to let a woman vent than to comment."

He grinned. "Is that in the Understanding Women Handbook, because I'd like a copy?"

Tension faded. He was too cute to stay mad at. Of course, she'd never tell him that. "Dude, you can read that book all day and never figure me out. I'm totally rad, gnarly, and awesome, but also mysterious," she said in her best surfer-stoner voice. "And I'm stoked to get this case closed, so let's hit it before the waves flatline."

His chuckle followed her into the car. "You've spent too much time with Chad."

"Not enough, in his mind." She leaned forward and pulled a slip of paper out of her back pocket. She held it up. Chad's name and cell number were written on it in sloppy handwriting. "He slipped me this as we left the apartment."

Rick's eyes narrowed. "You aren't seriously considering calling him?"

"He is the kind of guy I like: cute and uncomplicated." Cindi aside, she'd never date Chad even if he was single. His surfboard had a higher IQ. She just wanted to see Rick's reaction, for fun. It had been ages since a man expressed interest in her, outside of Dave. Her job kept her too busy to date. At least that's what she told herself.

A therapist would see things otherwise.

"I can't see you with a guy who uses 'dude' as nouns, verbs, and adjectives." Rick interrupted her thoughts. "How does he do that, anyway?"

Although he'd kept his tone light, she saw tightening around his mouth. She liked that the thought of her and Chad together irked him. Why remained a mystery. She certainly didn't want to date Agent Silva. Of course she didn't. And he didn't want her. Besides, they'd known each other less than twenty-four hours. There was nothing between them. At. All.

Then maybe she should call Chad. Not.

Firing up the car, she changed the subject. "Why don't we move on?" Leaving Rick's first question unanswered.

* * *

Taryn's pretty hazel eyes sparkled with mischief as she pulled out her phone and swiped the screen open. She scrolled around for a minute before jerking the car into drive.

"It looks like my coworker, Summer, has tracked the name of the wife right before your mother. Apparently she and Teddy bought a couch together, as the Clarks. Both names went into the store computer when he used an old credit card from one of his previous aliases."

"Idiot."

Nodding, Taryn said, "You'd think he'd be smart enough not to reuse names . . . and credit cards."

"He probably assumes he's bulletproof. I suspect he's been a sweetheart con for decades and knows the game. He's obviously gotten away with conning women for most of his life without getting caught." Rick shook his head. "I still can't believe he's married another wife since my mother. Does this man ever take a break?"

"He does like to rack them up." Taryn took the US-23 ramp south and hit the gas. "He's nearing retirement age now and has to be slowing down. I mean, how long can he bounce between wives before cataracts and incontinence get the better of him, and he no longer appeals to women? Maybe he now sees the wives, and their money, as a supplement to Social Security?"

"I'd like to supplement his face with my fist."

Taryn frowned. "Down, boy. Let's worry about finding him first."

Despite wanting to pound Brinkman into a bloody lump, he didn't want the guy dead. He'd rather the jackass spent years locked in a cage. He might even visit on family day, just to gloat.

"We're already in the car," Taryn said. "We might as well hit her up now. Toledo isn't that far."

"Mrs. Clark's marriage was a few years back," Rick said as he watched her brush hair out of her eyes. "She won't have anything current."

"True. However, at this point we're looking for names he may have dropped of old friends, or his favorite vacation destinations, even a childhood school or teacher. Little things become a big clue, when grouped together to form a picture of his history. Once we know his real name, we might be able to track him through government records or a family link."

It was easy to see why she liked being a PI, despite occasional grumbling to the contrary. Her eyes lit up when she talked shop.

"This is like building a criminal case against a drug cartel, only without the executions," he joked.

"Sort of." She smiled.

Excitement took root in him. He'd been given a four-week vacation block after five years spent mostly undercover. If not for his mom and her case, he'd be bored stupid during the remaining weeks left on his leave. He loved action over relaxation. Working this was like getting back into the game, on a smaller and less dangerous scale, of course.

"Summer did find a house loan, from the early eighties, under the name Nolan Marshal. He took the note out with a woman she thinks was his first ex-wife," Taryn said. "Unfortunately, she died five years ago from cancer. However, the loan contains what might be his actual Social Security number."

"Socials can be faked."

"Yes, but if that woman was his first wife, then he might not yet have turned criminal and this could be real," she said. "Oddly, he still uses that Social but with different names. That's how Summer dug it up. Even a good con leaves a grain of truth in his phony history, if you know where to look, and how to piece them together. Summer's still searching for his childhood records and any other wives."

"Some wives may be in hiding," Rick said. "Men who con women are often regarded as sociopaths."

"True. It's heartbreaking to think of how many lives he's ruined." Her expression turned pensive. "He's likely used a variety of names over the years. That was before he started internet dating and became Teddy Brinkman. In his early years, he could escape arrest as long as he moved around. With the arrival of the internet, it's harder for him to hide."

"Your friend found a lot of information in less than a day." He was impressed by how much further ahead the case was in fifteen or so hours. "If she finds him, I'm treating her to a spa day."

"Summer is a kick-butt tech and loves to hunt down criminals. Any little bit of information on Brinkman leads her to another piece of his life. The dating site and your mother's information on Teddy got her started. She lives for a challenge."

Another thought came up. "Maybe we should try and set a trap for him online. Like offer you up as a decoy?"

Taryn nodded. "Summer is keeping watch for a new profile for him on Match-Mate. There's nothing so far. So, for now, we're doing background work. If this doesn't net results, we'll try to catfish him."

"Catfish?"

"You know. Put up a fake profile and picture online and try to get him to bite." His face stayed blank. She stared.

"You really were out of touch while undercover, weren't you?" She followed a big rig blocking the passing lane for several muttering-under-her-breath miles, then passed it in a burst of speed and a horn honk, when the driver finally returned to the right lane. He instinctively reached for the strap as the other driver flipped her off.

"Okay, when someone catfishes," she continued, "they lie about themselves in profiles to hook other people into online relationships. They may put up a fake photo or give themselves an exciting hobby or job. Heck, some lie about their looks or even their gender. It's all about being a more exciting person. There's a TV show about this."

"And you think you can do this to Brinkman?" It was an interesting concept. He should watch more TV.

"Maybe. But we need to find him first. If he goes back on Match-Mate, it'll be easy. We'll compile a profile that he can't resist. Then we'll hook him. Otherwise, we'll set up a Match-Mate profile anyway and hope he surfaces. It's harder that way, with so many women for him to dig through."

She weaved left and right around several cars at a high rate of speed. He didn't bother to release the strap when she finally settled in the right lane. There were more slow-moving cars ahead.

"Better yet, if he's a fellow crappy driver, maybe you could run into him at court-mandated driving school?"

Taryn shot him a sideways glance. "Remind me again why I let you tag along?"

"Because I'm paying you?"

"Not enough, clearly."

Despite the slim odds of Brinkman heading back to the dating site under his current alias, Rick had a feeling the man would screw up somehow and get caught by the Brash team. The guy may be married to Honey, but Taryn was wrong about one thing. Rick had worked around felons long enough to know that creaking bones and fading eyesight wouldn't get Brinkman out of the game. Eventually, he'd be back hunting on familiar ground and they'd get him.

"Brinkman doesn't stand a chance against Brash & Brazen girls."

She made a face and braked at a stop sign. "I'm not a brash girl, Agent Silva."

"I never thought you were."

Their eyes met and held. Taryn looked away first.

He'd done right by hiring Taryn and her team. He was confident they'd find Brinkman and drag his sorry ass to jail.

"I agree that the Social Security number could be a huge lead, if it's real," he said. "Any time Brinkman uses it, Summer will be on him. He can't hide."

"Yes, but he hasn't used it since before your mother," she said, tamping down her earlier excitement. "He's either using a new ID and Social, or perhaps he recently died. You never know. 'Hot' Honey may have given the guy a heart attack."

"I've already considered the possibility Brinkman was dead. That would be too easy, and unfortunate. I want him alive."

"Still, we can't rule that out," she said.

"They haven't been seen together, before or after the wedding, by any neighbors and I didn't find obituaries under his aliases." He paused and a dark thought emerged. "Worst case, he might have killed her."

"He hasn't been violent in the past, that we know of, so let's think positively. I'm hoping Mrs. Clark can give us more insight into your Casanova."

Rick hoped so, too. The longer Brinkman was on the run, the better his chances of spending all the stolen money. "Where does she live?"

"About three miles outside of Toledo."

Forty-five minutes and a fast food breakfast drive-through stop for Rick later, they drove into a quiet neighborhood of large houses, landscaped yards, and a narrow meandering road gilded in gold. Okay, not really gold, but he was convinced they were in a sparkling Oz for wealthy people, with not one house on the street coming in at less than a million dollars.

A woman pushing a stroller stared, suspiciously, as if they were burglars looking for a house to rob. The car certainly fit that bill. His tattooed arm perched in the open window further confirmed that they didn't belong.

Rick gave her a little wave and wondered if she'd be calling 911 before they even rounded the first bend.

Taryn slowed to check the address on a mailbox and pulled up the driveway to a house with a front lawn that rivaled the land mass of Central Park. The cost of yearly landscape maintenance alone must have supported several businesses.

"We're not in Kansas anymore, Dorothy," he quipped.

The house itself was huge. Reddish brick, white columns, and black window trim. Set back and to the right was a four-car garage in the same red brick. Rick half expected to see fields of beautiful thoroughbreds chewing on bluegrass, flicking off flies with their cropped tails, and waiting for their turn on the track at Churchill Downs.

His mom loved horse racing.

"Is this right?" Taryn's voice broke in, as she double and triple checked the address to confirm they hadn't gotten the wrong place. "I bet she pays her lawn guy more than I make in a year."

"I was thinking the same thing," he said. "Brinkman financially downgraded to Mom after this one. Our entire house would fit on this porch."

They parked the Olds in front and walked across cobblestone pavers to the porch and the high black door. Huge pots of pink and red flowers sat on either side of the door and matched fancy outdoor furniture was laid out like a magazine spread. The only thing missing was Scarlett and mint juleps.

Taryn paused. "I wonder if I should park out back so as not to bring down the neighborhood real estate values."

He glanced back at the car.

"Why do you drive that wreck, anyway? Can't the agency afford to get you a better car?"

"I did have a better car. I usually use the Olds only for stakeouts in rough neighborhoods. But I had a little road rage incident a couple of weeks ago with an irate husband. He ran over my Edge with his monster truck and totaled it. Irving has a new vehicle on order." She bit her lip, then added, "He's putting in bulletproof glass and reinforced everything, to keep me safe. I refused to drive a used military Humvee." At his look, she shrugged. "Too hard to park."

Rick took in this new information and rubbed his hands over his face. He was starting to see a pattern here. There was something seriously wrong with Taryn. The woman was trouble in tight t-shirts.

"No wonder you need good insurance."

"Hey, it wasn't my fault the jerk had a temper," Taryn protested. "I was hired to find the monster truck and I did. It's Gibby Parnell's only asset worth anything and his estranged wife deserves half of its value. She put the down payment on the truck and bought its first set of monster tires. He wouldn't be on the show circuit without her."

"Hmmm." What do you say to that?

Taryn rang the doorbell. A stout woman with gray hair and a stern expression answered. She wore a pale gray uniform, white apron, and sensible black shoes.

"May I help you?"

"Were here to see Jane Clark," Taryn said as she looked past the maid into the foyer. The maid stared at Rick, or rather his snake tattoo, with a strained frown. He grinned. She blanched, recovered, and lifted her nose.

"Mrs. Clark is not taking visitors." She choked on "Clark" and her thin lips came together into a lemon-sucking pucker. Clearly she wasn't a fan of the missing Joe Clark.

"We have news about her husband," Rick said.

The maid hesitated for a moment in mid–door close. Taryn pressed forward. "It's very important we speak to her. It's urgent. We think she might be able to help us find him and save other women from a similar fate."

Rick was impressed with the way Taryn spun their visit with a serious tone. Although it was unlikely this wife had anything useful to add to what they already knew, Taryn made it sound like the ripped-off Mrs. Clark would be the key to solving a mystery, as big as the missing persons cases of Amelia Earhart or Jimmy Hoffa.

No wonder she had an excellent reputation.

Even if she was trouble.

"She's not feeling well today. Let me see if she'll see you. Wait here." She closed the door to a crack and strolled away, with a *squish-squish* sound of her shoes, on cream-and-gray marble. Without hesitation, Taryn pushed the large panel open and quietly hurried off behind her.

Rick followed them through a large white foyer, where what he thought looked like an original Warhol hung, and down a long hallway to a sunny room at the back of the house. The room was big and open, with floor-to-ceiling windows. Fancy artwork covered the pale yellow walls and added color to the space.

Oddly, there was a darker yellow rectangular spot over the fireplace mantel where he assumed a painting had once hung. On a white couch with her back to them was a woman with dark brown hair, her face turned up toward the fireplace.

Rick shifted and his boot made a scuffing sound.

The maid spun, realizing they were right behind her, and scowled. "I told you to wait outside," she whispered to Taryn, who shrugged innocently. Since the woman obviously sensed Taryn was staying put, she sighed dramatically and said, "Mrs. Clark, you have visitors."

A loud sniff followed as Mrs. Clark unfolded from the couch, turned, and faced them.

Rick grimaced.

Chapter 5

Taryn managed not to react, outwardly anyway, though she may have winced inwardly. Mrs. Clark was a mess; a huge understatement, for lack of a better word. Her curly brown hair frizzed out like springs around her head, having escaped the bun someone had carefully constructed at the nape of her neck. Mascara smudged around her watery eyes in spots of black goo with a few streaks of the product making a southern dash down her face.

Her lower lip trembled as she dabbed her eyes with a handkerchief, making the damage worse. A sob caught in her throat, leading to a trio of dainty hiccups.

"Oh, dear," she said, visibly distressed, and patted the couch springs with her free hand. "I wasn't expecting visitors. I must be a sight."

The maid scowled at Taryn, as if she'd somehow failed her mistress. Taryn was contrite. They should have waited outside.

"You look fine, Mrs. Clark," Taryn said, her contrition continuing with the lie. She didn't know Mrs. Clark's full story but understood what it felt like to marry the wrong man. "We should have called first. But this was urgent."

The woman was in her seventies, widowed after a long marriage, and probably lonely; a common theme among Brinkman's victims. She'd been a perfect mark for a charmer like Joe Clark/Teddy Brinkman/etc. From her expensive white pantsuit to the pearls around her neck, she was a walking invitation for a rip-off by a skilled con man.

"We came to talk to you about Joe Clark," Rick said gently.

A sob shook Jane Clark. She sat back on the couch. "That bastard."

"I'll bring tea." The maid hurried off.

Taryn gave her a minute to collect herself before they joined her, Taryn on the couch and Rick in the nearby chair. He shifted uncomfortably in the spindly, vintage Victorian era piece, looking very out of place. She suspected he was more the ratty-recliner-and-a-beer sort of guy.

Taryn explained who they were. "The reason we're here is that we're looking for the man you know as Joe Clark in connection to another case. You were not his only victim. There were other women he married and conned over many years."

Mrs. Clark sniffed into her monogramed handkerchief. This woman bore no resemblance to the photo Summer had found and texted to Taryn, off a Who's Who of Toledo online profile. That Mrs. Clark had looked years younger than her birth age, was well dressed, and had ruled as grand dame of her local society and its cultural epicenter. Heck, she even knew the governor.

"I'm not surprised," Mrs. Clark said, shaking.

Without understanding how the woman could be so devastated over losing that rotten con, and not knowing what to say to stop a possible meltdown, Taryn reached out to touch her arm.

"I'm sorry for your loss," she said gently. "But he isn't worth your tears."

Mrs. Clark stiffened, then lifted her head.

"You think I'm this upset about losing Joe?" She snorted and anger flashed. "I've already rounded up several local hunters to execute him by firing squad if my PIs find him." She blew her nose. "No, I'm grieving the loss of my Edward Cucuel."

Taryn and Rick shared a look. "Edward who?" Taryn said.

The woman pointed a finger at the empty spot over the fireplace. "My Edward Cucuel. He was a famous portrait painter. I met him when I was sixteen and he was nearing the end of his life. He asked to paint me and I said yes. After those few days of posing, I never heard from him again and never knew what happened to my painting."

She dabbed her eyes and stared off. "My beautiful husband, William, hunted the painting down and purchased it for my fiftieth birthday. He paid a premium, as the owner did not want to part with it. That beauty had hung up there for decades, until Joe Clark stole it from me."

Taryn wasn't a sentimental person but she felt for her. The treasured gift was both a memory of a youthful moment and a loving remembrance of how Jane was once a cherished wife.

"We'll do everything we can to get your painting back for you," Taryn promised. "And see your husband arrested."

A sad smile tugged at Mrs. Clark's mouth.

"He isn't my husband. I've had the marriage annulled. Well, it was never legal anyway. That much information my lawyers do know. They found a previous wife and her online web page. They never divorced." She scrubbed her handkerchief under her eyes. "The reason I'm still Mrs. Jane Clark is that I haven't had the energy to go to the court and have my name changed back to Ellington. It's humiliating to get duped."

"That wasn't your fault," Rick said. "My mother was another of his victims."

They shared a glance. "The poor dear," Mrs. Clark said. "Give me her address and I'll send her one of the voodoo dolls I have of him."

Rick hiked up a brow. She nodded. "My friend sewed them as a joke, but I do find jabbing him with pins therapeutic."

Despite her current appearance, the lady had a thread of steel in her, Taryn thought. She had little doubt that the firing squad was happily at the ready to take Teddy Brinkman/Joe Clark out at Jane's call.

"Why did you marry him in the first place?" Rick asked and shifted on the small seat.

"Great sex."

Taryn glanced to Rick, back, and quipped, "There are worse reasons to marry."

The comment earned a full smile from Mrs. Clark. She twisted her pearls with one finger. "Yes, there are."

For the next half hour, they sipped tea and ate little sandwiches and learned nothing more than that the couple had met online, had a rushed courtship, and the marriage ended in Joe stealing numerous treasures. Brinkman did like to keep to familiar patterns.

"Did Teddy-slash-Joe bring anything to the marriage that might tell us more about him?" Taryn asked.

Jane shook her head. "All he had with him were two suitcases full of clothes and a laptop in his Ford Pinto. When he snuck out, he took his clothes and laptop with him, along with my painting and two thousand dollars out of my safe."

"Two suitcases isn't much," Rick said. "A week or so worth of clothing, tops."

"When I asked him about that, he said he'd lost everything else in a fire," Jane added. "I'm sorry now that I never pressed him on his history or had him checked out. I wanted to believe he was everything he said he was. The scoundrel."

The comment brought Taryn upright. "No. Don't apologize. I think you just gave us our first solid lead." She stood and went to the window and looked out over the expansive grounds. Flowers bloomed everywhere. "If he came with almost nothing, then he hid his stolen items, personal papers and such somewhere."

"In a storage locker," Rick said, without pause.

She turned and nodded. "Exactly. We just have to find the right one."

Jane Clark had nothing more to add as they finished their visit. By the time they drove off, the lady seemed in much better spirits. Taryn no longer worried about her.

"I think she's on the mend," Taryn said, as the car rolled its way down the driveway and into the street.

"A trip to the bathroom repaired her face and her disposition," Rick agreed. "I think she was happy to have provided us with a clue."

"She did seem hopeful of getting her painting back." Taryn shot him a grin. "She even flirted with you near the end. I think she'll be Mrs. Ellington and back to her old life soon. A con like Teddy can't keep a good woman down."

Satisfied with the morning, and their one new clue for the case, she sped down the road and hit the highway north. Silent in thought, Rick watched the scenery pass as Taryn weaved in and out of traffic going well beyond the speed limit. She liked to drive fast. Jess called her a lead-foot. Summer lectured her on obeying traffic laws. Irving just shook his head.

They had passed back into Washtenaw County when blue and red lights flashed behind them.

Taryn's stomach dropped. "Damn."

Rick turned to look out the back window, as Taryn eased the Olds off to the side of the road with the crunch of wheels on the cracked pavement. The state trooper pulled off behind them and parked. Rick shifted his attention to the sideview mirror, as the officer settled his hat on his head and stepped from the vehicle.

Damn was right.

"How fast were you going?" Rick asked and reached for the glove box. After the morning he'd spent with her at the wheel, he imagined a huge stack of crumpled speeding tickets shoved into the glove box and forgotten. When he popped it open there was nothing but the registration and proof of insurance.

He collected both.

Taryn made a face and pulled her bag off the floor. She scrounged around for her wallet. "I don't know. Eighty, eighty-five maybe?"

Before he could poke at her, again, about her bad driving, she found her wallet, turned, and smiled brightly for the trooper. "Hello, officer. Nice day, huh?"

The trooper scowled and crossed a pair of massive arms over his massive chest. Though not overly tall, he'd certainly scare wayward motorists. "Cut the crap, Taryn. How many times do I need to lecture you about your speed?"

This took Rick aback. They knew each other?

Intimately, it appeared. The trooper was too familiar with Taryn to be a casual acquaintance. Were they a couple?

Up came a flare of male competitiveness that led him to size the guy up further. And he wasn't happy with what he saw.

The trooper looked like he'd walked off a *Twelve Months of Michigan State Trooper Hunks* calendar. He was what women would consider good-looking, clearly having won out in the gene pool. His biceps alone left little doubt that the man could bench-press a Mini Cooper. This left Rick thinking he spent all his free time working out. And Taryn had on a flirty expression so he knew she noticed, too.

"Come on, Hunter," she said sweetly and fingered her driver's license. "You know I don't speed on purpose. If they didn't make these roads so straight and flat, I wouldn't accidently go so fast."

Hunter? Seriously? Rick hated him already.

"So your law-breaking is the fault of the road commission for building straight roads?"

"See, you get it," she gushed.

Rick shook his head. Where had the real Taryn gone and who was this flirt? Whoever she was, he didn't like her. Or maybe he just didn't like the way she looked at Hunter the Trooper and his bulging biceps. The man needed a bigger shirt.

Hunter finally grunted and leaned down, putting his folded arms on the window frame, and grinned. Rick barely warranted a two-second look. He watched the trooper glance down Taryn's V-neck; then he flicked a smug glance at Rick, knowing he'd been caught looking. Ass. The guy was clearly hooked on Taryn and wasn't against staking a claim.

As long as Trooper Hunter didn't piddle on her shoe, Rick could deal with a little competition. If he were in the market for a relationship, that was.

Hell, what unattached male wouldn't be hooked on her? She was sexy as hell.

"I should give you a ticket," Trooper Hunter said and stared down at her mouth. "Several tickets."

"You should," she said, smiling.

"What I'd rather do is take you out to a movie," Hunter said. He reached out to touch her shoulder with his index finger. "One of those chick flicks you like."

Here we go, Rick thought. The guy casually flexed his pecs, as if to remind her of what dating him would get her: a testosterone-filled cave man. The feat of flexing was hard to pull off in a too-small polyester shirt under a bulletproof vest. But the trooper managed.

Thankfully, the seams of the shirt held. Just what they needed was a shirtless trooper to further entice Taryn.

Rick bit back a snort. He returned to trying to find faults with the Ken-doll–law-enforcement-professional. And failed. Damn, Hunter *was* perfect, Rick grudgingly conceded.

If you liked that type.

"Hunter, you know we don't mix," Taryn was saying with a frown and a scold. "Our previous date was a disaster. You tried to pick up our cute waitress during the fried cheese sticks appetizer. Right in front of me. That wasn't cool."

Hunter's grin widened. "You're right. I was a jerk. That's why I didn't ticket you the last two times I pulled you over. This is your third strike, though. So slow down."

"I'll try.

"Good. And if you change your mind about that date, you have my number. Call me." He drew a hand over his wide chest but stopped short of expelling a Tarzan yell.

Rick was grateful for an end to the encounter. And annoyed. At least Taryn hadn't giggled.

"I do have it," she said and slid her driver's license back into her wallet. "Thanks."

Hunter gave Rick one last glance, smirked arrogantly like he believed himself the dominant male, then pushed off the car and walked away. Taryn smiled a Cheshire cat smile and dropped her wallet back in her bag.

Rick wanted to beat the hell out of the trooper. Just for fun . . . and for looking down her shirt.

Instead, he focused on her. "You are a confirmed menace on the road," Rick said and tried to settle his temper. It wasn't working very well. "How many tickets have you racked up anyway?"

She looked at him sidelong. "Zero."

It figured.

"Life isn't fair, you know that?" he said and expelled a harsh breath. "Hot women get all the breaks."

"You think I'm hot?"

"Don't go there." He settled back in his seat, frustrated more at himself for caring who she dated than her driving. After all, he barely knew her and wasn't interested in her outside of work. Why did he care if she went out with Hunter the Trooper god?

He knew he should forget the muscle-neck, and surfer boy before him, and move on. Instead, he cut loose with, "I can't believe you went out with that jerk. I suspect he spent your evening with him looking at his reflection in his soup spoon."

Her brows shot up. "Are you jealous?"

"I'm not jealous."

"Uh-huh." Taryn started the car and carefully pulled back onto the expressway. "For your information, Hunter is a nice guy. He's just used to women falling at his feet."

"Including you."

She frowned. "I do not fall at anyone's feet."

He'd hit a nerve. Curiosity took over and the trooper was forgotten. "I don't believe that. You must have fallen at least once. What about a previous boyfriend? Fiancé? Everyone has someone in their past that they thought was The One."

Was she grinding her teeth? "Look, Silva. One date is all a guy like Hunter gets. I don't get involved with men who have tendencies to cheat. And, besides, my personal life is none of your business. Move on."

Huh. He'd kicked a wasp's nest. Someone had hurt her. Badly. He didn't like the sadness in her eyes, so he changed tactics. "Fine. But if you ever want to talk about the jerk who screwed you over, I'll lie and tell you I'm a good listener," he joked to lighten the tension. "But unless you want to talk sports or beer over a good belly scratching, I really don't care. Go find a girlfriend to talk feelings to."

A smile broke the frown. "At least you're honest." Then she laughed. "I've always suspected men only talk about their feelings to get women into bed. Thanks for confirming that theory."

Rick grinned. "Trust me. It takes a lot less than relationship talk to get a woman into bed."

That husky laugh about did him in. She should be offended by his bullshit. Instead she found him funny. He liked that damn laugh. Hell, if she wanted to watch a girly movie, or make him hold her purse while she tried on clothes, he was all in. She was the kind of woman men fell for, fast and hard.

Somewhere some dope was thinking about her and crying into his beer, knowing she was the one that got away.

"You are an insult to women," she said. "Yet, strangely enough, I think you're yanking my chain. I'm convinced that at least once in your life, you've had the 'feelings' talk and liked it, alpha-boy."

How quickly she'd twisted his earlier comment around and back on him. She was sharp.

"Touché."

An AC/DC song came on the radio and ended their conversation. She cranked up "Back in Black" to an ear-ringing level and sang at the top of her lungs. She likely got the love of vintage rock from her parents, and her singing voice from mimicking feral cats fighting. But she sang with enthusiasm and he liked that, too.

Shit, he liked several things about her. Her intelligence, her energy, her attitude, and the way she filled out her clothes. Taryn was no salad-only stick figure but a woman with curves. And he wasn't happy that he'd noticed. He'd been off the grid for years and had just started to get his life back. He didn't need a woman right now, even one who made his body ache.

They had to get this case closed, before he forgot all of his resolutions and got thoroughly hooked on Taryn Hall.

Chapter 6

Ten minutes later, Taryn was swaying in her seat to the final notes of "What I Like About You" by the Romantics, while Rick was probably mourning the loss of his hearing. Singing to window-rattling music always lifted her mood.

She pulled off the expressway, behind a semi-truck, and headed toward a small cluster of buildings that included a gas station and a big-box warehouse. She aimed the car for an uninteresting looking little brown restaurant at the end of the mini mall that promised, according to their signage, the best fried chicken in the state.

Her stomach rumbled happily. "I need food," she said and lowered the volume. "I hope you like chicken."

"I love chicken," Rick replied and stretched his back with a groan. The poor guy was probably stiff from sitting in Jane Clark's cramped antique chair. He'd looked pretty funny trying to keep the spindly thing from tipping over.

It was sort of fun to see him uncomfortable after his comments about Hunter. As if the trooper was any of his business. She pulled into the parking lot and found an open spot.

Yes, focus on something other than the emotions he'd dredged up from their previous conversation. She didn't want to think of Tim, The One, in her life. If her ex hadn't suddenly decided to become her texting friend, she might actually get over the hurt he'd caused and forget him.

"Good. I'm buying." Stopping in a parking space, she collected her laptop and notepad, and led the way inside.

"Do you ever stop working?" Rick asked, as they waited at the hostess stand. There was censure in his tone. This was odd for a man who had spent five solid years undercover.

"I can rest when I'm dead."

The restaurant smelled of fried food and cinnamon potpourri. The tables and chairs were solid wood, shellacked to a shiny sheen, and scarred up to give the place a down-home country kitchen feel. A middle-aged woman wearing a long beige-and-pink floral peasant dress hurried around a lunch buffet and headed toward them.

"Two for lunch?"

"Yes, please." Taryn didn't care about the atmosphere as long as the food was good. Those mini sandwiches at the Clark house hadn't lasted long. Her stomach was scraping her spine.

The hostess led them to a corner table and Taryn spread her things out, ignoring Rick in favor of keeping her sanity, and fired up her laptop. With him in close proximity, concentrating on work was better that staring into his pretty gray eyes and feeling all warm and dopey.

Their waitress brought menus and water glasses. The woman stared openly at Rick, like he was covered in chocolate syrup and sprinkles and she had a craving for both.

"I'll give you a few minutes to decide your order," the woman said. To Rick. There was some hair twirling.

"No thanks. I'm ready to order. I'll have the special and a choco-late milkshake," Taryn said and pointed at the folded card on the table without touching the menu. She turned back to her laptop and signed in. The screen saver popped up of a boat marooned on a beach in some far-off tropical island.

Someday she'd hit that beach, or one just like it, when she had time for a real vacation.

"I'll have the special, too. And a Coke. Thank you." Rick leaned back on the hard bench seat and stretched an arm along the back. She felt him staring, leaving her unsteady on her feet, like a case of ver-tigo, but worse. Thankfully, she was sitting down.

"I hope you don't expect me to converse with you. I have some-thing to take care of," she said and reached for her notebook and pen-cil. Keeping her hands busy and away from her own hair meant no twirling for her. The man was a menace to her vow to avoid any sort of bad boy.

"Of course you do."

She sent him an impatient glance. "I'm working on finding that storage locker. You should appreciate my dedication."

"I'd appreciate lunch without an open laptop in my face."

He did have a very nice face. Even when scowling.

Damn the attraction she had for the guy. Even Hunter the law enforcement god didn't compare. Rick was rough-edged and tough, but also had the ability to make her laugh. When he looked at her, she felt off-kilter.

Get it together, Taryn, she scolded herself. Rick was trouble. She didn't need trouble.

"I have to work our clues before they get cold," she said tightly. "Not entertain you with amusing chatter."

"I've been amused enough today just watching you drive."

She glared. "Ha. You're so funny. By the way, I've already proven I'm a good driver. I've never had an accident that I've caused. I bet you can't say that."

He chuckled. "I'll keep that in mind, Danica Patrick."

"Thanks. I'll take that as a compliment." She shoved her bag across the table and reached to click open a file. "I have a paperback thriller in there if you get bored."

Minutes ticked by and their drinks came. Without turning away from the file, she stuffed the straw into the thick shake and tried to pretend that she didn't know he was staring. And she did know. The weight of his attention spanned from her head to her toes, and in all her good parts along the way.

A lobotomy was the only way to get him out of her head.

More minutes ticked by. Finally, she lost her patience and lifted her eyes to his face. "Must you stare?"

"I'm bored."

"I told you I have a book you can read."

"Thanks, but I'd rather talk."

Her eyes narrowed. His crossed arms and set expression showed that he wasn't about to be put off. So she sighed and closed her laptop.

"Okay, Silva. What do you want to talk about?"

His eyes widened, as if he'd just been given the keys to her secret candy stash. She quickly added the caveat, "Anything within reason. I'm not answering questions that are too personal."

That should keep him coloring within the lines.

"Okay." He tapped his palms on the table. The wheels in his brain started turning. What would he come up with?

"I understand you were a pro football cheerleader."

Figures he'd lead with that, Taryn thought. All men found that fantasy-worthy. He's just another guy with a hard-on for cheerleaders. He'd probably Googled her last night and now had old photos of her bent-over butt or barely covered breasts as his screen saver.

This knowledge would make it easier to deal with him on an impersonal level. She couldn't stand a shallow man. "See, you're a typical male. Every man I meet wants to know if I still have my uniform and if I'll model it for him. You men are all alike."

"Do you still have your uniform?" He held up his hands in surrender at her frown. "I'm kidding. Geez. Get over yourself. What I wanted to know is how you got into that business. You don't look like a pom-pom waver."

Huh. "And what does a pom-pom waver look like?" She crossed her arms, matching his, and silently dared him to insult her.

One side of his mouth curled up. "Oh, I don't know. Perky?"

Despite wanting to kick him under the table, and realizing that maybe he wasn't shallow after all, she shook her head and smiled evilly. "You think I'm not perky?"

"You are perky's brooding Goth sister."

She snort-laughed. "I'm offended. I am neither Goth nor brooding. I used to kick butt on the sidelines. I was the cheerleader who got thrown in the air and always stuck my landings. Had I not gotten fired, I'd probably still be riling up the crowds at the games. It was a fun gig."

She'd been damn good at her job. Short-lived as it was.

"I still don't see it," Rick said. "Maybe you should model the uniform for me. Wave a pom-pom. Do a cheer."

Sigh.

"That's because you don't know me." She uncrossed her arms and disregarded his effort to tweak her temper. He did like to mess with her. "Ask me something else and we'll see if your preconceived notions match with reality."

"How did you get into cheerleading?"

"A high school friend dragged me to tryouts. We both thought cheering would help us nerds attract guys."

"Did it work?"

"What do you think?" she said with a sexy hair flip.

"I'll take that as a yes." He took a sip of Coke and paused, as the waitress brought their food and left. He tore off a piece of fried chicken with his fork. "Next question. Why were you fired?"

"My boss groped me and I Maced him. My lawsuit is still slogging through the courts."

"Would you like me to beat him up?"

"My friend Jess already has dibs."

"I have bigger fists."

"She's scarier."

Rick shrugged, leaving the offer open.

They ate in silence for several minutes. The sign outside hadn't lied. The food was really good. She shook some salt on her potatoes and waited for the grilling to continue.

After another gulp of Coke, he fired off questions in rapid succession. "What's your favorite color?"

"Black," she said and stabbed her fork into a small mound of buttered corn. He made a face. "Ha. Gotcha. It's red."

"Your favorite food?"

"Apple pie with a crumble top." At his brow lift, she explained. "My mom makes the best crusts."

"Favorite pet?"

"Tasmanian devil."

That stopped him. "First, I don't think it's legal to own one and I've heard that they stink like an outhouse."

"Oh, then I'll change my favorite to an anaconda."

"You are not normal."

"So I've been told."

He leaned his elbows on the table and bent his arms. He had very nicely muscled arms. Better than Hunter. Hunter was well built, but over the top. Rick likely got his build from carrying car parts around. Or women into his man cave for ravishing. Probably the latter, she figured.

"My turn," Taryn said. "What do you do when you're not arresting drug dealers and chasing con men?"

"I ride my bike, get into fights, and eat raw meat."

"Sounds fun. Anything else?"

"I like to play tickle monster." At her questioning glance, he said, "My niece is four and she loves when the tickle monster chases her around the house."

Awww. Taryn imagined him, all six-plus feet of tattoos and muscle, racing after a giggling four-year-old and giving tickles. She pictured his little niece on his back in a kiddie carrier and wearing a tiny pink or black helmet, as he roared down US-23 on his Triumph toward grandma's house.

Nope. The image didn't fit the man in front of her. Bikes were too dangerous for babies. Rick was too dangerous for everything else.

"I bet she's adorable," she said. He was adorable while talking about the girl. This topic was pushing her onto thin ice. She needed to get back to safer ground.

"Becca is the best." He whipped out his phone and scrolled through his pictures. "Here we are last week during tea party day at her house. They live in Montana so I don't see them often."

Don't look! She was already crossing a line with him by getting personal and imagining him naked.

Danger ahead! Abort! Abort!

She looked. The selfie showed a smiling little girl wearing a pink boa and smeared red lipstick, clutched cheek to cheek with Rick, who wore a purple barrette clinging to a few strands of his cropped hair, as she pressed a kiss on his unshaven cheek.

The pair was the cutest thing. There was some internal melting. Some going gooey. Damn.

Get a grip, Taryn. "She loves you."

"I love her." He clicked off. "My sister, Sarah, thought she couldn't have kids. Becca was her miracle."

Taryn nodded. Their eyes met. She felt her emotions slide out of whack. Since Tim dumped her for Gloria, she hadn't felt more than casual interest in men, and had only slept with one since she'd moved out of their house: Dave the race car driver, and that was never meant to be long-term.

Worse, she'd only known this guy a few hours. What was with all this hormonal craziness? She was too young for menopause and too old for raging teenage emotions. So what was the explanation for wanting to see him naked?

Pure visceral attraction, she suspected.

She hated feeling out of control. Tim had been her first real love. She'd thought they were forever. He'd thought they had an open marriage. She didn't remember agreeing to that in their wedding vows.

Perhaps it was time to cut to the chase and get Rick to stop looking, well, like he was interested in seeing her without clothes. Men usually ran off when confronted by brutal honesty about relationship and emotional stuff. If she couldn't control her attraction, let him think sleeping with her would be a serious train wreck.

So she let him have it with both barrels. "My ex-husband seduced our maid. In our bed. I caught them in the act," she blurted out. Her face flamed. Was it too late to take that all back? There was something to be said about too much honesty.

Nope. Too late.

"Wow." He sat back, stunned. "That's way beyond favorite colors."

She gathered her things and threw money on the table.

"That's why I don't date and don't have emotional attachments, and why I'm giving up men forever. Even you and your sexy tattoos are off the radar." Okay, giving up men wasn't true. She liked sex. She was just avoiding relationships and heartbreak like a communicable rash. Rick wasn't the kind of man for the former and certainly would cause the latter.

Yep, she was right to lay out her marital misery. He should be ready to run now.

"Shit," he said.

Taryn bolted for the door. By the time he caught up, she'd dumped half of her stuff onto the backseat of the Olds. And she felt less triumphant than she'd expected after the emotional blast. She'd wanted to warn him off. Not make him think she was a flake. Or emotionally stunted.

Instead he moved up behind her. She froze.

Rick leaned one hand on the roof of the car and bent around to look into her face. The expected panic wasn't there. Rather a mix of anger and concern.

"The maid? That's cold." He put his other hand on the open door frame and trapped her. His warm scent roiled around in her senses and made her forget almost everything else but him.

She bit her lip. Hell, it looked like he might not flee. Darn. Admitting to her husband cheating was the best ammo she had to scare him off. That meant she'd have to find another way to get a grip on this stupid attraction.

He shifted slightly. He was very close. Too close. "He didn't deserve you."

She dropped her notebook onto the seat and turned to face him.

"You don't know me well enough to make that determination. I was probably a crappy wife."

"Maybe," he said, clearly attempting to distract her. "I can't judge. I don't know anything about your marriage, but you still didn't deserve to be cheated on."

"Um, thanks. I think." She hadn't been a crappy wife, just a naive one. She had that in common with Rick's mother and Mrs. Clark. Tim was a podiatrist and not a con man, but he'd betrayed her nonetheless. And the betrayal still hurt.

"I thought love and sex and devotion were enough to keep my husband happy," she said. "He wanted to do other women. How could I compete with that?"

He reached out to touch her face. His rough fingertips scraped her skin, but not in a bad way. Next to him, she felt very feminine.

Images of him using those hands on her naked body crept in. She forced them back out. Lust didn't last. Eventually, she'd fall for him and then he'd move on, or cheat, and she didn't want another Tim in her life.

"You shouldn't have to compete for your own husband," he said. "That guy's an ass."

There was no argument to that statement. "I don't want to talk about him anymore. He's Gloria's problem now. They're made for each other."

"What shall we talk about then?" he said and slid his fingertip along her jaw and his eyes locked onto her mouth. "I know. I'd like to discuss the part where you've been thinking dirty thoughts about me."

Chapter 7

"I said you had sexy tattoos. I never said I was having dirty thoughts about you." He was just ridiculous. And funny. And dangerous. A man couldn't carry himself in the cocky way he did and wear all those tats around without getting into trouble: bar fights, street racing, perhaps even jaywalking. There was no telling what kind of darkness lived inside Rick.

"It's okay if you're hot for me," he said and leaned in to whisper in her ear. His breath tickled her lobe. "Most women are."

A shiver went down her spine and bloomed into a fireworks display south of her belly button. The man was too damn confident of his charms, even if he was teasing her to get a reaction, which he clearly liked to do. Often.

"Stop making me laugh." She'd stopped laughing because she couldn't breathe under his overwhelming closeness. His mouth was inches from hers. A slight head turn and they'd be kissing.

"You're my client," she said, forcing the words past a tightening of her throat. "I'm a professional PI."

"I see that." He looked down to where her flattened hand had somehow made its way to his warm, muscled chest.

Surprised, she yanked it back, gulped, and said somewhat breathlessly, "Just get into the car."

Rick's expression turned from sexy to concerned, as if the danger of following her directive might lead to his death in a fiery car crash.

Lust vanished. "Really? I'm not a bad driver."

He slowly stepped back, grinning. Released from the circle of his arms, Taryn wanted to grab his shirt with both hands and yank him back. Kiss him. Grab his butt. Kick his ass. Instead, she brushed past him and slipped into the car. The bucket seats would provide a safety zone between them.

He joined her.

"We need to get on the storage locker angle." She inhaled and exhaled slowly, until her heart calmed. The man was exasperating and all too attractive. Unfortunately, her body wanted to behave badly. All over him. All night. Darn it!

Rick said nothing but she felt his amusement.

Even now, with the console between them, she could catch occasional sniffs of his scent and still felt the brush of his breath on her ear when he'd whispered to her.

Damn. She needed a lobotomy. Or maybe she should bring up Tim again. Or maybe not. That hadn't worked the last time.

Taryn shook her head, jammed the car into drive, and took off in a squawk of brand-new tires, letting the breeze blowing through the open windows cool off her overheated . . . well, everything. She was speeding toward a wall of trouble with Rick and wasn't sure how to avoid the crash.

Since they were closer to Rick's motel room than the office, Taryn suggested, in a momentary lapse of sanity, that they go there. The space was no more than one decent-sized room split into a bedroom, a small attached kitchenette, and a bathroom. The carpet was a dingy red and orange shag and the bedspread a golden harvest yellow.

The stale odor of old cigarettes and damp permeated the room. "Nice room."

"I didn't want to waste my money on something fancy, when all I need is a bed and shower." He scooped up a few discarded clothing items off the bed and shoved them into a dresser drawer. "I didn't expect a guest or I'd have picked up."

"Then we both should lower our expectations. I didn't think I'd ever be in a motel room with you," she quipped, without thinking, and immediately wanted to take it back.

He grinned. "Didn't you?"

Instead of answering, she turned sideways and sidestepped past the queen-size bed, went to the particleboard desk, and set up her laptop. The room was so small that pulling out the chair put the wooden legs in contact with the bed. Maybe she should have taken him to the office. The intimacy of this setting made her nervous. Being near a mattress with Rick made her nervous.

Ugh.

"Okay, let's see how many storage facilities are in and around Ann Arbor." She slipped into work mode. Rick took a seat on the bed to her left. "It looks like there are seven with Ann Arbor addresses, one in Saline, and six more in a ten-mile radius of the city. I'm assuming since Teddy's victim, Honey, was from Ann Arbor, he'd set up nearby."

Taryn started searching. She didn't have Summer's deep web skills, but she excelled at the basics.

"Are you hacking into computers?" Rick slid closer and looked over her shoulder.

"I wouldn't use that word." She wanted to put some distance between them but there was no room. Besides, it might clue him in that he affected her and she couldn't do that. The guy was already too confident. "I'm just taking a peek at a few files. If these storage facilities didn't want anyone looking, they'd upgrade their online security."

Rick snorted but said nothing. It took her almost an hour to realize that Brinkman hadn't rented a storage unit under his name or in any of the aliases they knew. At least not in the Ann Arbor area, and she was almost to the end of their list.

"I thought we had something here." Disappointed, she moved to close the file on Affordable U-Store. "Another dead end."

"Wait," Rick said. "Go back. Scroll up." She scrolled up. "Look, right there. Comstock. Joey Comstock. That's the name of one of Honey's sons."

"Are you sure?"

"I'm sure. When I uncovered her as Brinkman's latest wife, I had a friend run her history. Her sons came up. The other one is Ronnie. There is no mention of their father. "

Returning to feeling hopeful, Taryn clicked open the file. "Let's see. Joey Comstock, age twenty-eight. He paid with a credit card." She lifted the card number, texted it to Summer, then scanned the rental agreement. "This is odd. He rented the unit a few days after his mother married Brinkman."

"Maybe with a combined household, they had too much stuff and something had to go."

"Possibly. But Jane Clark said he came to her with almost nothing but a suitcase. I can't imagine he's turned to schlepping around a living room furniture set in the back of his Pinto."

"Point taken."

Her phone pinged. That was quick. "Summer says the credit card was opened up four months ago under Honey's name. But the address traces back to a nail salon that closed up last year."

"That's probably around the time that Brinkman started romancing Honey."

She turned her head to meet his eyes. "I'm getting a funny inkling here. Something's not right."

Rick nodded slowly. "Could Brinkman have opened up the card in her name and rented the unit under Joey's? It seems like whoever managed the facility would check the name on an ID against the card. Brinkman is almost twice Joey's age."

"That would make sense," she said. "But not everyone does. Why give up a sale over a detail like a stolen credit card or ID?"

Scanning the page, Taryn suspected the address and phone numbers linked to the card were bogus, too. "Again, why would Brinkman use real names that could be traced to him?" She tapped her fingers on the desk. "He's getting sloppy."

"Possibly. Or because he knew no one would kick up a fuss, that's why," he said. "If anyone was hunting him, they'd only be looking for Honey, not her kids. And by the time the credit card company, or Honey, got wind of the scam, he'd be gone."

"I agree. Or there could be another, darker, reason." Taryn's stomach tightened, as she stared blankly at the screen. Her thoughts raced to places she hadn't considered earlier in the case. "Honey and her sons might already be in danger."

Rick understood where her focus was going. He needed to rein her in, before in her mind she turned Brinkman into a serial killer. "Brinkman has never shown signs of violence. Why would he hurt this wife?" He leaned back to put some distance between them. The scent of her shampoo was spinning around in his head.

"Who knows? He's a sociopath. Maybe he does have dead wives somewhere. We don't know for sure. And if Honey discovered his game, she may have threatened him with arrest. Or she might have made some innocent comment that set him off. I've watched enough murder shows to know that there could be a number of reasons a husband, or wife, can snap. Add a sociopathic personality and Brinkman could explode."

Yes, she did watch too many murder shows.

"Or he may be living happily somewhere off the proceeds of his thefts," he countered. Yep, Taryn had molded Brinkman into a serial killer. "Until we find signs that she's been harmed, you shouldn't jump to the conclusion she was murdered. Let's focus on finding them and forget the rest, for now."

Taryn returned to the screen and sighed. "You're right. I'm letting my imagination run crazy. Why don't we check out this unit and see what we find?"

A quick mobile mapping app gave them directions to the facility. It wasn't far. They also did internet searches for more information on Honey and her sons. Taryn got a hit on Honey, but found nothing on Joey and Ronnie. At least not the Joey and Ronnie Comstocks they were looking for. The Facebook ages and pictures, under both names, didn't match. "Odd. Joey and Ronnie have no online presence."

"Some people don't use social media," Rick said.

"True. However, it's unusual for their age group. Even my mom, who's in her sixties, has a Facebook account."

She pulled up the link to Honey. "She still has an active Match-Mate page, though it shows no recent activity." Honey was slightly weathered looking, under overly processed blond hair, but her smile was engaging. "No wonder Surfer Chad found her hot. She doesn't look like any mom I know."

Rick didn't disagree. He leaned in for a better look. "She claims to be forty-three. Unless she had Joey when she was fifteen, she's shaved a few years off her profile," he said. Ten if he were to guess.

"She likes long walks on the beach and drinking wine in front of a fireplace." Taryn made a face. "What a cliché."

"Yes, but she's had over a hundred hits. Something about her profile drew the men in."

"Her low-cut top, perhaps?" she said.

Rick couldn't argue that one. The picture showed Honey in distressed jeans and a tight white halter top. The top enhanced her surgically modified assets. "Brinkman may have met the love of his life."

Having spent years hanging with low-life drug dealers and gangbangers, he'd seen many women with Honey's hard look. Without knowing anything about her, he felt sure that he could make up a fairly accurate profile anyway.

"I suspect the new Mrs. Brinkman has spent some time on a stripper pole. If I'm right, then Brinkman may have gotten in over his head with her. She'd be streetwise and not easily duped."

"Then we're back to her being in danger." Taryn closed the laptop. "Let's go and stake out the storage facility. We may get lucky and Brinkman will show up."

They both knew that was unlikely. Still, it was their best lead so far. At this point, nothing should be dismissed.

They left the motel and stopped for coffee on the way.

The facility consisted of a gated fence to keep undesirables out, a small white office building that sat off to the left side, and four long rows of orange and gray connecting metal units. An open field ran up to the fence on one side and, behind the property, in an upside down L, a community of duplexes sat on the other side.

Although they had the number of Joey's unit, they couldn't get close enough to find the exact location without getting on the property and alerting the owner of the white Ford Fiesta parked outside the office.

"I guess we wait until dark and sneak in," she said. Taryn pulled the Olds across the street and parked next to a closed furniture store. From there, they could see the entrance of Affordable U-Store, if not much else. "You're about to find out what it's like to watch grass grow."

Remembering her earlier comment about the boredom of stakeouts, he finished his coffee and settled back for a long couple of hours, as Taryn pulled out and opened up her laptop. From the intense look on her face, he figured she wouldn't be up for another round of twenty get-to-know-you questions, so he leaned his head against the seat and closed his eyes.

Looking up from her laptop a little while later, to see why Rick was so quiet, Taryn shook her head. "Some PI you are," she whispered to her sleeping companion. "Five minutes and you're out."

She glanced back across the street and saw a red pickup leaving the facility, with a bed full of boxes and a rolled-up rug. The man behind the wheel was big and bald with a runaway gray beard. The woman beside him appeared to be in her sixties. Distance kept her from concluding anything more, but either way, they weren't the Comstocks or Brinkman.

Satisfied, she dropped her eyes back to the computer screen.

Another hour of digging around found nothing on the Comstock boys and only one more hit on Honey. She was mentioned in a four-year-old obituary, listed as the wife of the decedent, one Arthur Prinz, of Westland, Michigan.

Forty-seven-year-old Arthur Prinz.

This caught her attention. She scanned the obituary and discovered that Arthur had died in a freak car accident with a runaway cement truck. The couple had only been married for six weeks. Honey Comstock had kept her name. Either that or hadn't had time to change it over. The ink hadn't yet dried on her marriage license before she was widowed.

"From widow to con victim. Poor Honey." This was consistent with what had happened to several of Brinkman's other wives. They'd all been widowed when he'd duped them. This showed a pattern of familiar behavior he'd used for decades.

Teddy was a consummate con. He swooped in when the women were vulnerable. And if Honey collected on a lawsuit or insurance payout, he'd be all over that like a shark on blood in the water.

She hated him already.

Rick slept on.

Time ticked by slowly. She updated the file, played an online game of Scrabble, watched the sunset, and waited for the lights to go off in the office of Affordable U-Store. Finally, a shadowy figure walked from the small building to the Fiesta, climbed in, and drove off. The gate closed behind him.

"Rick, wake up." She poked him.

One gray eye opened. "I was just resting my eyes."

"Uh-huh. For the last three hours?"

He grinned and sat up, scratching his jaw. The back of his hair stuck up in an endearing sort of way. "I'd apologize but you're the one getting paid to watch the grass grow. I'm just along for the ride."

"Then you want to stay in the car?"

"Not a chance."

Taryn filled him in on Honey's widowhood, popped the trunk, and climbed from the Olds. She stretched her back as she walked around the car to retrieve her stakeout kit. Inside the plastic toolbox were all the things she needed when on stakeout, including a couple of extra water bottles and a half-finished paperback. She pulled out two flashlights and handed Rick the smaller one.

"An heir and a spare in case the batteries die in my Maglite. And these are for you." She pulled out two pairs of latex gloves and gave him a pair. "In case we find evidence of anything criminal." She collected a hand-sized black zipped pouch and closed the box. She took her Mace but left her Glock behind in its locked case. It would be hard to climb a fence with it and, after all, what kind of trouble could there be in a closed storage facility? "Let's go."

It wasn't quite dark enough to hide them from neighbors in the duplex complex, so they waited for a break in traffic to run across the street and make their way to the field side of the fence. The vegetation was mostly wild grass and a few clumps of something taller, a weed with lacy white flowers on top. Queen Anne's Lace, she thought.

"Keep close to the fence," she said softly.

Rick stepped in behind her. "Why are you whispering? This isn't the Watergate break-in. And I don't see guards or dogs."

She glared over her shoulder. "Yes, but someone might call the cops if they hear us or see us lurking around. Why take that chance? I don't want to go to jail for breaking and entering."

Summer and Jess would find her incarceration amusing.

"If you do get arrested, I'm sure Hunter will bake you a cake with a file in it, or throw you over the prison wall to freedom with his big biceps."

Taryn squelched a snort of laughter, but shook silently with good humor. "I don't know why he bothers you so much. We only had one unsuccessful date."

"He doesn't bother me."

"Sure. You stick with that story." She rounded the fence to the back of the property and looked for a place to go over. A row of parked campers and trailers would hide them from the street so she stopped there. She handed him the flashlight, grabbed the fence, and stuck her toe in a chain link. "I like that you're jealous. Just don't mark your territory by humping my leg or piddling on my boots. It would be embarrassing for both of us."

He grunted in response as she pushed off the ground. His free hand clamped under her butt and shoved her up.

"I can do this myself," she said and gripped the top of the fence for stability.

"I just want to be helpful."

"How? By checking the fit of my jeans?"

"Something like that."

The man did have big, strong hands. What do they say about a man with big hands? Never mind. She pivoted on top of the fence and jumped down on the other side.

She accepted the flashlights through the fence and waited for him to climb over. He dropped to the ground, grinned wickedly, and stepped close. Too close.

Taryn's stomach fluttered as he reached for her.

"Sweetheart, if I wanted to mark my territory, it would go something like this . . ." His hand slipped around her neck and his warm mouth came down on hers.

The kiss was firm and too brief but when he released her seconds later, she was all warm and fuzzy inside.

"Hunter who?" she said.

His soft laughter filled the night.

Chapter 8

Damn, Taryn tasted good. As he'd suspected she would. Like cinnamon gum and a chocolate bar. No, really. Cinnamon. Chocolate. She'd been snacking while he was sleeping.

Maybe that was a normal part of her stakeouts. What wasn't part of a watching-the-grass-grow stakeout, and subsequent breaking and entering plan, was kissing his PI. That was all him. And he knew it was a mistake. But thinking that and being sorry were two different things; common sense warred with wanting to kiss her again. Neither came out a winner.

The kiss had stirred up the sleeping beast in his briefs and he had to step back or risk seducing her on the cracked concrete pad that ran beneath the nearby campers. Cement would be hell on his bare knees.

Better yet, a camper would make a perfect place for seduction. For a moment, he wondered if any of them were unlocked. Campers had beds, and privacy. If he ever got Taryn naked, he wanted a mattress, not cement, beneath them.

Before he could formulate a really hot fantasy about rocking the camper off its wheels, she quickly walked away with a sexy hip sway, leaving him and his lusty thoughts behind. But she couldn't distance herself from the reaction he'd felt with the kiss. She'd been just as into it as he'd been.

Oh, hell. He was falling into familiar patterns when it came to women. Through no fault of her own, Rick was spending more time thinking of Taryn than planning the demise of Teddy Brinkman. That's what got his mother into trouble the first time. His inattention.

Focus, Silva, he told himself. Focus.

A tall streetlight stood on each end of the lot, giving off just enough dim light to chase off total darkness and discourage burglars. Crickets sang in the field and he swore he heard a bullfrog in the distance. Making a quick sweep of the area with his eyes, he relaxed a bit. Thankfully, there was no sign of human life forms. Or dogs. So far, so good.

He caught up with Taryn in the middle section of the units, as she examined the numbers on the doors.

"I think we need to go one row over." She casually brushed past him, as if the kiss hadn't happened. He glanced down at her butt as she moved away. He couldn't help himself.

"Keep your mind on business, Special Agent Silva," she said.

His eyes snapped up. Damn. She was one hell of a mind reader. He grinned and followed her around the building.

Certainly one kiss couldn't hurt the case?

Taryn scanned the numbers and stopped at a unit three from the end. "This is forty-five. Here, hold this." She passed over her Maglite then reached into her pocket for the zipped pouch, dropped to her knees in front of the padlock, and went to work.

"What you're doing is illegal." And fascinating. He settled back on his heels to watch. She was quite the criminal for a PI. "Is there any law you won't break in the search for justice?"

"I've done worse than lock-picking. You can turn away if it bothers you to watch."

He stayed put.

Approximately two minutes later, the lock snapped open. She stood, put the kit in her pocket, and retrieved her flashlight. "Let's see what we have."

Rick did the honors and pushed up the wide metal door.

Inside, front and center, was an old cream-colored Pinto with a dented and rusted fender and peeling paint on the hood. A pair of faded fuzzy red dice and a drooping dream catcher hung from the rearview mirror. What was once a stone chip had turned into a crack that went from the center of the windshield all across the passenger side to disappear into some old rubber window trim. All this added to the creepy feeling emanating from the Ford.

They both stood and stared.

Rick broke the silence. "I believe we've found Brinkman's car." He clicked on his own flashlight and stepped into the darkened unit. There wasn't much else in there. A few boxes, some loose paper scattered on the floor, and a mummified dead mouse on its back with its feet in the air in the far corner. A back tire on the Pinto was flat.

"I can't believe the women didn't take one look at this piece of shit and flee," he said. "Only a deadbeat would drive a car like this."

He looked down at the back fender and a cracked bumper sticker that proclaimed, "McGovern for President."

"Jane Clark did say he was good in bed." Taryn touched the hood. "Why would he leave the car here? He must love this piece of junk to keep it around. He probably bought it new."

"It may have died. Or he worried Jane Clark had filed a theft report on her painting and the police were on the lookout for his car. There are not many old Pintos still on the road."

They both donned their gloves and aimed their beams inside the car. "I half expected to find a dead Teddy Brinkman buckled in and rotting behind the wheel," he said.

"One could hope."

Instead were only more loose papers, some odds and ends of junk, and a couple of cases of motor oil on the floor behind the driver's seat. The Pinto probably guzzled the stuff.

"The key's in the ignition," Rick said. He couldn't shake the feeling that something wasn't right about the scene. "So it probably wasn't towed here."

"Hmm. No sign of Jane's painting." Taryn tugged open the passenger side door to a loud squawk of protest from the rusty hinges. She clicked a few photos of the interior with her phone. "I don't see anything of value in here."

Rick opened his door. The handle fell off in his hand and clattered onto the floor. He kicked it aside. "Brinkman probably pawned the expensive stuff and tossed the rest in here." He leaned inside and made a face. "The interior smells like dirty jockstraps and sweaty feet."

A brow went up. "Should I ask how you know what used jockstraps smell like?"

"High school hockey." He lifted a sheet of paper to the flashlight beam. It was a dry cleaner receipt. He folded and pocketed it. "After the game, the uniform smell was brutal. Mom used the heavy-duty laundry detergent to get the stuff clean."

"Ick. Hey, I found a half-eaten French fry." She made a face and threw it over her shoulder. "And a hotel room key. That might be something." She slid it into her back pocket.

They dug around for a while, finding little of evidentiary value, if the case ever went to court. Brinkman had cleared out the car, leaving only junk behind.

She slammed the glove box closed. "No registration. Where's a confession letter or incriminating photos when you need them?" Taryn asked. She tossed aside a gum wrapper.

The boxes held a bunch of trinkets of a life lived mostly in his car: maps, matchbooks, takeout menus from all over, some personal items, an unopened package of tighty-whities, a blanket, all sorts of nothing. She photographed it all.

Rick held up a pencil with a well-chewed eraser. "I'm keeping this in case we need DNA." He added the pencil to the laundry receipt, then stood back and took photos of the car. Taryn joined him.

"Let me see if I can get a VIN," Rick said and came around to her side. "If he did buy this new, the information could lead to his real name."

"I'll text Irving and see if we can get a warrant for a more thorough search."

Rick grabbed her arm. "Did you hear that?"

They fell silent. "I don't hear anything," she whispered.

Then came the muffled sound of slowly approaching footsteps and Rick froze. In unison, they clicked off their flashlights and fell silent. The unit went dark.

"A guard?" Taryn whispered.

"Probably." Damn. Rick put a finger to his lips. His heart thudded. If there was a guard, they were toast. The open door was a giveaway to their presence and there was nowhere to hide. Hopefully he could badge their way out of an arrest. "Stay here." He walked silently to the door, stopped for a moment to listen, then peeked out.

A bullet nearly took off his head.

Taryn cried out as he spun back into the building. A second shot went wide and hit the metal doorframe with a loud snap. They dove behind the Pinto and came up on their hands and knees.

"Shit!" Rick said and did a quick assessment for injuries.

"Are you okay?" she whispered and touched his arm. Her eyes went over him but it was hard to see anything with the flashlights off.

"I'm okay." He peered around the car. Dim light from outside etched shadows into lines on Taryn's worried face. He wanted to assure her that they'd be okay, but he was confused by this turn of events and had no answers. "Who in the hell is shooting?"

"Another burglar?" she offered. "Wait. I swear I just heard the muted sound of two male voices arguing outside."

When he strained to confirm, there was nothing but silence.

"Most thieves don't carry guns." He crawled out from behind the car and headed back to the door. Dropping to his stomach, he carefully looked out. His eyes didn't have time to focus when another pair of shots rang out and bullets hit the outer wall above him. Whoever had the gun wasn't a skilled marksman.

He pushed backward and rejoined Taryn. "We're trapped."

Turning, he sat back and leaned on a tire. "Where's your Glock?"

"In the Olds." At his look, she snapped, "We're searching a storage unit. What would I need a gun for? Shooting spiders?"

She had a point. He hadn't expected danger, either. "Sorry. You're right. I'm unarmed too."

Frustrated, he knew they had to get out of here, but how? There was only the one door for escape. And that wasn't an option. Even if they did get out, they had no protection against bullets in the open alley between the units. But he had to save himself and Taryn. The idea of her being hurt soured his gut.

Before he could get past that grim thought, she nudged him with her elbow, turning his attention to her.

"I have an idea," Taryn said. She stood, went around to the driver's side door, and slid inside. He kneeled and, through the window, watched her put the car in neutral, then step out. "If we push it outside, we can use the car as cover."

He stood and met her at the back of the Pinto. Staring into her shadowed eyes, he said, "Amazing."

A smile split her face. "Thanks." Her hand caught his t-shirt and she pulled him in for a brief kiss. "If we don't survive, it's been nice knowing you, Special Agent Silva."

Rick brushed her chin with his thumb, then pulled back and formulated a quick plan. "Stay low and go right, keeping against the wall. You circle back around on the north side of this unit and head for the front gate. I'll go around the trailers to draw the shooter's attention. We'll meet back at the Olds."

"Got it," she said and added, "Be careful."

"You too."

And they rolled the car out.

The car wobbled to a stop halfway out of the unit on the flat tire. That was the best they had. There was no time to adjust the plan. "Now!" Rick called out in a harsh whisper.

Taryn slid between the car and the door frame, crouched and bolted for safety, Rick on her tail. Shots blasted behind them but the car proved to be an effective barrier. Ancient auto glass shattered and metal pinged as bullets tore into the already damaged Pinto. She took a fast right around the building and then another into the row to the north.

And ran.

Gunfire erupted from the back of the lot and her heart raced over the sound of her rubber soles pounding on the pavement. Her heart twisted with the sound. Let Rick be safe!

It was probably ten seconds to the gate, but seemed more like hours, when trying not to draw the attention of a killer. She was almost to safety when she heard running feet behind her. Panicked, she dove under the gate and rolled to her feet in a fighting stance only to watch Rick slide out under the gate next to her on his stomach. He scrambled to his feet.

"Go!" he yelled. He didn't have to repeat the order.

Shouts and another shot sounded behind them, as they hit the street and raced across. Taryn sighted the shadowy shape of the Olds and took off in that direction. She heard Rick's uneven breathing as he matched her strides. He'd positioned himself behind her as her shield.

Her normally kick-ass PI sensibilities should have been insulted that he thought she needed protection, but at the moment, she appreciated the effort.

When she reached the car, she yanked open the door and jumped inside. The keys were tucked in the visor and she fired up the engine as Rick landed on the seat beside her. "Hang on!"

Rick grabbed the dashboard and strap when she hit the gas and the car jerked forward. Two men in dark hoodies scrambled to a stop in the middle of the street, one firing the gun at the moving car. Taryn banked right and ducked, as several shots hit the battered Olds. The men jumped out of the way as the car bore down on them.

The Olds fishtailed left. She righted the beast and punched the gas pedal, narrowly avoiding an oncoming panel truck. Within seconds, they were out of bullet range. She waited until they were miles from the storage facility and out of the city before letting herself relax and ease back on the gas.

The high-beams split the darkness, as she kept a look out behind them in case they were being followed. When she was sure they were in the clear, she pulled off on a quiet dirt road bracketed by cornfields and put the car in park. Her breath came in shattered gasps through an invisible weight on her chest.

She'd never been shot at before.

"What in the hell just happened?" She glanced at Rick and found him slumped in the seat and grinning. "Have you lost your mind? We almost got murdered and you find that amusing?"

"Sweetheart, I've never been so happy to have you behind the wheel. That was one hell of a getaway. Thank God for the crazy woman driver."

"I'm not a crazy—" The rest of her admonishment died, when something out of place caught her attention in the glowing green light from the dashboard; a red smear on his upper arm. A sickening dread turned her cold.

"Oh no. Rick, you're bleeding! You've been shot!"

Chapter 9

Taryn flicked on the tiny penlight dangling from her keychain and aimed it at Rick. Blood seeped from his upper left arm to cause spots of red on his shirt. They were hard to see with the backdrop of the black tee, but clear enough to confirm her assessment. This wasn't a scratch. He'd been hit.

Her stomach clenched. "Take off your shirt and let me see the damage."

He looked down at his arm and gently probed the spot with his fingertip. The only reaction was an almost imperceptible wince. "It's nothing."

Stubborn man. "It isn't nothing. We have to get you to the hospital before you bleed out."

"No hospital." He made a face. "I'm not going to bleed out, Taryn. I've had worse."

"You've been shot before?"

"Grazed." He grinned. "That doesn't count."

Great. She turned off the car and pulled the trunk latch. Facing him straight on with her best "I'm not taking any bullshit from you" glare, she ordered, "Then get out of the car. I'll take care of it myself."

Without waiting for him to obey her command, she went in search of her toolkit. Without the flashlights, which had been left at the storage unit, her options for lighting the area were limited. Thankfully, she had the penlight and the headlights. Between the two, there should be enough light to patch Rick up. Hopefully.

"You should see a doctor." She walked to where he'd taken a seat on the hood. She dropped the toolkit beside him with a thump to show her aggravation. "There is only so much I can do if you have a bullet lodged inside your arm. If you get an infection and your arm falls off, don't blame me."

"I trust you, Doctor Brash." His half smile and the warmth of his knee against her hip almost made her forget the gravity of the situation.

"I'm not brash."

"Certainly you are . . . while driving."

Instead of arguing, she got to work. "The first aid kit is meant for bug bites and scraped knees. Not bullet wounds." She took out an antiseptic pad and ripped the foil wrapper open with her teeth. "Take off your shirt."

Wincing, he got it up far enough to expose a seriously ripped stomach and stopped. "I think I need help."

From the look in his eyes, she wondered if he needed assistance or just wanted her to undress him. Either way, she couldn't work without it off.

She laid the antiseptic pad on the discarded wrapper.

Without hesitation, she tugged at the hem. Keeping her manner clinical, she tried to ignore the tattoo resembling some sort of hieroglyphic on his upper right arm. It was all one color, blackish, and very cool. She struggled not to trace her fingertip over it, but her eyes followed it down from shoulder to elbow.

The muscle beneath it flexed. Once. Twice. Three times.

"I'm not looking," she said, jerking her eyes away.

He chuckled. "I didn't think so."

Frowning, she maneuvered the shirt over his head, leaving the damaged arm covered. Her eyes kept getting drawn back to the tattoo. She'd never been a fan of ink, but on Rick it upped his sexual appeal.

Geez. Did the man have any flaws?

Move on, Taryn. "I'm going to ease the shirt off your arm." She held it bunched in her hands. "I'll go slowly. Hopefully, it won't hurt too much."

A little at a time, she slid the shirt down over his left arm, exposing the head of a large scorpion, then its body and tail. Every nerve ending inside her buzzed, her breath caught, and her lips parted. She barely registered the seeping wound inside the curled tail.

"Like it?" he said softly.

"I, um." Not only did she like it, she had the sudden urge to rip off her clothes. And his. "It's, ah, okay. If you enjoy that sort of thing."

Rick chuckled again. "Good thing you're immune, then. I wouldn't want you to start thinking sexy thoughts about me."

Heat flashed up her body, taking up residence in her face. How could he know what she was thinking? Did he see heat in her eyes or was it just a good guess?

Biting back a frustrated groan, she disregarded the teasing, dropped the shirt on the hood beside him, and reached for the pad.

Unfortunately, Rick wasn't finished flirting with her. "If you wanted to see me shirtless, all you had to do was ask."

"I have no interest in you *sans* clothing."

"Then why did you kiss me?"

One brow lifted. "A kiss in the heat of the moment is all that was. We were in danger. I thought we were about to die."

"If you say so."

Choosing to let the comment drop, she went into doctor mode. Even in the low light, his chest was amazing: hard, scarred, with just a light dusting of hair to play with. Just right.

If not for the blood slowly seeping from his arm, she might well have forgotten all about that whole client-PI thing and done something really stupid, like a full body exploration. With her mouth. That would be a disaster.

"Is that where you were shot?" She pressed the pad gently on the wound and looked over the rest of him for any other damage. She pointed to a puckered scar that marred an otherwise perfectly muscled stomach.

"Stabbed." He touched the spot. "Shanked, actually. A gangbanger wanted my mashed potatoes. I said no. He politely asked again with a sharpened toothbrush. I didn't react quickly enough to the warning signs. I got four stitches and he got a compound fracture of the tibia."

"And the potatoes?" She brushed aside his hand and touched the scar. His skin was warm and soft beneath her fingertips.

"Lumpy and dry. I should've let him have them." He twisted to the left and pointed to a scar the shape of a caterpillar right below his rib cage. "This was from a bullet."

"Should I ask?" She touched the old wound.

"Drive-by."

Releasing a breath through pursed lips, she shook her head and said, "Interesting."

And he'd called her a menace.

Before her hand turned the touch into a caress, she returned her attention back to his arm.

"I thought you said you stayed out of the general population?" She drew the wipe over the wound. The antiseptic pad cleared away the blood so she could examine the wound. Rick was right. It wasn't fatal. "And yet you got shanked."

"True. But I still had to show up enough to establish a presence. The man I was hunting had eyes everywhere. Getting stabbed was actually good. It gave me prison cred."

Men. Only a man would take pride in getting stabbed.

She lifted the penlight and squinted for a better view of the torn tissue. "This doesn't look like a bullet wound. Hand me the needle-nose pliers. There's something under the skin."

"You stock pliers in your PI kit?"

"Yes, and two screwdrivers, a small pry bar, and a hammer. I'm always prepared for any eventuality." She cleaned the pliers with a second antiseptic wipe. "If I have to play field surgeon, I don't want to give you a fatal infection."

"I appreciate your concern." He rattled around in the box with his free hand, while she unhooked the penlight from the keychain and put it between her teeth.

"Here you go, Girl Scout," he said. Taryn handed him the first aid kit and he gave her the pliers.

With the light illuminating the shallow wound, she could just see the edge of what looked like broken glass. She gently probed the wedge and after two tries, managed to get a hold on the slippery edge and pull it out.

Rick didn't flinch.

"Got it," she said, slightly slurring her words around the flash-light, and laid the shard and pliers on the hood.

Blood trickled out of the cut. "Hand me the big pad." With him acting as her surgical assistant, and Taryn using the skills she'd picked up from watching hospital dramas on TV, they managed to patch him up with gauze and medical tape.

"Not bad." She removed the flashlight and stepped back to examine her work. Even the scorpion seemed happy with the final outcome.

"Not bad at all, with no medical training. I may have picked the wrong profession."

"I'd like to see you in hospital whites." His hand caressed her hip, before moving up to hook his thumb in her belt loop.

She looked up to see him staring at her, his eyes soft and smiling. Darn, he was way too handsome for comfort.

A couple of steps to the left and she'd be in his arms and kissing him again. Instead, she moved back, collected the semi-clean discarded wipe she'd used on the pliers and cleaned his blood off her hands.

"You shouldn't look at me like that," she said. "We're working partners. That's it."

"I think you like me looking at you like that."

"You're delusional."

"And yet you kissed me."

There was that. "We've already covered this. Kisses during a life-and-death situation don't count."

He slid off the hood and leaned his hard butt against the car. Crossing his arms caused his upper arms to flex, showcasing the tattoos and causing heat to flow back through her body.

Was it wrong to want to unzip his Levi's and answer the burning question foremost in her mind: boxers or briefs?

Well, that wasn't the foremost thought keeping her awake at night. It was more about a part of his anatomy that was covered by said skivvies.

Lord, she needed alcohol, and lots of it.

"So you don't want to kiss me again?" he said.

Anything she said at this point would be a lie. She wanted to throw her heated body against his long muscled self and kiss the hell out of him, explore his tattoos, cup his butt, and test the size of the backseat with their naked bodies. Rick was everything she wanted but didn't need—another bad boy to run over her heart with his big, bad motorcycle.

The next man she took to bed would be stable and settled; a relationship kind of guy.

No more bad boys for her.

And this man was bad. Very, very bad.

"Kissing you was a mistake. You kissing me was your mistake."

She collected her things and tucked everything back into her PI kit, all while squelching the silent command from her body to forget caution and have some really great sex. Because a guy like Rick wouldn't leave her unsatisfied.

Yet she couldn't take that leap. Not now. Not with this man and his sexy tattoos. "From now on, no kissing."

All sorts of emotions filtered through his eyes. When he finally spoke, the words were a surprise.

"I agree. Kissing and sex are a distraction from the case." He reached for his shirt and eased it over his head. Taryn stayed back and didn't help. "Our focus is catching Brinkman."

Although she wasn't certain he was serious—the attitude adjustment had been awfully quick—but she had to take him at his word. Life would be a lot easier if he wasn't looking at her like she was his favorite snack food.

"I think we should call it a night. If you feel feverish and need to go to the hospital, phone me."

"I will."

She dropped Rick at his hotel and headed home. She slowed to turn into her driveway, when a large figure darted across the road, in a flash of her headlights, and vanished behind a hedge that fronted the red brick ranch opposite her house.

Strange. Her mind reached for but couldn't grasp why someone would be out at this hour without a dog to walk or a backpack full of college books. Crime was low in the neighborhood, outside of petty thefts of stuff like lawn furniture or car stereos.

She pulled in and parked. There was something familiar about the way the man carried himself. But she couldn't place him among the neighbors. She was too tired to put the pieces together so she let it go. The guy was probably someone new to the neighborhood out chasing his cat.

Taryn was not entirely surprised to see Andrew sitting in the darkness on her front steps after she got her stuff out of the car and headed for the front door. The fact that he wouldn't look her in the eye as she approached was concerning.

"Hey, kid." She sat beside him. "What's up? More panties in my tree?"

Chapter 10

Andrew stared at his feet through his thick glasses, his worried face illuminated by his cell phone. Whatever troubled him was serious and he'd come to her for advice. It made her feel sort of sisterly toward the nerdy panty-peeper.

She leaned sideways and nudged him with her shoulder. "Look, Andrew. You'll feel better if you get out what's bothering you. We bonded the other day over beer cans and thongs. You can tell me anything."

While she watched his inward struggle, she hoped he wasn't going to tell her about something gross, like STDs or foot fungus. With hormonal teen boys, one never knew.

"I'm afraid you might hurt me," he blurted out.

Not gross. Worse.

"What have you done?" She turned on the step to face him. He shifted his upper half away from her and seemed poised to bolt. Instead, he pulled out his phone, swiped a finger across the screen, and slowly turned it to face her.

Taryn watched in horror as a ten-second video clip played out in full, clear color.

Someone had caught her the other day with her boot on Andrew's chest, her hair in disarray around her angry face, and her finger pointed in his direction. Wearing all black and acting seriously badass, she'd looked like an outraged warrior princess.

"What in the heck?" She yanked the phone out of his hand and hit replay. If not for the clear invasion of her privacy, she'd have appreciated that she did look kind of good. Sexy, even. She never realized how much she rocked dressed in boots and black jeans.

But that wasn't the point. "Who took this? Take it down!"

Andrew shook his head, his face morose, like he was worried she'd hate him. Or hurt him. She was leaning toward the latter. "It's too late. The video's gone viral. You already have one hundred twelve thousand hits."

She gaped. "One hundred twelve thousand?"

"Guys think you're hot," he rushed on. "Women want to be you. At least that's what the eight thousand four hundred and two comments say."

Shocked, she felt the blood rush from her head and pool at her feet. "Is this a joke? Please tell me that one percent of the entire American population is not watching me kick your ass."

"Well, the percentage isn't that high." At her glare he gulped and rushed on, "Sorry. Taryn, it's not bad to be viral. Really. You're even cooler than kitten videos."

Great. As if that helped. She was the YouTube flavor of the week and couldn't do a darn thing about it.

The irony of the situation was not lost on her. She'd taken her share of videos of cheating spouses and other such nonsense, but that was business. This wasn't the same. Was it?

"At least you weren't naked," Andrew said helpfully.

Instead of freaking out over the idea of a hundred thousand people watching her threaten Andrew, while he was sprawled in a bed of panties, she leaned back and rubbed her eyes. "There is that." She didn't try to hide her sarcasm. "Who took this?"

"I d-don't know."

"I have a gun."

He paled, gingerly took the phone from her hand, and slid back a foot or so. Not enough for safety. He was still within reach, if she wanted to twist off his head.

"I can't tell you, Taryn. It's the bro code. We don't rat on each other."

Taryn knew several painful ways she could torture the information out of him. And thoroughly enjoy doing each. However, she liked Andrew and didn't seriously want to kill him. Well, maybe a little. Still, the damage was already done. And like he said, she wasn't naked. Still, she had to make sure this didn't happen again. She didn't want her neighbors spying on her for internet glory.

"Keep your secret then, Andrew. But I want you to go back over there to your fourteen bros and give them this message." She leaned forward, her eyes taking on a wicked gleam. "If anyone ever takes a video or pictures of me again, while I'm on my property, I'll make him very, very sorry." She leaned forward and whispered. "I know people."

His Adam's apple bobbed and his eyes went wide. "Okay." He jumped up and scurried off.

Taryn shook her head as the door next door slammed shut behind him. There was only one thing worse than college kids with cell phone cameras and that was their need to take pictures and videos of everything and post them online.

She pulled out her phone and loaded up the video. There was nothing indicating her name, where she lived, or the city of origin. She wouldn't have freaks chasing her around Ann Arbor. Well, hopefully not.

Standing, she forwarded the link on to Summer and Jess. They'd have a good laugh.

Once inside, she closed the curtains on Andrew's side of the house. No sense taking chances.

Her cell beeped. A text.

Jess: New boyfriend?

Summer: He's hot. ☺

Jess: Nerdy young stud.

Summer: Easy to train.

Jess: Youthful stamina.

Summer: Good point.

Taryn: You 2 are hysterical.

Taryn put her things on the end table and headed for the stairs. She liked living alone, but the one thing she missed was having someone to come home to at the end of the day. Though she knew she could call her friends anytime and chat, it wasn't the same as snuggling up to a partner and downloading her latest adventure. And tonight had been quite an adventure.

Rick. Her mind involuntarily went to him. She wondered if he gave good foot rubs with those strong hands.

The doorbell rang. "What now?" She was exhausted, had Rick's blood under her fingernails, and needed a shower.

Walking to the door, she peered out the window and saw a bouquet of flowers obscuring a male head. The dim light from the porch made it difficult to figure out whose. Rick? Nope, not tall enough. Andrew? God, she hoped not.

She swung the door open. The flowers swung right. The bearer of the blooms was blond with bright blue eyes, thin, and appeared to be about twelve. It was probably the braces. Or the oversize blue suit that hung on bony shoulders.

"Can I help you?"

The kid grinned, flashing blue wires and a pair of rubber bands pulling the braces back from what was probably once a severe, and still lingering, overbite.

"Hi. These are for you." He shoved what looked like a bronze urn stolen off a gravesite into her hands, slopping water over the rim and onto her sock-covered feet.

"Thank you?" What else could she say? She had nothing. "And you are?"

"Thurston Covington Weatherwax the Third." He beamed. "Of the New York Weatherwaxes."

"Um, okay." She held out the urn to keep water and damp potting soil from dripping on her shirt. Suspecting where this was going, she sighed inwardly and wished she'd ignored the bell. What was with her and men with roman numerals after their names?

"Do I know you?"

"I hope so," he said. He straightened up to an imposing five-six or so, just enough to look her in the eyes. "I brought you flowers with the hope that you'll do me the honor of having dinner with me this Friday night?"

Dinner? What? Happy meals? This had to be a joke. She wouldn't put it past Jess and Summer to set this up after hearing about her meeting with Andrew. She'd set them both up on blind dates that ended badly. This would be a perfect payback.

"Do your parents know you're here?" She looked out for a waiting parental car parked at the curb. Nope. Nothing. "Are you sure you have the right house? How did you get here?" School bus?

"I live next door."

No way. "You live with the college guys?"

"I am a college guy," he said proudly. "And you are Taryn, so I'm at the right house.

Yep, this was a joke. She stepped out onto the porch and looked around for Jess or Summer. There was no sign of them. Uh-oh, this wasn't a joke. "How old are you, Thurston?"

"Fourteen," he said and puffed up his narrow chest. "But I'm mature for my age."

Sigh. "Kid, you'll have to mature another four years for a romance between us to not be a crime in most states, and two in Michigan." She sat the urn on the porch next to a post. The flowers did dress up the peeling paint.

Thurston stepped closer, not at all put off by her comment about their age difference. "I'll take the risk if you will."

The cloying smell of an aftershave bath tickled her nose.

Outside of a clear case of boyish charm, and a puppy dog cuteness, it was impossible to find anything else in the youngster standing before her that would entice her to risk decades of incarceration in order to date a kid who couldn't even drive. And that was the least disturbing of all the reasons not to date a fourteen-year-old.

Taryn needed a beer. Or six.

"How can you live off campus at your age?" she said, hoping to distract him from any further attempts to ask her out. "Are you old enough to leave home?"

He shrugged. "My brother, Byron, lives with me. He's eighteen. I'm a genius, so I'm in college. What do you say? I have my mom's credit card. We can tear up the town."

Heartbreak was a lesson all youngsters would learn, but this was the first time she'd had to let down a boy under eighteen. It was his hopeful expression that tugged at her. Had she been born ten years later, she might have given him a chance. But she had panties older than him. And she enjoyed life outside of prison bars.

"Look, Thurston." She gentled her tone. If she was going to flat-out reject the kid, she'd be gentle. "I appreciate the flowers and the invitation. I really do. But you are eleven years younger than me. I can't date you."

His face fell. Desperation replaced hope. "I'll give you my *Star Wars* collectables if you say yes."

Taryn bit back a smile. He was a charming kid. "Not even for that, buddy."

"Darn." He walked to the stairs, paused, and turned back. "You can keep the flowers."

"Thank you, Thurston." She watched him shuffle down the steps, along the sidewalk, and vanish into the house.

Taryn hoped this was the last of the crazies from next door.

Chapter 11

Taryn walked past Gretchen, with a good morning and a perfunctory glance at her newest pre-Thanksgiving sweater. Against a bright orange backdrop, it appeared as if two smiling turkeys were fornicating on her breasts.

A second horrified glance assured her that they were actually dancing and not making baby turkeys. Yipes.

She hurried away.

"Hey." Summer's blue eyes turned away from the screen when Taryn stepped into her office. She gave Taryn an assessing once-over. "You look rested."

After sending Thurston away, she'd showered, dropped on her bed, and slept through the next fourteen hours. Surprisingly, Rick hadn't invaded her dreams. She'd taken that as a sign that keeping their relationship impersonal was the right way to go.

"I did." She ran through her day, keeping the kissing parts to herself. "It ended with my getting asked on a date."

Blue eyes lit up. "That's something good, right? Who is the guy? Where did you meet him?"

"He lives in the house next door and he's fourteen."

Summer snort-laughed and said in her best Texas drawl, "Darlin', you do like them young'uns."

"Sadly, his is the best offer I've had in months." Well, there was Rick. But his offer was more of the implied sexual variety and not the innocent date night sort. Telling Summer about that would only bring more drama, so she kept the topic on Thurston. "He brought flowers."

"What a sweetheart," Summer said. "Too bad my younger sister lives in Dallas. I'd ask you to fix her up with one of your teenage admirers."

Summer was blond, blue-eyed, and beautiful. She was built like a fifties pinup, which often led people to stereotype her. Well, men mostly. She was no bubblehead. And once she opened her mouth, they never made that mistake again.

This led her to a general aversion toward dating. She wanted to be appreciated for her brain, not her breasts.

"Did I miss my invite to the party?" Jess joined them and sat on the desk. She was dressed in camo pants and matching tee for a case involving a man poaching deer off-season. She looked like she was about to be shipped to Afghanistan. "What did I miss?"

Taryn filled her in. Jess smiled and shook her head. "It sounds like *Animal House* moved in next door."

"Geez, I hope not," Taryn said. "I'm too old for drunken keg parties."

"No one is that old," Jess said. She ran her hand through her messy and cropped brown hair. The cut was something new for her; edgy and fun. Taryn liked it. Jess had the face to pull off short hair.

Irving didn't prefer it. He wanted his women PIs to have long hair in memory of a 70s TV show.

"Irving is too old," Summer quipped.

"Irving was born at the same time as dirt," Jess said.

Taryn jumped in, "He's so old that his mother put mastodon milk in his bottles."

"I heard that!" Irving said from the hallway. The trio spun around and flushed guiltily, as Gretchen wheeled him past the open door. "For your information, it was saber-tooth tiger milk. Get your facts straight, young'uns."

The three laughed. Jess stood. "I have to go. I have a poacher to catch."

Once Summer and Taryn were alone again, they got to work.

"Have you found anything new about Teddy?" Taryn said.

"No, but I did contact three women he dated recently, before marrying his latest wife." She clicked three Match-Mate profiles up on the screen. Two were in their sixties and one was thirty-seven. "They all thought he was charming at first. It was his interest in their financial status that chased them off."

"Smart ladies."

"The youngest one said he bragged about owning a property in Vail, Colorado, but I found nothing to prove that. She thought he was too old for her anyway and cut him loose. He'd told her he was forty-five. She didn't buy that, either."

"He probably lied to look better in her eyes, once she realized he wasn't forty-five," Taryn said. "How did he think he could pass for that young?"

"I honestly think some people use fake information and pictures, hoping that their personalities will overcome the fibs once they're face to face with a date," Summer said. "They don't get that attraction can't be forced, and that there is someone out there for every size, age, and interest. So be honest."

"You're right. I suspect it seldom works out for the one lying."

Gretchen popped her head in. "Mr. Silva is here for you."

"Send him back," Summer said before Taryn could stand. At her frown, Summer shrugged. "What? I hear he's cute."

"He is cute," Gretchen said, and she and her fornicating turkeys left.

"I thought you were off men?" Taryn didn't know why she didn't want Rick to meet Summer. Oh, right. Every man turned into a slobbering idiot around her friend.

"It doesn't mean I can't look," Summer said.

Just this once, Taryn didn't want to be relegated to second place. Selfish, she knew, since she didn't want him for herself.

It wasn't that she resented Summer for what God gave her. And Summer would never go after anyone Taryn or Jess liked. But it was hard not to feel invisible when her friend was in a room.

And Rick would be no different than any other guy. Why that irked her had no explanation.

He appeared in the doorway.

Summer sighed.

Taryn scowled.

"You must be Rick Silva." Summer unfolded herself from her chair and stood to her full five foot eight. She wore a form-fitting blue sweater and cream slacks that, though modest, hugged every perfect curve. A ray of heavenly light beamed down and surrounded her blond head in a shimmering unearthly glow as she walked across the room to shake Rick's hand. "I'm Summer."

"Nice to meet you, Summer."

Okay, the glow came from bright fluorescent bulbs in the ceiling. Still, the effect was the same. Rick was grinning and Summer had on her brightest smile.

Taryn hoped Summer and Rick's wedding registry would contain affordable gifts and that her bridesmaid's dress wouldn't be hideous. At the same time, she knew she was being silly. And worse . . . jealous.

Rick's amused eyes darted her way. Her stomach tingled. "Taryn's told me all about you."

She'd done nothing of the sort. He'd obviously seen her reaction to his meeting Summer and was ruffling her up.

"I hope we can find Brinkman for you," Summer was saying as Taryn yanked her eyes away from him and returned her attention to Summer. "This man is a menace to society."

Summer's sweet drawl was doing its job. Rick turned back to her and was transfixed. At least that's how Taryn saw it. His eyes were locked onto her friend's face and he wore the dopey expression of love at first sight.

If anything good was to come of the pair's mutual attraction, it had snapped Taryn out of her growing crush and proved to her that Rick was only a client and nothing more. She was happy she'd gone no further than a couple of brief, though still yummy, kisses. They'd get through this case and he'd move on. That's the way it should be.

Rick leaned back against the doorframe, as Summer reclaimed her chair. "How is your arm, Special Agent Silva?"

He rotated the injured limb, exposing the bottom ridge of the taped pad. His bicep bunched beneath the sleeve of his dark blue tee and he winked at Taryn. "As good at new. Taryn does an excellent field dressing."

Summer glanced curiously between them. Taryn shot her a frown. Reading her friend, Summer moved on. "Taryn told me about the events of last night. What is your take on the shooting?"

Rick crossed his arms. "After Taryn dropped me off, I called an acquaintance who got me in touch with a local police detective. The police were already at the storage facility when I reached the officer on his cell and got permission to head over. Neighbors had called in the shots. I met the detective over there. He wasn't happy that we'd jumped the fence or broken into the unit, but I talked him down by promising I'd pay for any damages."

Taryn stewed. "And you didn't call me?"

"I didn't think we both needed to be there. The police found nothing other than spent shell casings to link to the shooter." He paused. "The car's VIN had been removed, so there was nothing new to learn from the Pinto."

If he thought to calm her temper, he failed. "You were the one who wanted to be a team. You came to me for help. Now you're cutting me out of the investigation?"

"I'm not cutting you out." Rick paused and took a deep breath. "You looked half dead on your feet last night. I thought one of us should get some sleep. Had they found something, I would have called. Right now, they're testing the shells and car for fingerprints. That's all."

What he said made sense. She'd been so exhausted that she hadn't thought about contacting the police. And that didn't make her feel any better. She didn't want to look like a second-rate PI in his eyes.

Rick must have read her mind. "I'm sorry. We don't even know if the shooters have anything to do with the case. They were more likely just overzealous burglars."

True. Taryn felt a little better with that reasoning. "What are the odds that someone connected to Brinkman, or Brinkman himself, showed up at the moment we were digging through his car?"

"A zillion to one," Summer offered.

"Still, if he was connected, then this changes the direction of the case." Taryn did a quick mental run-down of the clues. "We haven't had any luck tracking Brinkman the old-fashioned way and Summer hasn't gotten any current hits on his aliases." She leaned forward in her chair. "I think it's time to flush the bastard out online."

Chapter 12

Summer clapped her hands. "Let's do this." She spun in her chair and reached for her keyboard. Within seconds, she was on the Match-Mate site and clicking into the "Setting Up Your Profile" page. "We'll set you up and use the restaurants he used on his other three dates for meet-ups. I have a list."

"Slow down," Rick said, holding up his open hands. "Are you sure you're ready for this?" he asked Taryn. "We can still investigate more locally, without opening this can of worms."

Taryn bit the inside of her cheek.

"Once you put yourself online, you're setting yourself up for a lot of crazy," he added. "Every Tom, Dick, and Psycho will want to date you. We'll spend days, weeks, just slogging through the Catfishes. And Brinkman might not even show."

"You've been watching the show," Taryn said.

"A couple of episodes. Even though Brinkman is another level of con, *Catfish* does come across some unstable people. Do you want to open up your life to that?"

"What alternative do we have?" she said. "The police have our only evidence, and apparently the car wasn't leading us anywhere, anyway. Brinkman clearly hadn't been near the storage unit for quite some time. Jane Clark and the other wives had nothing current to offer, and it looks like our felon has gone underground."

She did have a point. He rubbed his neck and conceded to her argument. "Hell. How hard should it be to find one aging con man?"

Summer, without turning from the screen, piped in, "Very hard. Despite his Match-Mate presence, he's not online. No Facebook, no Instagram, no nothing with any of his aliases. I've set up a program to track his old Social Security number and aliases, if he uses them again, but otherwise I'm all out of leads."

Although Rick knew that eventually Brinkman would make a mistake and get caught, patience wasn't his best asset.

"Most of his old crimes have already elapsed their statute of limitations," Taryn said. "We may only get a few of these to court, including your mother's. If Brinkman's retired from conning and is sitting on the beach somewhere with Honey, he may never resurface. If he isn't retired, he'll be back online once he wipes out her assets."

"Don't forget the shooting," Summer said.

"That may be unconnected," Rick responded.

"Maybe," Summer said. "Maybe not."

He didn't like Summer's words. He didn't like his sense that the shooting was connected to the case and that they were missing a huge chunk of clues. And he didn't like putting Taryn in any sort of danger. However, if he didn't agree to putting her profile on Match-Mate, then she'd just do it anyway without him.

"Do it," he said.

With a nod and smiles from Taryn and Summer, they stepped off the cliff and into online dating.

"Name?" Summer said.

"Terry Jones," Rick said.

"Why?" Taryn asked.

"She was the girl who broke my heart in second grade."

Amused, Taryn turned to meet his eyes. "And you still aren't over her? You may need therapy."

If Summer weren't present, he'd show her how far he was over Terry Jones. He may have agreed last night to keeping things professional, but his body wasn't on board. He wanted Taryn badly. If he could find a way around her objections, he'd like to show her that all men weren't like her ass of an ex. Naked.

Taryn's eyes widened. She must have seen something in his expression, or the wolfish smile on his face, that led her to believe he was thinking naughty things about her. She reddened slightly and turned back to the screen.

"Age?"

"Twenty-five."

"That's too young," Rick said. "Make it thirty-five."

"She doesn't look thirty-five," Summer said.

"Thirty?" Taryn asked.

"This won't work," he grumbled. "Taryn is too young to have a big bank account and she isn't a widow or divorced. Brinkman won't take the bait."

"I'll put in forty and we'll fudge her picture." Summer clicked away. "Profession?"

"Pediatrician," Taryn said. "*Widowed* pediatrician."

At Rick's look she shrugged. "What? It's my profile. I can be what I want. I'll sound compassionate."

"A doctor would be too smart to fall for a con," he said.

"That's where you're wrong," Taryn said. "Women and men will overlook a lot of alarm bells for a shot at love. Besides, a widow is vulnerable and her doctor income will be a draw for Brinkman."

"She's right," Summer said. She added that. "Hobbies or interests?"

"Strolls on the beach, wine, fireplaces, and travel."

Rick cocked up a brow.

Taryn frowned. "Do you think scuba diving with sharks, skydiving, and murder mysteries will hook a guy like Brinkman? I thought not. Dr. Terry is boring and lonely and looking for a man to spice up her life."

Skydiving? Sharks?

Was it wrong that in this moment he wanted to drag her off into the nearest broom closet and kiss the hell out of her? And maybe more?

Was there anything about her he didn't find sexy?

Summer finished up the profile and reached for her phone. "Okay, stand back against the wall and smile."

"The wall is white." Taryn stood. "Won't that be sort of boring?"

"I thought you wanted to be boring?"

"Not enough to induce a catatonic state in my dates," Taryn said. "I have an idea. Follow me."

The three of them walked down the hallway to Irving's office. His door was open. He was lining up a golf ball with a putting thingy. His orange and red plaid pants and orange shirt could cause spontaneous brain seizures in even the heathiest human.

Rick's left eye twitched.

"I thought the doctor wanted you off your feet?" Taryn scolded. "A fractured foot takes time to heal."

"He fell into a sand trap two weeks ago," Summer whispered to Rick.

"What does the doctor know?" Irving made the putt. "I survived a plane crash over the South Pacific in '67. Broke seventeen bones in the landing and was almost eaten by cannibals, before swimming thirty miles to safety. I can survive one broken foot."

"You were also not one hundred and twenty-seven years old then," Taryn scolded. "You should be off your feet."

Irving grinned. "Someday you'll be my age and you'll regret calling me old, young lady. And I'll do as I please, so go mother someone else."

Despite his scolding, Rick heard no anger in his tone. In fact, he was looking at Taryn with fatherly affection. She was glaring back. It was Taryn who looked away first.

"Fine, but if your foot falls off, don't expect me to bandage your stump."

Chuckling, Irving nodded. "Deal."

A moment later, Irving noticed Rick, hobbled over on his walking boot, and stretched out his hand. "You must be a new client?"

"Rick Silva, sir. Nice to meet you."

"Silva?" The old man nodded. "You are working the sweetheart con with Taryn?"

"I am." They released hands.

Irving leaned in and said in a stage whisper, "You need to watch out for that one. If she doesn't kill you with her driving, she'll nag you to death about your health."

"Hey!"

"She is a driving menace," Rick agreed. "You must spend a fortune paying insurance for her car."

The other man nodded again. "Thankfully, I love her like a daughter, so I deduct her road costs on my taxes, as the price of doing business. Otherwise she'd be sorting mail in the basement."

Both men turned to find Taryn scowling and Summer snickering behind her hand. They chuckled.

"Neither one of you is funny," Taryn said. "Come, Summer. Let's get that picture and get out of here before Laurel and Hardy break into their 'Who's on First' routine."

She stalked over to a large painting of the Great Wall of China and stood in front of it. While Summer took several pictures, Irving stepped close to Rick and his voice dropped.

"Taryn is a great girl who's had some bad breaks," Irving said. "She needs some fun in her life and I can sense that she likes you. But if you hurt her, I'll split your skull with my nine iron and dump you in the swamp behind this building."

Rick suspected the senior would have one hell of an aim. They locked eyes and came to a silent understanding.

"Taryn and I are business associates. Nothing more."

The grin showed perfect teeth. "You keep telling yourself that if it helps you sleep better, Mr. Silva."

With that, the man winked and crossed back over to retrieve his golf ball.

"Are you ready to go?"

Rick's voice snapped Taryn back to the present. Summer was looking at her oddly and he had a half-smile on his face.

She didn't care for his expression. He looked like a storefront psychic wearing a cheap turban he'd bought online and waving his hands over a crystal ball, dreaming of bilking gullible clients out of their life savings. Only Rick was short one turban and one crystal ball.

But he certainly seemed to read her mind quite proficiently.

They'd just finished uploading the final file to Match-Mate. Using a photo altering program, Summer had made Taryn look fifteen years older. Rick had been leaning over Summer while they'd done a few last-minute tweaks and Taryn couldn't help but notice, again, how great they looked together.

They'd have stunning children.

After the teasing she'd endured from Rick and Irving, and a good ten minutes of reflection while watching the profile go up, she realized the truth. She had too many quirks to make someone like Rick an ideal match. Even in a temporary relationship. Rick would do far better with a sweetheart like Summer.

Heck, she hadn't kept her husband happy and she had been legally bound to him. This further proved her theory. She wasn't good at relationships. So why bother starting something new?

"I'm ready." She stood and walked out. Her head pounded and

she couldn't stop thinking about Rick kissing Summer the way he'd kissed her. Rick was probably thinking the same thing. Summer was every man's fantasy.

Taryn made it to the front door before he moved ahead of her and held open the door. They rode down the elevator in silence. They arrived at the car before he spoke again.

"You didn't tell me your friend was beautiful."

A prick of irritation slid up her spine. "So?"

"Do you think she'd go out with me? I'm free tomorrow night for drinks and . . . whatever."

The camel's back broke.

Taryn spun on a booted foot, ready to give him all the reasons why she was not a matchmaker, how Summer had better taste in men and would never go out with him, and why she didn't care what he did, when the look on his face stopped her.

Gray eyes danced with amusement.

He was messing with her. It seemed to be his game of choice, and she'd swallowed the bait like a starving carp taking a tasty worm on a hook. He knew she was jealous and used it to tease her.

Letting out an explosive breath, she wanted to Mace him. Too bad the can was in her bag. "You are one aggravating man, you know that?"

"So I've been told. And that's why you like me."

She pulled out her keys. "I don't like you, not even a little bit. I'd rather befriend Jack the Ripper than call you anything more than a temporary annoyance."

Rick caught her stare and his eyes narrowed. He stepped toward her, backing her up against the car. The sun-heated metal shimmered through her thin top and seared her skin. However, it was the heat in his eyes that burned the most. She hungered for his kisses, wanted him to kiss her again.

Taryn's breath caught and she tried to redirect her thoughts. The man knew how to both entice and intimidate her, and she didn't like that feeling. "Step back. I have Mace."

"I don't think you want to Mace me." He tipped his head and murmured in her ear, "I think you want to kiss me."

"You're crazy," she said, breathless, as he pulled back to let his attention linger on her mouth and remained close with a brush of warm breath on her lips. Shivers tingled through her. If she didn't get out of this ASAP, she'd lose all control.

Using a defensive maneuver that would make a Navy SEAL proud, Taryn avoided contact with his lips. She ducked, sidestepped, spun, and managed to get several feet away before he realized he'd lost the opportunity to kiss her and try again.

Chuckling, he straightened and turned. "You are one piece of work, Taryn Hall."

"Thank you. Now get back to work or I *will* Mace you."

Chapter 13

They drove slowly past the storage facility. Taryn wanted to get another look at the place. She just couldn't shake the feeling that getting shot at hadn't been random.

"It's unlikely that Affordable U-Store employs armed guards to protect a bunch of junk that will end up in garage sales when clients tire of paying rent," she said.

"True. This isn't Fort Knox."

She turned around and drove by again. The white car was back and the gate open for clients. It was as if the shooting had never happened.

"If we're correct, this comes back to how Brinkman knew we'd be here at the right moment discovering his car," Rick said when she clued him in to her thoughts on the matter. "Besides, there were two men. I don't think either of them was Brinkman."

"Perhaps he's moved up to having accomplices?" Right now, she was working in the dark. She could tell by his expression that he didn't agree. "Well, whoever did the shooting wanted us away from the storage locker."

Rick nodded. "They won. But what did they get out of it?"

"That remains a mystery."

The police were long gone and the facility back to business. There would be no more jumping the fence today.

Taryn drove on. It was hard to imagine a man on the verge of collecting Social Security hiding himself so well in this age of everyone living online. Yes, he'd had a Match-Mate profile. But the rest of Brinkman's life was conducted offline. He couldn't hide forever. Could he?

Jane Clark had PIs on his trail. She and Rick were hunting him.

And Summer was ready to pounce if he showed up on the web. Yet he was still a ghost.

"Where can he be?" She didn't realize she'd spoken aloud until Rick responded.

He stared out the window as Briarwood Mall came into view. "I doubt we'll find him here."

She drove onto the mall property and down an aisle to an open parking spot. "I need a couple of things for my dates. Most of my dressy clothes are too 'going clubbing' for a forty-year-old widow."

"You do realize that the dates won't believe you're forty."

"I know." She grabbed her bag and exited the car. "But I'm still playing the part."

She dragged him from store to store until he started to grumble under his breath. "Quiet down or I'll make you hold my purse." She found a pair of blue slacks and a white blouse with embroidered flowers on the collar.

"That looks like something a retiree would wear." He took the hangers out of her hands and returned the items to the racks.

Taryn crinkled her nose. "Too old?"

"A little." He walked to a selection of dresses and dug around. He pulled out a red halter dress with a flirty skirt. "I like this one. Classy but sexy."

"I thought I was supposed to be a mark, not a real date."

He handed over the dress. "Men will be open to grilling if they have a beautiful woman seated across the table."

"You think I'm beautiful?" She twirled her hair. He frowned. She laughed. It was fun to mess with him, too.

Digging back in the racks, she pulled out three more dresses and went into the fitting room. Five minutes later, she hung one dress up on the discard rack and led Rick to the checkout.

"That was quick," Rick said.

"I like to be efficient." She handed the three dresses to the clerk and pulled out her company credit card. "So what's next?"

"I assume your dates are already lining up. We'll need to get you wired up." He waited until the transaction was complete and took the bag from the clerk. He just couldn't shake his caveman DNA. She let him carry the bag. "Will the agency have what we need for surveillance?"

They left the store. "Who knows what Irving hides in that basement of his," she said. "He never lets us down there, though he always has excellent surveillance equipment when we need it. Let's go wrestle the key from him."

Fifteen minutes later, they pulled into the parking lot.

Gretchen waved as they passed her desk. They found Jess coming down the hallway as they headed for Irving's office.

"Hey, kids, what's up?" she said.

Taryn told her.

"Cool. Unfortunately, Irving is off getting a facial at the Fountain of Youth Spa. He won't be back for a couple of hours."

"Drat," Taryn said. "We'll have to get the spare key from Gretchen."

"She won't give it to you," Jess said. "She guards Irving's secrets like a bulldog."

A bulldog wearing ugly sweaters.

"What do you think is down there, anyway?" Taryn said. Her curiosity ramped up. "Dead bodies?"

"Maybe."

Rick snorted. "Speculation isn't getting us closer to discovery." Despite his casual posture, Taryn could see that he was curious, too. "We need a plan."

"I have an idea." Taryn sized Rick up. "Rick will distract her with his manly muscles and I'll steal the key."

"Right," Jess agreed and turned to Rick. "Flex something."

In the end, it was the scorpion tattoo and bandage on his arm that got them the key. He asked Gretchen about her disturbing turkeys-mating sweater, which somehow, in Gretchen land, led to a discussion about the tattoo and the injury, and that allowed Taryn to access her desk and a key ring. Given five more minutes, the assistant would have had his life story.

He never could figure out how women worked. One minute you ask a woman to point out the men's room, and the next, she's patting your hand and commiserating with you about your crappy childhood and absentee father. And you have no idea how you got to that subject.

Now he was following two giddy women down into the dungeon of the office building like they'd just discovered Ryan Gosling was living down there wearing nothing but a pair of boxers and a smile.

"Do you think Irving will fire us?" Jess said.

"Yes." Taryn rattled the keys. "But it'll be worth it." They came to a door marked STORAGE. "This has to be it. The other businesses don't have space down here." She tried four keys before she found the right one. As Taryn slowly pulled open the door, she and Jess huddled together like they expected a starving zombie to jump out and chew on their faces.

The block-and-tile room was empty.

Jess frowned and released Taryn. "Well, that's a disappointment."

"Wait, there's another door," Rick said in a whisper. "I bet there's something on the other side."

"Are you mocking us?" Taryn said.

He grinned. "Who, me?"

Earning a pair of narrowed eyes, Rick just kept smiling. Taryn went to work on that door. He liked how she bit her bottom lip when she concentrated. Inside was nothing but another door.

"Visions of Al Capone's vault," Rick joked.

"Not funny." Taryn walked to that door. "There has to be something down here. Irving is too secretive about this place for it to be empty."

"Or he's playing you ladies for his own amusement?"

The two women looked at each other. "Why did we invite him along?" Jess said. She ruffled her spiky hair.

"I've been asking myself the same thing," Taryn replied. She opened that door and again . . . nothing. "Okay, this is getting ridiculous. I think we're going around in circles."

"Yet we can't stop with an unopened door. Damn our curiosity." Jess pointed to the next one. And the next.

Taryn was ready to concede defeat when she spotted a sign on door seven that had a big red X on a white background and small lettering beneath it that said:

I KNEW YOU'D GET PAST GRETCHEN EVENTUALLY. I DIDN'T
HIRE YOU THREE FOR YOUR LOOKS. CONGRATS! IRVING.

"He *was* playing us," Jess said, smiling. "The old bugger."

"He could have just given us the key," Taryn said. She searched the ring for the right key. "The man clearly doesn't have enough to do. We should sign him up for bingo and shuffleboard at the senior center."

"Or put him up on Match-Mate," Rick offered. "Women will come running, once they see him rocking out with those orange plaid pants and alligator shoes."

Taryn rolled her eyes and pushed open the door.

Inside the sizeable room were several rows of gray metal shelves weighted with all sorts of gadgets, from cameras to body armor to stuff she'd have to Google later to find out what it was. The place was an electronics playground.

"The only thing missing is a tricked-out car with bulletproof glass and machine guns built into the bumpers," Taryn said, awed.

Rick let out a low whistle. "Irving is so cool."

"I'm going to start calling him Q." Taryn loved James Bond movies. She'd even cried a little when Desmond Llewelyn passed. To her he was the only real Q. "Where do we start?"

While Jess wandered off to explore, Taryn and Rick looked for audio wires. "If we do find a tricked-out car in here, I'm driving," he said and lifted up what resembled a thick cell phone. "You'd probably shoot yourself with the bumper guns."

"What is that?" she asked, ignoring the jab. Like a little kid who told the same joke fifty times because he got a laugh the first time, if she rose to the bait about her driving, he'd never stop.

"No idea." He turned the phone-thing over in his hands. "There must be an owner's manual somewhere."

They moved on. Jess went back upstairs. They found the listening devices at the end of the first shelf.

"I could spend all day down here," Rick said. He pulled out a device still in its original box. He held it up for her. "The A3000 audio and video package. It says it can pick up the sound of two gnats flying from a hundred yards away."

"Is that so?"

"Yep." He pointed to the small print on the bottom of the box. "Right here."

She leaned to look. Her breasts brushed his arm. He moved the item out of reach and glanced down to where their bodies made contact. A tremor zipped through him.

"Don't you trust me?" he said, low and deep.

Her eyes went soft. "No, I don't."

Were they still talking about the A3000?

As he handed her the box, their fingers touched, paused, then Taryn pulled back. Slowly. There was nothing about bugs written on the A3000, but it did guarantee excellent sound quality. However, it wasn't the audio and video devices causing his brain to misfire. The body-to-body contact made his hands itch to explore every inch of her and bury his face against her sweet-smelling neck.

All too damn aware that they were alone and she remained pressed against him, he struggled with whether he should go for it and the promise he'd made to keep his hands to himself.

"Maybe Irving will authorize a playdate for us in here," she said in a husky voice, and returned her eyes to his. "I'll bring the animal crackers and you can bring the juice boxes."

He wondered if she realized the signals she was giving off. Then her lips parted, her breathing turned uneven, and she swayed against him.

Whether her response was voluntary or some sort of primal instinct, the invitation was there. He'd throw a match on the fuel to see if Taryn combusted. "Honey, feed me animal crackers and I'll let you play with all my toys."

The charge snapping around the two of them should have sent Taryn fleeing for the door. Instead, she dropped the box on the shelf, grabbed his shirt with both fists, and kissed him.

Oh, hell. Maybe it was possible to work the case and kiss Taryn all he wanted in the process. She wasn't just any other woman or a casual conquest. She was so much more. And a damned good kisser.

Rick considered himself tough, but the softness of her mouth, the press of her curves against him, and the sweep of her tongue against his nearly brought him to his knees.

His hands went down to her butt and held her locked in place, as his tongue explored her mouth. There was something dark and reckless about kissing—deep, passionately kissing—this strong, muscled, tattooed man that made her feel alive!

Rick ran one hand from her butt up her back to her neck and deepened the kiss. He was all in. She was on fire.

If not for the unfortunate arrival of Jess, leading Summer, Taryn would have welcomed Rick to play in her sandbox with his monster truck. But their laughter as they approached was like jumping into frigid Lake Michigan, well, anytime.

She unwrapped her leg from behind his calf, not remembering how it got there, and tried to step back.

"We're not finished here," he said as she gulped for air.

She wanted to contradict the statement but knew anything she said would be a lie. If not for her friends, she'd be, in no time, splayed out on the bare white-speckled tile floor galloping headlong toward a screaming orgasm with Rick holding the reins.

That he could make her scream was not in doubt.

"This is so fun," Summer said, as she rounded the corner into their aisle. "Irving is the coolest boss ever."

If either woman noticed the tug that pulled her shirt back into place, or that Rick's tee had finger dents in it, they said nothing. Summer was too distracted by a disguise kit and Jess only shot her a quick questioning glance before turning away.

Taryn bent over and cleared her throat, reclaimed the box, and clutched it to her chest. "Audio. Video. I think this listening thing should be fine."

"Umm-hmm," Rick said. "Just fine."

And she knew he wasn't talking about electronics.

Chapter 14

Taryn adjusted the bodice of the red dress, careful to show the right amount of cleavage without giving the men heart attacks (Summer's words). Although she did dress up when she and her friends went out, she usually did not show so much skin. But now she did feel kind of sexy in this dress. Very sexy, in fact.

And Rick thought so, too, if the low growl-grumble in the back of his throat when she'd met him outside the restaurant had been any indication. Luckily, Summer and Jess hadn't been close enough to see or hear his visceral reaction. They'd gone off to get a table inside.

She squelched a grin. Ever since the earlier kiss, he'd been grumpy. Taryn knew why. There would be no romance between him and Summer, no wedding with ugly bridesmaids, and no perfect children. He wasn't interested in her friend. He was interested in her. The kiss and his body's response proved he wanted her. His current state of frustration confirmed that conclusion.

Where she should be worried, she was oddly content. But the dress was killing him.

With her skimpy cheerleading uniform days behind her, she liked keeping her outfits to mostly jeans and tees for work and skirts and tops for play. This dress was something else. She did a little twirl to flutter out the skirt and felt very feminine, like Marilyn Monroe on the grate.

"I like it," she said.

"I don't." He took the A3000 off the seat of his motorcycle. She stepped into range.

"You picked out the dress," she said innocently.

He slid his fingers under the fabric just enough to clip the device onto the top of her lacy red bra. His teeth gnashed. "I changed my mind."

She shivered, as his knuckles brushed her skin.

"Too bad. I don't have time to go home and change." Knowing the dress might be too much for him, she'd avoided meeting him at her house or his motel. Had she been alone with him, without her friends around to counter the effects of the dress, they wouldn't have made it to the restaurant.

She didn't have enough willpower to resist him on her own. Kisses were one thing, full-blown sex was another. The man was a sex magnet; a north to her south. They were driven together by an invisible magnetic force.

It seemed he was having trouble getting the device properly placed in her bra. "Do you need help?"

His fingertips on the skin between her breasts were warm and rough. Naughty images danced through her head like sugarplums at Christmas.

Nope, no spending any more time alone with him.

"I've got this." He leaned back, closed his eyes for a second, and seemed to pull himself together. Then he adjusted the device one last time and his fingers slid abruptly out of her dress. "No one will see it now."

Was it wrong to want to ask him to double-check?

Was it wrong that she wanted to see if two people really could have sex on a motorcycle and not fall off?

Yes, it was wrong. So wrong. She pretended to smooth out the dress. "What about the camera?"

"I've already set it up here." He pointed to the pin on his collar. He put the listening earbud in his ear and the recorder in his shirt pocket. "I didn't want to risk detection by trying to hide it on you."

He'd left the metal band tees behind and was wearing a medium blue button-up shirt and jeans. The loose fit of the shirt hid his gun. Since the shooting, he'd kept it on him at all times.

She had no room under the dress to wear hers, but she did have pepper spray. Just in case. And her gun was in her purse.

Taryn walked ten feet away and turned her back to him. "Can you hear me?" she said softly.

"Yes."

"Then we're ready."

The cafe was already half filled when they entered. It smelled of coffee and baked goods. Jess and Summer had claimed a table and Taryn took one with a clear view of them. Rick veered off at the door and joined the two women. He sat facing her.

Several men looked appreciatively her way. Taryn ignored them. "Can you still hear me?"

He gave a slight nod. She reached for the menu card. Although only two of her dates, based on their profile pictures, somewhat resembled the sketchy Brinkman photo, she knew that many people either posted photos of their much younger selves or pictures that weren't even theirs. With Brinkman and his criminal past, he'd probably be cautious and lean toward the latter.

His previous photos were likely of him, but at angles or Photoshopped to make them shadowy. They couldn't chance missing him due to faulty information.

Taryn didn't have to wait long for her first date. A balding man of about forty-five entered, scanned the room, hustled over, and dropped into the chair beside her. He was sweating from his temples and dabbed his round cheeks with a paper napkin. A smile revealed that his right canine was partially missing and what was left was a brownish stump.

"You must be Terry? You look younger than forty. Did you have work done?"

And so it began.

A headache crept into Rick's brain and refused to leave. One after another, a group of dimwits, pervs, and oddballs had come and gone over the past two hours, all of them more focused on Taryn's cleavage than her face. And each time, after a few minutes of this crap, and after confirming they weren't Brinkman, he'd appear at her side, pretending to be a jealous ex and chase them off. Since she had ten "dates" that afternoon, the men couldn't linger.

Number six even stopped on his way out to hit on Summer. She politely and firmly told him to get lost. Rick wasn't so polite.

"That one looks thirty years older than his picture," Summer said. "Not one of the eight so far has matched their profile photo."

"I'm glad I don't date," Jess said.

Rick shut out their conversation. He was focused on Taryn. The latest arrival was leaning over the table, gripping her hand, and grinning like he'd won the lottery, while she worked to discreetly extricate her hand.

"Please let go," she said through gritted teeth, and tugged.

"I have a house in Cabo, baby doll," suitor nine said and tried to bring her hand to his lips. "I'll buy you anything you want, if you play nice with me."

Rick stood.

Jess and Summer pulled him back down. "Don't ruin our fun," Jess said, smiling. "Watch."

Taryn stopped tugging and reached for her purse with her free hand. She pulled out a lipstick and worked off the cap.

"I know this nude beach," the guy continued. "Me, you, naked. Sun, sand in our—" His icky sentiment was cut off by a quick burst of pepper spray to the face. "Ack!"

Like a wasp hit with d-Con, he started to writhe in his chair, letting loose of Taryn, as his hands went to his eyes.

"Bitch!"

A pair of old ladies at a table in the far corner clapped, having watched the procession of dates come and go with interest.

Rick was at her side in a second. He clamped a hand over Number Nine's mouth and dragged him backward off his chair. Across the restaurant they went, past the bathrooms, and out the emergency door, which failed to buzz, thankfully.

He spread the guy out on the ground and made sure he was breathing. He bent and looked into red and watery eyes. The man whimpered.

"When a woman says no, she means no." Low moans assured him that the dumbass would live, so he went back inside and reclaimed his seat with the women.

Taryn sat with a hint of a serene smile on her perfect mouth, as if nothing had happened, and casually checked her watch, despite curious looks sent her way.

God, she was something else.

In that moment, Rick realized he was toast. He was falling for her and fast. She was everything wrong for him, and everything right: brains, beauty, and fire. But a terrible driver. And an all-out pain in the ass.

Damn, he wanted her.

"He's got it bad," Jess said, from some far-off place.

"He's hooked," Summer agreed.

Rick pulled his mind back to his companions. They were both staring at him and smiling.

"I hope Taryn doesn't pick yellow for our bridesmaids' dresses," Jess said. "I look terrible in yellow."

"I like peach," Summer said. "Or blue."

It took him a moment to get clued in to their conversation. He scowled. "You think you're amusing, do you?"

"We're just calling it like we see it," Jess said. She and Summer shared a nod. "If you could see the way you look at Taryn, you'd be amused, too."

The arrival of Number Ten kept him from responding. The guy had slipped past him while he wasn't paying attention, so Rick hadn't gotten a look at his face. From the back, he could be Brinkman. The guy had salt-and-pepper hair and a lean build.

Rick tensed.

"Hi, I'm Terry," Taryn said and took his hand.

"Chuck. Nice to meet you."

Chuck? If this was Brinkman, he was using a new alias. Rick glanced at Taryn. Her face revealed nothing.

"You don't look forty, Terry," Chuck said.

Taryn leaned forward taking him into her confidence. "Don't tell anyone, but I've had work done."

"You have?" Chuck said, worshipful. "Your surgeon was a genius."

"Thank you." While Chuck ordered a coffee, Taryn looked at Rick and winked. He grinned, realized he had an audience, and then frowned without taking his eyes off Taryn.

"Don't say a word, ladies," he threatened.

Their laughter ground up his nerves.

Chapter 15

Chuck turned out to be a bust. Although Chuck and the other men were old enough to be her father, they were not Brinkman.

Taryn was ready to crash by the time she extricated herself from the sweet and charming Chuck and paid her coffee bill. Ten partial cups of the brew had sent her to the bathroom three times and made her slightly manic.

"You're twitching," Rick said as he walked her out.

"I've had enough caffeine to rev up a sloth." His hand went to her bare back as he held open the door for her. She liked his touch. She wanted to invite him back to her place to help bring her down from her coffee high, but thought better of it. Sex would only lead to heartache. She already liked Rick too much for her peace of mind.

Besides, Jess and Summer were waiting by the Olds. She couldn't kiss him good night, even if she wanted to.

"Well, good night," she said and headed to her car.

"Hey, Taryn." She turned around and found him grinning. "You look damn sexy in that dress."

With his compliment cemented in her mind, Taryn longed for the relaxation of a hot bath and a steamy romance novel. Whenever she needed to chill, she liked to read. If she couldn't have Rick in her bed, a wicked duke or hunky FBI agent was the next best thing. Well, sort of.

Overdosed on caffeine and Rick, she had to do something to unwind or risk calling him up and inviting him over. A long, hot bath should do the trick.

Thankfully, there were no teenage suitors on her porch or calls from her ex, as she tromped up the stairs and put her key into the lock. Her fried brain took a full ten seconds to process the sounds of footsteps behind her, and another one or two to figure, wrongly, that one of the wolf cubs next door had indeed found her.

She spun to shoo him off, startled at the massive bulk of the man before her, and dragged her eyes up to his unshaven face; a face she knew well.

She took only a half second to complete a full and almost fatal heart failure.

"Hello, Taryn."

Alvin the Ape.

She tried to scream but only a strangled squeak came out. However, she did manage through the panicked spinning of her mind to reach into the side pocket of her purse for the lipstick Mace. Closing a fist over the tube, she whipped it out and aimed. She shot him full in the right eye with enough noxious chemicals to take down a grizzly.

Nothing.

She shot him in the left eye.

Again. *Nada.* The third strike was a pitiful stream from the nearly empty can. It hit him midchest.

She was going to die.

He blinked, shook his head, but looked more annoyed than damaged. "I need to talk to you," he said in his deep, deep, serial-killer voice.

She held up the can and sprayed, sputtering liquid back and forth across his wide face, like a hyped-up mom treating her pasty white kid with spray-on sunscreen at the beach.

Instead of dropping down in pain, Alvin sighed deeply and he reached out. Resigned to death, she slowly placed the empty lipstick can onto his ginormous hairy paw; the same hand that would soon choke the breath out of her.

Twenty-five was a long and successful life, right? She'd had some fun and made friends, and could have slept with Rick, the sexiest man on the planet. He'd wanted her and not Summer. That was enough. She was ready to go to God.

Closing her eyes, she waited.

A second sigh opened them back up.

He was staring at her like she was a moron.

"I'm not here to kill you, though I could if I wanted to. I could break you in half with one hand and not even sprain a finger." He flexed said hand as proof.

"It is a big hand," she agreed. What?

He shook his head like a dog. Clumps of drying chemical went flying. "Look, can we talk inside?"

"Sure." She didn't want to traumatize her next-door neighbors by letting them watch her be murdered. She wasn't entirely convinced that wasn't Alvin's end game despite his assurance, and she couldn't chance the boys taking the opportunity to upload the video to the web. Boys would be boys and all that.

She unlocked the door and led him in. He had to dip his head so as not to conk his forehead on the doorframe.

Taryn thought about her gun. It was in its case in her purse. But she suspected in the time it would take to retrieve it, he'd probably snap off her head. She thought about those many hours of self-defense training. But Alvin was a trained bodyguard, at least six foot seven, and probably had a good one hundred and fifty pounds on her. Why waste the energy trying to raise her foot up over her head to kick him in the groin? A peaceful murdering was preferable over blood and gore.

So she waited and covertly looked around for a weapon.

Alvin crossed his arms and leaned back on his heels. "Willard wants you dead."

"I know. He said so in court." Her stomach soured. "It's on record."

"No. I'm supposed to kill you and make it look like an accident."

Well, this was a turn. She'd thought Willard's threats were as empty as his morality. The bastard. "That's why you're here? I thought you said you wouldn't kill me. Just a minute ago, I heard it. You promised."

"I'm not . . ." He blinked and sucked in and released a deep breath. It took a moment before he spoke again. "My therapist says that I have anger issues. I'm trying to change." He scratched his scruffy black beard. "I can't be a better person and murder you, too. So I told Willard no."

There were moments in life when it felt as if *Candid Camera* was about to pounce. While she waited for Peter Funt to jump out and shout, "Smile, you're on *Candid Camera,*" she wobbled backward into the living room and perched on the arm of the couch.

"I knew Willard was angry." She met his eyes. "I can't believe this."

"Believe it."

Murder. "All this trouble over a rejection and a lawsuit?"

"He thinks you'll be awarded his team. He's seriously pissed. He loves being a team owner. He's been to the White House. He bags groupies. Without the team, he'll have to go back to Utah and raise chickens with his wife, and hang out with the Mormons. His words."

Wow. Willard was a bigger lunatic than she'd thought. "Do you have evidence of this murder plot?"

"Nope. Just my word."

Darn. Knowing how close she'd been to real death left her unsettled and ticked off. She took a moment to think it all over. At least she'd been warned. And if Alvin agreed to testify about the murder plot, Willard would be sunk. But first, she wanted him out of her house. After all, who could take the word of a hired assassin that she was safe?

"Well, thank you for the warning." She pushed off the couch arm and headed for the front door. "My lawyer will be in touch."

He frowned. "I can't leave."

"Why not?"

"I have nowhere to go."

She waited for him to explain. He obliged.

"When we stopped for gas in Atlanta, I took a pee break. When I came out, the bus was gone." He dug in his pocket, pulled out a business card, and handed it over. Gold embossing gave Willard's name and information. "The clerk gave me that."

Taryn turned it over.

YOU'RE FIRED!

Willard did have a flair for the dramatic. "Okay. I'm sorry you lost your job, but what does that have to do with me? If you've forgotten, you ejected me and my friends from his bus and left us stranded in the boonies. We could have died of exposure or starvation. That wasn't nice."

That may have been a bit of an exaggeration, but it had been a hot day and they'd had no water. Death by dehydration had been a real threat.

"I apologize for that." He managed to look sheepish. "I was much crankier then."

Taryn's brain hurt. She was chatting up her assassin, in her living room, like they were old friends. She wanted him gone. She wanted a bath. And Heather and Brandon were awaiting their first kiss on her nightstand. She was just getting to the sexy part of the book.

"Alvin. Let's cut to the chase. What do you want?"

"I want to stay here."

"Are you crazy? No!" She paused. "Was that you I saw the other night, running for the bushes across the street?"

"Maybe. Look, I have nowhere to go and no money." Despite his size and scary face, he looked sort of pitiful standing there. Still, it wasn't happening. She shook her head.

He made a pinched face, sort of like a baby filling its diaper, and his bottom lip trembled.

"What are you doing?"

"Trying to show emotion. My therapist says it's healthy." He tried to summon up a tear, failed, and gave up. "I walked a long way to get here."

"You walked from Atlanta?" At his nod, her eyes widened. "That's, like, six hundred miles."

"Seven hundred and nine. Give or take. I slept in woods and culverts. Do you know there are black bears in Kentucky?"

Shocked, Taryn ran her eyes over him. For the first time she noticed how disheveled he was and that his left big toe poked out of one black dress shoe. Bits of plants and dust stuck to his black suit and an old (and new) sweat stain circled his dress shirt's collar.

His jacket looked a bit chewed.

Pressing a palm to her forehead, she knew Heather and Brandon's love story would have to wait.

Seven hundred and nine miles.

"Just for a few days."

He smiled. One front tooth was missing.

Alvin was a melting pot of species and cultures and hair. Black tufts of fur stuck up from beneath his shirt collar and on the backs of his hands. And after who knows how many weeks of walking, he was sporting some serious black beard growth, and the last time he'd taken a shower was a mystery. In a squabble with a Kentucky black bear, she was sure he'd be the victor. The bear was probably still licking his wounds.

And now, Alvin was all hers.

Chapter 16

Taryn overslept. Full sunlight streamed through her eastern facing window as she rolled over to check her clock. Ten a.m. She groaned and flopped back onto her pillow. The urge to cover her head and go back to sleep fought with the need to get up and moving before Rick arrived at her door.

She was too tired to fight about Alvin. She'd made her decision and that was that.

After tucking Alvin into the spare bedroom with the biggest bed, and leaving him towels for a shower, she'd locked her door, in case he reconsidered the whole murder thing, and she tossed and turned all night. Now she was late meeting Rick.

Reaching for her phone, she checked her texts. He'd sent three, the last more urgent that the first two. She quickly whipped off an assurance that she'd not been abducted but that she'd overslept.

Rolling from her bed, she padded to the bathroom. After taking care of business, she stared in the mirror at the haggard face peering out from beneath a tangle of hair.

Before she could attack the tresses with a brush, and then shower, the doorbell rang.

Great.

Things got better when she discovered Rick on her doorstep with a bag of doughnuts and a pair of coffees. "Jess said you hadn't been in and Summer was worried you might be sick." He stared. "Were you in an accident with a lawn mower?"

"Ha. Always a comedian." She stepped back and let him in. He smelled freshly showered and yummy. "I didn't sleep well and I just sent you a text. Sorry."

"It's fine." He handed her a coffee. "Why don't you get ready and I'll put the doughnuts in the kitchen."

He wandered off. She had reached to the bottom of the staircase when his voice stopped her. "Do you know you have a primate in your backyard, in boxers, barbecuing hot dogs on your grill?"

"Damn." Alvin. She hurried into the kitchen and out the back door. Rick followed. Dressed only in blue-and-white-striped boxers and wielding a pair of semi-rusty tongs, Alvin had a row of dogs sizzling over low heat. He must have dug them out of her freezer. But what took her aback was the trio of boys sitting on her deck railing, also in boxers, with cans of beer in their hands.

"What in the hell?"

Andrew grinned. "Taryn, you throw the best parties." He popped the can tab and took a drink.

She scowled at Alvin. "You can't let them drink beer."

He waved the tongs at the trio. "They're college students. College students drink beer."

She pointed to Thurston. "That one is fourteen, that one is eighteen, and that one—" She paused and looked the guy over. She'd never seen him before, but he was sporting a tangle of brown curly hair and a soul patch, and looked way over twenty-one. "And he may actually be legal. But still. It's ten a.m. No beer."

Thurston reached for Andrew's beer. Alvin snatched it from him, crushed the can, spilling beer on the faded deck, and tossed it over the railing and into the bushes.

"You didn't tell me you were fourteen."

"You didn't ask." Thurston sent Taryn a puppy-dog glance. "I'm mature for my age."

Rick chuckled behind her.

She collected the opened cans and the rest of the six-pack. "No drinking, and put on pants." She stomped into the house and dumped the beer into the trashcan. "Watch them," she called back to Rick and headed up for a shower. She couldn't think straight in her PJs.

Twenty minutes later, she was refreshed, dressed, and ready to take on the issues in her backyard.

Alvin and the boys, all still sporting their boxers, were eating plain hot dogs speared on forks, while Rick stood in the open doorway, arms crossed, watching over the foursome as she'd ordered.

When he saw her coming, he cocked up a brow and smiled at her frowning face.

"Andrew was right. You do throw the best parties."

"Hmmm." She brushed past him and shooed the boys, and soul patch guy, off her porch, then helped Alvin clean up. Once finished, she grabbed her bag and keys. "I'll stop by the big and tall store today and get you something to wear. Until then, stay out of mischief."

Rick waited until they were away from the house before finally giving in to his curiosity. "Would you like to explain why you have a large, half-naked man in your backyard?"

"He's my assassin."

"Right." It took him a second to realize she was serious. He pulled the SUV to the curb and faced her. She popped the last bite of a doughnut into her open mouth. "Is there anything about you that's normal?"

"My parents are retired school teachers from Iowa?"

Smart. Beautiful. Crazy. "Why don't we start with Alvin."

So she did. Taryn told him about the harassment, the bus, the lawsuit, and the murder-for-hire. When she was finished, his gut was in knots. "You let a killer live in your house?"

"He's really just a bodyguard, and he promised not to kill me." She was so matter-of-fact about trusting the thug that he wasn't sure if he should take her arms and shake some sense into her or go back and extricate Alvin from her house before the guy changed his mind.

"And you believe him?"

She played with the end of her ponytail. "He's trying to change. He's in therapy."

Yep. Crazy. "Maybe you two can get a group rate."

As she swiveled in the seat, her hazel eyes blazed and she snapped, "What was I supposed to do? He walked seven hundred miles to warn me that Willard wanted to kill me. If anyone deserves a little compassion, it's Alvin."

The knot stayed. He wasn't comforted at all by the Alvin-in-therapy thing. The guy looked like a stereotypical Hollywood movie killer. And he was living with Taryn.

"I think you're making a mistake," he said. By the stubborn jaw clench, continuing the argument would be a useless gesture. She had her mind set.

"It's mine to make." She crossed her arms and stared out the windshield. The subject was closed. There might not be anything he could do now, but he intended to keep a close eye on Alvin the Assassin.

They hit the big and tall store for shirts and slacks. Then they went to the office for an update from Summer. There was still no sign of Brinkman online, but she had a full roster of dates for that evening.

His phone pinged with a new text. "It's the detective investigating the shooting. They got prints off the Pinto. The same prints were found on a receipt for a rented Lincoln out of Livonia." He scrolled down. "When the car wasn't returned, the company reported it stolen and hunted it down by GPS. It took a while to find the car. It was at the bottom of Lake Erie."

"The renter was Brinkman? If it was, then Brinkman was likely the renter of the storage unit, too."

"Yes. Video at the car leasing place and a copy of his driver's license confirmed it's him. The manager from Affordable U-Store also confirmed he rented the unit. Brinkman moved up from the Pinto."

"To impress Honey, perhaps?" she said. "I'm beginning to think that Honey might not be in danger at all. He's never tried to impress any other wives. There must be something about her that made him change his routine."

"He might be in love," Rick said.

Taryn refused to make eye contact with Rick since she was still annoyed with him. He refused to give in on the Alvin thing.

"I guess we won't know until we find them," she said.

Rick treated Taryn to a strained lunch and took her back to her house. He walked her in, offered her guest, still in his boxers, a warning, in front of her, and left with all sorts of reservations dogging at his heels.

Taryn slammed the door behind him.

Taryn sipped her coffee, determined to ignore Rick, who was seated with Summer and Jess a few tables over. The Salty Pretzel was a karaoke bar with loud music and a festive atmosphere. She wore her new flirty sundress with a pair of cute low boots from the back of her closet that she'd dusted off. She'd twisted her hair up in the back, leaving some tendrils to fall down around her neck and shoulders.

The table was off in a corner, and it was the first time she'd been there, so there was little chance she'd run into anyone she knew.

The comment Rick made about Brinkman being in love stuck with her; she hoped that wasn't the case, or the con man wouldn't be out trolling for new victims. Although she didn't want him loose on the female population of Michigan, if he had settled down and was happily wed, it would make this stakeout a waste of time. They might never find him.

Rick was dressed in a loose red shirt to hide his gun, and his caveman club, if she were to guess. His warning to Alvin had ratcheted up her annoyance level again, just as she was starting to get past the first overprotective lecture. As if she couldn't take care of herself.

Date one approached and Taryn turned her attention to business. He was short, round, and overly effusive with his praise of her beauty. He talked marriage, kids, and station wagons, all in the first two minutes. Rick had to drag him off before he dropped to one knee and proposed.

Guy two was a college professor with wispy brown hair and a severe overbite. He was the first to realize they weren't a match and left after finishing his coffee.

Number three was well into his seventies, a good ten years older that his profile claimed, and appeared to want a nurse more than a wife. Jess shuffled him off and into a cab.

And on and on it went with no sign of Brinkman. Date six was convinced God was speaking to him through his hearing aids. Date seven was hunting for his eighth wife. None of the men seemed overly concerned that Taryn looked twenty years younger than her profile picture. A couple of the men thought dating online was a game and lying about themselves was not a deal breaker. They expected her to accept them for their winning personalities and overlook the fact that they were not the male models whose photos they'd lifted online.

By the time her last date came and went, she was ready for some fun. Pushing up to her feet, she wandered over to join Rick and her friends. The small round table was crowded with four of them seated there.

"Another bust," she said and slumped in a chair at the four-top table. "I could use a cocktail." She ordered a cosmopolitan. "I'm starting to think Rick is right and our felon is in love. Brinkman loaded Honey up and left town with her, to a life of sipping fruity drinks on a beach somewhere."

"If he has, he'll be harder to find," Rick said.

Taryn ignored his knee pressed against hers. Well, tried to, anyway. She didn't need therapy, or him, to protect her from Alvin. Although she wasn't sure he'd completely changed from the thug who'd tossed the three of them off the bus, Alvin had shown no sign that he was dangerous.

"You know you can't stay mad forever," he said, just loud enough to be heard over the music.

"I can and I may."

"I'm right about Alvin. The guy is a menace."

Her chin went up. "You don't know him."

"I've been an agent for eight years and I know guys like him. All you need is a match and he'll explode."

Here he went again, trying to boss her around. "You're wrong. Alvin can change. He wants to change."

Taryn didn't realize her voice had gone up until Summer made a distressed sound. She turned to find her friends gaping like a couple of carp.

"You can't be talking about Alvin the Ape?" Jess said, wide-eyed and disbelieving.

"Alvin is here in Ann Arbor?" Summer's voice was high and her expression freaked out.

Silence confirmed her question. Rick tossed in the gasoline. "He is and he's living with Taryn."

For the next ten minutes the three women argued while Rick drank a second beer. He'd hoped Summer and Jess would talk some sense into Taryn, but she was just as determined to help Alvin as she had been before her friends got involved.

"Please trust me on this," Taryn pleaded as the arguing died down. "If I'm wrong, you can gloat. Until then, he stays."

There was more grumbling, but Taryn won the battle in time for the lights to lower in the bar and a man to take the small stage to announce the start of karaoke. Summer and Jess shared a worried glance, but kept silent. If Rick needed allies in the future, he could count on them.

Clapping erupted from the crowd.

"We have a lot of future singing stars with us tonight, so let's get started." The emcee called out a name and a pair of women took the stage to belt out a Shania Twain song. One was off key. The other did a decent job of mimicking Shania.

"We should go," Summer said after the second act, and grabbed her purse.

"Yes, let's," Jess agreed. There was an undercurrent of desperation in her tone that caught Rick's attention.

"I don't want to go," Taryn said. "This is fun."

Rick watched a slightly panicked look pass between Summer and Jess. Taryn didn't seem to notice.

"Next up is . . ." The host pulled a name out of a box. "Taryn!"

"Oh, no." Summer slid down in her chair, as Taryn jumped to her feet and hurried for the stage. "Jess, when did she enter?"

"It must have been when she went to the restroom," Jess said, her eyes accusing. "I thought you were watching her."

"Me?" Summer turned defensive. "I thought it was your turn. I drove us past that bar in Dexter, before she spotted the sign. That counts."

"Is there a problem here?" he asked. They leveled pitying stares his way.

"Please don't let it be Whitney," Jess said and grabbed for her purse. The brunette frantically dug around in the bottom of the bag. Relief flooded her pretty features when she found what she was hunting for.

"What will you sing tonight, young lady?" the emcee said.

" 'I Will Always Love You' by Whitney Houston."

Summer whimpered.

Jess groaned. "Dear lord, by all that is holy, no." She removed a small tin and popped it open. Reaching inside, she handed Summer and Rick each a pair of gummy orange earplugs.

"Come on. She can't be that bad," Rick piped in. He'd heard her sing in the car and she wasn't very good, but she wasn't earplug horrible either.

Shaking her head, Jess clicked her tongue. He dropped the plugs on the table. "I'll take my chances."

Summer pushed earplugs into her ears. "Your funeral."

The music swelled. Taryn sang. What started out okay swelled into a karaoke nightmare of epic proportions when she summoned up everything in her and hit high notes that dolphins off the coast of Maine could hear. Dogs howled, babies cried, and glasses shattered. Rick dove for the plugs, but it was too late. He'd already suffered irreversible damage.

"I will always love youuuuuuuuuuuuuu!!!!" Taryn wailed. Several people leapt to their feet and ran for the exit. When the off-key crescendo faded away, and Taryn took her bow, Rick suspected that the frenzied clapping as she left the stage was because the horror was over and not because they thought her the next Taylor Swift.

"That was so much fun!" Taryn said breathlessly, as she hurried back and dropped onto her seat. Her dress skirt fluttered around her in a poof of pastel flowers. All her tension and annoyance with him was gone. She was happy and relaxed when she reached for her drink. "How was I?"

"Whitney had nothing on you," Rick said. What else could he say that wouldn't hurt her feelings? Anything more would cause a heavenly lightning strike on his head for lying. "I've never seen such an enthusiastic performance."

"It was great!" Summer exclaimed.

"Your best rendition yet!" Jess said and clapped.

Rick was sure the three of them were doomed to a heaven-sent electrical jolt to the head the minute they stepped outside. But Taryn's eyes softened and she sent her friends a sweet smile.

"Thanks." Taryn sipped her drink and peered at him over the rim. After a few more acts came and went, Summer and Jess headed off to speak to someone they recognized—or to discreetly ditch the earplugs. Probably both.

They promised to meet Taryn outside.

Trying not to look at the way her dress rode up to mid-thigh revealing creamy skin, Rick could see how much Taryn loved her friends and they loved her. To sit through karaoke at its worst proved their love and loyalty.

"Ready?" he said.

She finished her drink and nodded. He pulled out her chair for her. A curl led his eyes to the back of her neck as she stood. Despite causing him an inner ear bleed, she was still damn sexy. He wanted to kiss the soft skin on her shoulder, her neck, and her breasts. Hell, he wanted to kiss her all over.

Yep, he was toast. His promise to behave until the case was con-cluded had its limits when it came to Taryn. Loving his mother and being a loyal son meant closing the case. Anything outside of that was his business.

When they got outside, she paused on the sidewalk. "Did you really like my singing?"

What he said at this moment would either make or break any fu-ture chance of getting her into bed. He struggled inwardly for a beat before shaking his head. "No."

Instead of taking insult, she laughed. "I know I'm bad, but I love to sing. I won't apologize for that."

"You shouldn't." If singing made her happy, he was all for it. This was yet another thing to admire about the pretty PI: her fear-lessness.

"If anyone complains, I'll have Jess pass out earplugs," she said, her laughter deepening. When his brow went up, she shrugged. "What? You think I don't know? How else could they sit through karaoke with me and not go mad?"

Chapter 17

Taryn enjoyed his deep rich laughter. She liked the way his eyes crinkled at the corners. She liked the way his shirt fit his excellent body. And she loved the way he kissed.

All those were good reasons to avoid any sort of serious physical contact with him. Each time a momentary bout of weakness hit and she thought a "no commitments" romance with Rick wasn't a terrible idea, Tim's texts brought all the hurt from her divorce back to the present. Rick was the kind of guy who'd never want anything more than sex and she wasn't certain that she could keep her emotions in check with him.

It wasn't that she didn't like sex. She and Dave the race car driver had had a fun, no-strings time together for a few days. But there was never any threat of loving him. Rick, on the other hand, already had the ability to make her heart race just by showing up.

If she didn't fight to keep her heart protected, he could be next in line to break it.

Glancing at her watch to disconnect from staring longingly into his eyes, she pulled herself together. "It's only nine-thirty?" There, neutral topic. Add work: "I'm thinking I might do some recon on another case that Irving put me on. A friend of his thinks her ex-boyfriend stole her dog. I want to go by and see what I can find out."

"Dognapping?" He grinned. "That sounds like a high-end case. What's next, kitty espionage?"

"Ha. Ha. For your information, we take a lot of unusual cases. They don't all involve cheating spouses or felonious con men." She could see that he wasn't going to let this one go. "People love their pets. If this guy has Karen's dog, she wants her back."

A heartbeat passed. Then he said, "I guess you're right. I'd be ticked off if someone hijacked my pooch. Can I come with you?"

"I'll have to go home and get my car."

"We can take my bike."

How she wanted to say no. But it was the first time he'd asked, instead of told her what to do, and she thought he should be rewarded. Besides, what could a few minutes pressed against him on the back of his vintage Triumph hurt?

"Fine." She looked down at the dress. "I need to change first. I have a bag in the back of Summer's car."

They walked over to join Jess and Summer at Summer's convertible. Taryn and Jess teasingly called the car the Cotton Candy Mobile because of its light blue color. But it fit her personality and the three had spent many a day in it cruising the highways and byways of Michigan searching for mischief.

Taryn filled them in on the plan. "Rick can take me home later." She noticed the glance that passed between her two friends. They were all too knowing for comfort.

"Move on," she warned. Both grinned.

"I'll get the second round of dates set up for tomorrow night at someplace new," Summer said and unlocked the car. "We'll catch him. I know we will."

"I hope so," Taryn said. Climbing into the back of the car, she slumped in the white seat and watched Rick walk to his Triumph to give her privacy. It was criminal how good he looked in jeans.

Summer and Jess were both watching him, too.

"I think I just had an orgasm," Summer said.

Jess sighed. "I know I did."

Taryn made a face. Lusting after him was one thing. Having her friends do so in front of her was another.

Summer turned on the car and cranked up the air conditioning. "That is one hot man. I wanted to run my foot up his leg under the table for the last three hours."

"Too bad he's already taken," Jess said. They both turned around in their seats.

Obviously, they weren't finished with the subject of her and Rick. Maybe she should cut them off and make Alvin her new BFF. She sensed he'd be less likely to probe into her personal life than her other so-called friends.

Taryn want to tell them to mind their own business but knew that no matter what denials she came up with, it wouldn't keep them from believing she and Rick were headed for a passionate love affair. Instead, she unzipped her duffel and dragged out a pair of jeans and a slightly wrinkled blue t-shirt.

"Do you mind?" She scowled. They turned back around.

The halter bra was not meant for t-shirts but it worked okay. Taryn slipped out of the dress and into her dark jeans and tee. She put her sandals on the floor, laid the dress out on the backseat, and reclaimed the duffel. She kept a camera, her gun, and a few other emergency items inside it in the event a last-minute case came up. The dognapping situation was not an official case, even if she led Rick to believe so.

"I'll see you tomorrow," she said and got out before they could talk smack or try to slip her a condom. With those two, anything was possible.

Summer drove off as she joined Rick.

"Ready?" he asked.

"Ready." She gave the bike a look over and felt a tingle of apprehension/excitement. The bike was vintage; blue, black, and silver; and very Rick. She frowned while imagining how many other women may have ridden on it with him. "It's been years since I've been on a bike. And that one was actually a moped."

Rick chuckled and opened a pack that was lashed to the back of the seat with bungee cords. "Mopeds don't count." He pulled out a blue helmet and handed it over. Metallic sparkles embedded in blue shimmered in the streetlamp's light.

"This looks new," she said. His expression confirmed her suspicion. "Obviously, you planned for a passenger."

His smile lit the dim light. "Obviously."

Ah, so much weight in that one word. He knew he'd get her on his bike someday. The helmet was for her.

That was kind of sweet.

She handed over the duffel and put on the helmet. Rick tucked the duffel into the pack while she adjusted to the feel and weight of the helmet and tried to hook the straps together.

He stepped in front of her. "Here, let me."

Tipping up her face, he reached under her chin. "If you don't get this right, it won't stay on properly."

"Are you the highway safety monitor?" His fingers brushed the skin on her neck. She gulped.

"I am, so do what I say." The smile stayed as he threaded the straps, adjusted the helmet, and finished the job. Leaning back, he examined the fit. "Good. You look like a biker babe."

He unbuttoned his shirt and shucked it off. Beneath was a black AC/DC concert shirt. Figured.

"How many concerts have you gone to?" she asked.

"A lot." His eyes glittered. "I could go about two months without wearing the same shirt twice."

She shook her head. "And you call me crazy."

"You are crazy."

"And yet you're obsessed with heavy metal t-shirts." They locked eyes. She whipped out her phone. "Fine. Let's call a tie. But I still think you're crazier."

His snort answered that.

A mapping app gave them directions to Karen's ex's house. It was roughly ten minutes away. Darkness would offer cover as Taryn poked around looking for the dog. Despite Rick picking on her about this case, she liked taking breaks from cheating spouses and other more serious cases.

"Why doesn't Karen just go over and demand the dog back?" Rick asked. He pulled his t-shirt over his gun.

"Because she knows that he gets off on face-to-face angry confrontations. This way, she doesn't have to see his ugly mug or smell his bad breath. Her words."

"Then let's go get that dog."

When Rick lifted his arms to put on his own helmet, his tee slipped up and his jeans were just low enough to give her a glimpse of part of a muscled six-pack. Her hands twitched to follow his waistband with her hands along the strip where white and tanned skin intersected just below his navel.

Her mouth went dry and her mind went back to what Jess and Summer joked about in the car, about having spontaneous orgasms just from looking at him. She was already halfway there.

Rick swung a leg over the Triumph. He positioned himself on the seat before turning back to her. "Put your foot on the foot peg there and climb on. There is another peg on the other side for your right foot. Hold on to me and you won't fall off."

She did as told and climbed behind him. There was room between him and the back, but not much. Her hips were cradled against his tight butt as she held onto his waist. "Good?" She nodded. He turned away and fired up the bike. The engine rumbled beneath her and kind of turned her on. Rick drove slowly through the parking lot and down a slight incline to the street. "You okay?"

"Yes!"

"Then hold on!" he said, and they took off.

Taryn's breath caught. She scrambled to get her hands tighter around his waist, sure she was about to be ejected from the bike. Nervous energy and something primitive and exciting mixed inside her, as the man and bike roared through the dimly lit streets of Ann Arbor. It didn't take long to understand the free feeling that came from being out on the open road with the wind surrounding your body.

Beneath her hands, she felt the play of his muscles as he adjusted to each turn, and her heart beat a little faster.

Taryn looked damn beautiful in the helmet and jeans. Too beautiful. First that red dress, the girly sundress, and now this. She was locked against him like they were one person, her breasts pressed to his back. He tried to refocus on something other than what their closeness was doing to him as she tightened her grip on him and snuggled even closer. How, he couldn't figure out.

He wanted to find a quiet place to peel her jeans off and show her all the things they could do naked, but refrained, not out of a sense of duty, but because of something deeper. He knew that if he got involved with her other than professionally it would make going back to L.A. nearly impossible. And he didn't want to hurt her when he walked away.

Besides, his mom deserved his focus and her justice. He'd already gotten sidetracked from the case by kissing Taryn. If he got her naked, he'd likely never get out of bed.

Once they got intel on the dog, he'd drive her home, drop her off, and get the hell out of there, before temptation got the worst of him.

Taryn pointed right and he slowed for the corner. He followed her directions until they found themselves on a quiet suburban street. The houses were a mix of brick ranches, all tweaked a bit to not be exactly alike. The ex's house was fifth in the row and looked as if some genius had decided to whitewash the brick and had done a shitty job. The peeling paint and a rusted-out Cutlass up on blocks lent a shabby look to the place. He suspected that the neighbors, with their kept-up yards and neatly tended houses, saw this guy's house as the neighborhood eyesore.

Steering to the curb a few houses down, he parked in front of a row of yews and removed his helmet. She did the same.

As she peeled off his back, he felt the loss. Rather than do something stupid, like kiss her, he climbed off the bike and took her helmet.

"So what's the plan, brash girl?" He wanted Taryn annoyed in order to make resisting her mouth easier.

"A butt-kicking if you call me that again." She swung her leg over and got off the bike. She adjusted her clothing and looked around. It was getting pretty dark. The streetlamps worked but were probably energy efficient, therefore not putting out a lot of light. "Why don't we walk past the house and look for nosy neighbors who might call 911 on us. From the looks of Caleb's house, I wouldn't be surprised if a block watch wasn't formed, just to keep tabs on him."

"Good point." Rick pocketed the bike key, dug out her camera bag, and handed it over. "Lead on."

Taryn headed for the sidewalk. "Sweet'ums is a show dog and Karen is worried that she isn't being cared for properly. We need to get the dog back ASAP before Caleb harms her."

"Sweet'ums? Are you kidding?"

"I wish I was." She slowed past the house. Lights were on in the living room. A shadow passed the sheer curtains. "Someone's home. Listen for barking and look for dog poop in the grass. He may have more than one dog."

Dog poop? "Should I go to the minimart for evidence bags? We can test for doggie DNA to confirm we have the right dog."

"Funny." She walked to the far end of the property line. "I wish we knew what the dog looked like. Irving tried to send a photo, but he's computer challenged. All I got from the picture was a gray and black blur of fur."

A floodlight across the street, like the kind found at a professional sports stadium, clicked on, blinding them. A shout followed. "Is someone out there?"

"Damn!" Taryn said. "Hide!"

Chapter 18

The only place not covered in alien spaceship white light was the backyard. Taryn darted past Caleb's rusty car and into the half mowed grass, half weedy patch between the two houses. Rick briefly lost her in the darkness as his eyes adjusted from the spotlight to night vision.

"Here," she hissed from behind a patch of daylilies at the back of the next-door neighbor's garden. Rick joined her, crouching out of sight. This proved difficult for him, as the flowers were only about two and a half feet tall.

They waited for a couple of minutes for the cops to discover them. When that didn't happen, Rick shifted up to his knees and looked around.

"See anything?" she whispered. It was hard to hear over her racing heart. With all the running she'd been doing lately, she considered taking up jogging for better fitness. What could it hurt? Sitting in her car all day watching hotels wasn't doing anything positive for her butt.

"A bare patch of dirt and what looks like piles of aging dog crap," Rick said.

"Are you sure?"

"It's too dark to confirm, but I think so." He squinted. "Otherwise they have one hell of a mole population."

Taryn started to get up to investigate when a pale yellow back porch light flicked on. She dropped back and Rick slid silently down beside her. The light flickered and sizzled like the bulb was going out. Poo-poo-gate would wait. She held her breath as the screen door popped open and a figure in a ratty nightgown appeared with a dog at her side.

"Hurry up and do your business!" The voice was harsh and female. "I don't have all day to wait." A pause, then, "Sweet'ums! Go!"

Doggie toenails tapped down wooden stairs to the backyard and headed out about a dozen feet, the dog's nose to the ground. Taryn and Rick each made surprised faces at each other. Could it be this easy? Would the dog get close enough to snatch? Should she call Karen for approval to nab the dog?

The woman backed inside and let the door slam shut behind her. Evidently, she wasn't worried about Sweet'ums wandering out of the unfenced yard.

Taryn and Rick got to their knees and peered through the daylilies. Shadowed along the fenceline of the house on the opposite side was a small dog shape intently sniffing along the grassy edge, as if looking for something gross to roll in.

"What should we do?" Rick said.

"I'll try and call her over. You catch her." Taryn let out a low whistle. The dog went ballistic. Darting across the yard, she stopped six feet away and released a shrill round of barking. From her shape and size, they wouldn't have trouble carting her off.

From inside the house, a male voice yelled, "Shut up, you stupid dog!"

"Well, that wasn't nice," Taryn said, but the dog went silent and sat. When no further activity came from inside, she whistled again. The dog stayed where she was. "Come, Sweet'ums."

Nothing.

"Hand me my camera bag." Rick obliged. Taryn dug around for something to entice the mutt. She pulled out a package of beef jerky. Rick's brow lifted. "They taste funky but kill hunger during long stakeouts."

She peeled the plastic wrapper back and broke off a piece. She tossed it toward the dog, and the mutt took a sniff. And sat back down. In the shadow, her skinny body quivered.

"I don't have caviar, mutt." She rifled in the bag and found an old half-eaten and dried-out string cheese chunk. Nope. She tossed it behind her. A pack of Skittles, a piece of gum, and a nail file all got set aside. "Shoot."

"I could make a run for her," Rick said.

"Yes, and get us caught. I'm still looking." Finally, her hand closed around an unopened package of peanut butter crackers. She held it up like she'd found the Holy Grail. "This should work." She ripped it open and broke a cracker in half, then threw it to the dog.

Sweet'ums, stood, walked over, sniffed, lifted her leg, and piddled on the treat. Taryn gasped.

"I suspect Sweet'ums is a boy." Rick chuckled. "And he doesn't like crackers."

"This is not funny," she said, laughing quietly beside him. "We're never going to retrieve him before that woman comes back." She was running out of ideas.

"Let me try." He cleared his throat. "Come, dumbass!" he said in a tone stern and low. The dog stood. "Come, stupid!"

Sweet'ums trotted over. Rick snatched him, clamping a hand around his nose to cut off a strangled bark. The dog went crazy, fighting to get free.

"Let's go!" He jumped to his feet, Taryn bolting after him. They made it between the two houses before a shout went up.

"Sweet'ums! Hey! Where are you, you dumb mutt!"

Rick and Taryn raced to the sidewalk and took off toward the bike. Once there, he spun and shoved the dog and his jacket at her. She pressed Sweet'ums to her chest with one hand and jammed her free arm into the jacket. In seconds, she and the dog were zipped inside and on the bike. Rick didn't bother with helmets as he fired up the bike and took off, just as the dognapper and his accomplice rounded the house.

They were still confused over the missing dog. Taryn gave the pair a salute as they sped by, clueing them to what had happened to Sweet'ums. Caleb wasn't as dumb as she'd been led to believe.

Swearing followed. Taryn's laughter drowned it out. She buried her face in the open neck of the jacket and made soft cooing noises. The dog shook, terrified. "It's okay, baby. We'll get you home to your mommy."

After a stop at a closed gas station to call Karen, who unfortunately wasn't home, Taryn left a message and gave Rick instructions to get them to her house from there. He shoved the helmet on her head and donned his before heading off again.

They arrived at the house. All was quiet from next door, except for lights on in what she assumed were late-night study sessions in bedrooms. Her porch was boy and assassin free.

A first.

Rick pulled up the driveway and shut off the bike. He helped her remove her helmet so she wouldn't drop the dog. Sweet'ums let out a low growl deep in his battered bomber jacket, clearly unforgiving of the earlier manhandling.

"It's okay, precious. I won't let the big bad man hurt you," Taryn said and patted the dog through the coat as Rick hooked both helmets onto the bike. "He's just a meanie."

"I don't think it's me who's the bad guy here," Rick countered. "I'd be surly too if my owner had named me Sweet'ums. It's emasculating." He helped her off the bike.

Taryn assured the dog that he was the manliest dog ever born, despite his name, and headed for the house. Once inside, she walked through to the kitchen table and flicked on the light. The house was quiet and there was no sign of grilling in the backyard or Alvin sharpening the cutlery for her assassination. So far, so good.

"Alvin is either sleeping or out," she said, as Rick joined her at the table.

She couldn't imagine where Alvin would go. He didn't know anyone in town. But she wasn't his babysitter and his life was his own. He'd show up eventually. The dog was the priority.

"Let's see what a fancy show dog looks like, Sweet'ums." She unzipped the coat and the dog tumbled out in a tangle of legs and paws.

She went still with shock.

"Good God, what is that?" Rick said and put his hand on his gun. "Step back, the dog has mange."

The entirety of his gray fur was located on his head and tail, with a few tufts between his toes. His eyes were watery and bulging and his lower jaw was not aligned with the upper, so his tongue hung out and to the right. A few upper teeth appeared to be missing and the lowers were crooked. His skin was a grayish color with a few black spots.

Rick clicked off the safety. Taryn stepped between them.

"Stop it. He isn't sick." She examined the dog as it wagged its bald stick of a tail. "I've seen these online. It's a Chinese something or another. They win ugly dog contests."

Scowling, he flicked on the safety and returned the gun to his waistband. He didn't appear convinced. "This is a breed? Someone mates them together on purpose?"

She reached out to run her hand down Sweet'ums's smooth bald back. He was pretty soft. "Don't be rude. He can't help the way he looks. All dogs need love."

In response, the dog gave her wrist a lick. "Aren't you precious? Yes, you are." She scooped him up and he laid his head on her shoulder. "Are you hungry? I think I have a can of cat food in the cupboard from when my parents visited with Fluffy and Bob."

The dog let out a low growl at Rick. She turned her head to see dog and man lock eyes, the latter making the sign of the cross over his metal band t-shirt.

"Pay no attention to him, Sweet'ums." She rubbed his bald neck. "We'll find you some food and wait until your mommy comes to get you."

Rick grunted. Sweet'ums growled again. Then he laid his head on her shoulder and sighed.

He was the ugliest thing on four legs, but he was sweet. More to her amusement, he hated Rick, so that alone was worth something. It was fun to watch the big bad biker unsettled by a fifteen-pound dog.

After scrounging for a can of Friskies, she fed the dog from a bowl on the floor. As Sweet'ums happily devoured fish-flavored shreds, she stood watch over him, concerned about the look in Rick's eyes. He'd grumbled under his breath the entire time it took to feed the dog. She'd heard everything.

"Sweet'ums does not need an exorcism," she said when he took a breath. "And a holy water bath will not cure what ails him. Don't be a meanie."

"I'm just being proactive. You don't want to unleash the hound from hell on this house. Demon spirits are hard to eject, once they've crossed the threshold. I know. I've seen several exorcism movies."

"Shhh." She bit her twitching bottom lip. "You'll hurt his feelings. Dogs are sensitive."

"With a name like his, he's probably heard worse on the doggie playground."

The dog dribbled a few bits of food out of the side of his crooked mouth. "Poor baby. He really could use dental work."

She dropped onto a kitchen chair. A prickle of a thought came into her head. "Hold up." She pushed some papers aside and reached for her laptop lying on the table, which also served as her desk when she was home.

"What's up?" Rick took a seat beside her.

"One second." She opened her emails to all the links Summer had forwarded to her about Brinkman and Honey. She scrolled through the headers and clicked on one email.

Honey's inactive profile picture popped up. She scanned it and grinned. "I think Sweet'ums just cracked this case."

Chapter 19

Rick stared at the screen. "I don't see what you're seeing." Taryn touched the photo. In the background on the Match-Mate page, and to the right of the smiling Honey, was half of a fluffy white dog sitting on a pillow in the screened porch behind her. Most of the background had been cropped out, leaving Honey and her, um, sizeable assets as the focal point(s) of the picture.

"So? Honey likes dogs."

"No." Taryn turned to him. Excitement filled her face. "Don't you get it? Dogs, especially small, high-maintenance dogs, require frequent grooming, and vet care." She pointed at Sweet'ums. "The way to find our missing lovebirds might be through her dog."

She was right. His mother once had a Pomeranian and it required a lot of grooming. The ladies at her local Cut and Fluff knew them like old friends. "If Sweet'ums leads us to Honey, I may develop a grudging appreciation for the hell hound." He had a higher, and not at all grudging, appreciation for his PI.

"I knew I hired you for a reason," he said. She was one hell of an investigator. "And it wasn't for the way you fill out your jeans."

Her eyes danced. "Are you hitting on me, Special Agent Silva?"

"Only if you want me to."

Those same eyes indicated she was game for a kiss. He leaned in. Sweet'ums growled. Rick swore and glanced down. The mutt had his rump on her foot and was staring up at him with its upper lip curled back from its crooked teeth. He couldn't tell if it was surly or smiling. Either way, the dog had won the battle for the damsel.

The moment was lost. There'd be no kissing while her watchdog was around. "I saved you, mutt. Show a little gratitude."

Taryn laughed and scooped up the dog. "Come, baby. We'll find you a place to sleep for tonight. I'm sure your mommy will call in the morning."

They left the kitchen. Rick took the opportunity to call his mother with an update. She liked to stay up late watching QVC so he wouldn't be waking her up.

"Hey, Mom."

"Rick, honey, what's wrong?"

Always surprised by how easily she could read him, Rick leaned back on the chair. He wanted to confess his transgressions with Taryn and ask for advice, but held back. He should be working the case and the case only. Not playing around with his PI. Not that his mom wouldn't like the thought of him in a relationship.

"Nothing. I just got bested by the devil."

"Do I want to know what that means?" She took a deep breath. "Have you been drinking?"

"I haven't been drinking." His father, Ed, had been a weekend drunk. He'd started on Friday after work and stopped at bedtime on Sunday. Although he'd been nonviolent and a jovial drunk, he'd nonetheless killed off his liver and died at age fifty-two, devastating his wife and kids. "Have you heard from Ryan lately?"

"He's still in the Middle East somewhere. That's all I know. I wish he'd stop re-upping and come home."

"Me too." There was nothing he could say to comfort a mother who worried about her Special Forces son in a war zone, so he changed the subject. "I hired a PI to help with your case. We've worked some leads, but no Brinkman yet."

There was a lengthy silence. Although Brinkman had screwed her over, Rick knew his mother had loved him. Or rather the man she thought he was. She was still hurting.

He wanted to crush the con man.

Instead, he filled her in on the hunt, leaving out the shooting and kissing parts. "Tomorrow we're looking into vets and groomers. Hopefully, we'll get a lead."

"This Taryn sounds like a competent PI. Is she cute?"

"Mom."

"What? I'm just curious. Is it wrong to want to see my son happy?"

Happy in Joyce Silva's mind was him married to a nice woman, settled in a house next door to her, and his wife pregnant with quintuplets. The idea of that made him shudder.

"Moving on." He loved his mother, but she had her own plans for her sons. Those plans made her trouble. The one time she fixed him up was a surprise home-cooked dinner with a woman who had "childbearing hips." He'd fled before dessert and spent five years working undercover out of state. "I'll call you if this dog thing pans out."

"I feel bad that you're missing your vacation to do this. You should be on a beach somewhere."

His mind flashed to Taryn in a bikini. Maybe he'd suggest a trip after this was over, as a thank-you for all her hard work. Seeing her in a swimsuit would be his reward.

"You know I wouldn't do this if I didn't want to." He listened to the quiet of the house. The place was old and worn, but it suited Taryn. He yawned. "Listen, it's getting late. I have to go. I'll call you again soon."

"I love you, honey."

"Love you, too, Mom. Night."

He shoved the phone into his pocket. To hell with her guard dog. Somewhere in the house was the woman who made him crazy and he wanted to know if he could steal another kiss before he went back to his lonely motel.

A quick sweep left him confident she wasn't downstairs. So he took the steps up two at a time. The second floor had several bedrooms, and two bathrooms, all of them empty. In the biggest room at the end of the hallway, he found Taryn.

She was curled up fully clothed on the bed, with the dog wrapped in her arms, sleeping. Well, *she* was sleeping. Devil dog gave him the evil eye as he entered her bedroom. Rick frowned. He was too damn tired to fight with the mutt. He ignored Sweet'ums and focused on Taryn.

Damn. She was beautiful. Her lashes fanned out to cover her eyes and her mouth parted slightly as she breathed. He knew he should go, but discovered that the idea of sleeping alone tonight didn't appeal to him, nor did leaving her alone with Alvin the assassin and the mangy mutt. And knowing that she'd probably kick his butt for taking advantage didn't stop him from taking off his boots, placing his Glock on the nightstand, and climbing in beside her.

Sweet'ums growled. Rick glared. The dog looked away first.

Satisfied with the win, Rick snuggled up behind her and promptly fell asleep.

Something odd brought Taryn awake. Surprisingly, it wasn't finding Rick spooned up against her back with a sleep erection that caused her discomfort, though it should, or the glow of her phone with a text from Tim. Nor was it the low grumble coming from the dog. No, it was an unfamiliar creak in the house that caused her to tense up on the bed. After almost three years of living here, she knew the place intimately.

The energy in the house was wrong. It was an unfamiliar creak on the stairs that kicked up an alarm.

She awkwardly turned on the bed, dislodging the dog from the crook of her knees and rousing Rick. She clamped a hand over his mouth. "Shhh," she whispered. "Someone is in the house."

Taryn released him.

"Are you sure?" he whispered back. "It's probably your killer."

"It isn't Alvin," she assured him. "He has a thudding and lumbering gait. This one is lighter."

A protesting stair confirmed a presence. Whoever the intruder was, he was unfamiliar with the old bones of the house. Not even stealth helped him avoid making noise on protesting stairs.

Rick reached for his gun, as Taryn silently rolled from the bed and went for hers. The feel of the weapon in her hand gave her confidence. She'd never had to use it, but was well trained with years of practice behind her.

"Follow me and we'll sneak up on him," she whispered.

She left the room in stocking feet and stayed to the left of the hall, where the boards didn't creak. Rick was silent behind her. There was no need for lights to guide them. She could get from her room to the kitchen and back for a midnight snack without flicking on a single light.

They just about made it to the top of the stairs, when a clatter of toenails raced past them, followed by high-pitched barking. "Sweet-'ums, no!" Taryn cried.

"Shit!" came a voice, followed by the sound of a man run-stumbling down the stairs.

The dog went nuts. Rick rounded her and gave chase. Taryn dove for the hallway light switch. Unfortunately, the intruder had a head start and was already out the open front door before the illumination could clue them to his identity.

She bolted after the two men and out onto the porch.

The street was quiet but for a chorus of crickets and Sweet'ums's barking from the open doorway. Taryn could see Rick's outline and headed that way. He darted between two houses across the street and vanished. She caught up with him on the next street over, gun in his hand, barefoot, and spinning to look for the suspect.

"Where is he?" she asked and came to a stop beside him.

"I have no idea." The streetlights were bright enough to be seen from Mars but there was no sign of the burglar. "Damn. He's gone."

They wandered up and down the street to the end of each block for another ten minutes without success. "Whoever he was, he had his escape well planned," Rick said, when they reconvened on the corner.

She nodded. "I'm now convinced the shooting was connected to this. This is the second strange occurrence since I took this case. I'm not one for coincidences.

"I agree." He tucked his Glock into his waistband. "Our sweetheart con may have upgraded from swindler to killer."

Chapter 20

Trudging back to the house, they found the dog whining and shivering in the open doorway. Taryn scooped him up. "His little doggie heart is racing. It's okay, pup. You're fine."

Sweet'ums gave her a lick. Yuck.

"Some watchdog you have," Rick grumbled. "And where's your bodyguard? I though he took a blood oath to protect you from the evil Willard and his murdering minions? He's doing a bang-up job tonight."

As if on cue, Alvin shuffled up the sidewalk, turned onto her property, and clomped up the stairs to the porch.

He glanced between them and stared down at Rick still holding his Glock. "What's happening?"

"Someone broke into the house," Rick said, scowling.

"Shit." Alvin turned to scan the darkness. "Did he try to kill you?"

"He didn't have the chance," Rick said. As much as he disagreed with Alvin staying with Taryn, it angered him to know that if he hadn't decided to spend the night, the evening could have turned out much worse for Taryn. Although she was fully able to take care of herself, a killer with a gun lowered the odds of a successful outcome to a confrontation. "We chased him off."

Alvin looked over at Taryn and the dog. If he was curious about the pooch, he said nothing. Instead, his eyes went hard and his hands closed into fists. "I'm going to hunt down Willard and break him into little pieces."

So much for anger management therapy. She'd have to find him a new therapist before he slid back to the dark side.

"You will do no such thing," Taryn said. "We don't know if he's behind this. Houses get burglarized all the time. For all we know, our burglar could have been looking for cash for drugs." She glanced at Rick. "Why were you in my bed anyway?"

"I like to spoon after doggy kidnappings," he said dryly. He turned on Alvin. "Where were you? I thought you were watching her."

"I don't need watching." She waited for a response. When that failed, she faced the dog. "The two vessels of bubbling testosterone continue to glare at each other as if I hadn't spoken. At least you are a male who appreciates a competent woman, sweet boy."

Rick frowned. He continued to stare at the large bodyguard. He was good at staring down bad guys.

After ten seconds, Alvin's expression finally turned sheepish. "I was getting some sex."

"From who?" Taryn said.

"The lady in the blue house." He pointed down the street with a crooked finger. "She saw me fixing your porch swing and invited me over."

At Rick's puzzled look, Taryn explained. "Kitty Henderson. Her husband is away a lot. She likes to entertain strange men she picks up . . . wherever."

Alvin fit that profile. He was strange.

"Before we get off topic, let's get the housebreak taken care of." Rick pulled out his phone and called the police. He wasn't taking chances with Taryn's safety. Whether it was a burglar or a killer, Taryn wasn't safe. Maybe the presence of the cops would deter further break-ins or attempts on her life.

"No."

"Yes."

Taryn stood with her bare foot braced behind the door early the next morning, determined to keep Rick and his duffel from crossing the threshold and into her house. She knew he had strength over her, yet she was convinced that if she let him in, things would change in their relationship. It would flip from professional to personal.

They were already on shaky ground in that regard anyway.

"We covered this last night after the police left and you agreed that I don't need a bodyguard. Not even Alvin and his giant knuckles," she snapped. "I can take care of myself."

"I know you're capable of taking care of yourself under normal circumstances." He flattened a hand on the panel above her head to keep the door open. "But this isn't a normal case. Twice you've been put in danger. Let's think of me as backup, your partner in safety."

She raked her eyes down him. He did have a point. Sort of. Still, the partnership didn't have to spill over into her personal space.

"You know I'm right," he said.

"No. I'm sizing you up for a fur Speedo, Cro-Magnon man, since you clearly haven't evolved enough over the last gazillion years to know that women don't need men to protect them anymore."

He grinned. "Serve me up a slab of raw meat and I'll let you see what's under my pelt, sweet thing."

Her eyes rolled up. The man could argue the paint off the house. "I'm not going to get rid of you, am I?"

"Nope." He ran a finger down her arm. "You're cute when you go all tough-girl."

"You're a pain. Always."

He glanced at her worn and slightly crooked porch swing. Clearly Alvin had been taken away for sex with Kitty prior to finishing the job. Rick couldn't fault him there.

"I'll make you a deal. You don't have to let me in. It's your house, your decision." He picked up the duffel. "I'd be happy to camp out here. A sleeping bag and a few blasts of mosquito repellent and I'll be all set."

The idea of him stretching his over six-foot frame out on a four-foot swing did appeal to her. He'd be walking like a stooped octogenarian after one night sleeping there. However, that wasn't her biggest concern.

"The neighbors will get a kick out of that. They're already fleeing into their houses when Alvin steps outside. More crazy hijinks and they'll run me out of town." With the largest long-suffering sigh ever expelled from a pair of lips, Taryn stepped back and opened the door. "If you try anything shady, you're out. Got it?"

"Got it."

The dog trotted after her. "Pick any room that isn't mine. You can even bunk with Alvin if you don't mind spooning." He made a face. Now that image brought her a smile. "I'll feed Sweet'ums and then we'll go. I've narrowed down to three vets and two groomers, as possible candidates to start with. We might as well get moving early."

* * *

Rick chose the room across the hall from her, dumped the duffel on the bed, and went in search of Taryn. He found her already seated in his rented SUV. He climbed in. A snuffling noise from the backseat turned him around.

"Oh, hell no." Seated dead center of the bench seat was the devil in dog form. Sweet'ums blinked his watery eyes, bent to lick his equipment enthusiastically for a full ten seconds, and then lifted his head to smile at Rick through crooked teeth, as if silently challenging him to repeat that neat trick. Rick had to resist crossing himself again. The dog was disturbing.

"Oh, hell yes," Taryn countered. "Dr. Karen had an emergency surgery come up in Traverse City. If all goes well, she'll be back for Sweet'ums in two days. Until then, where I go, he goes, or I'll work this case by myself."

"Why can't your felon watch him?"

"He's spending the day having sex with Kitty. She's allergic to dogs."

Damn. She had him trapped.

Why was it that Alvin was the clear winner in all this? Rick wanted to have sex with Taryn and all he got was the dog drooling all over his backseat. How was this fair?

He'd won the battle over staying with her. But by the stubborn tilt of her chin, he knew she'd not let him win this skirmish. She was punishing him for invading her house.

"Fine. But he'd better behave."

Rick plugged the address of the first groomer into his GPS and they pulled away from the curb. "How did you narrow the list of vets and groomers? In this town, there's one on every street corner."

"There are a lot," she agreed. "I chose the closest ones to Honey's former apartment and called them all. I described her and the dog. Honey did use the Groom and Go a couple of times, but it's been months since they've seen Brutus. So I assume she's gone elsewhere."

"Brutus? What's with women and dog names? Just being seen around a dog like Honey's voids any man points, even with a man like Alvin. Calling him Brutus doesn't help."

"A man shouldn't need a mastiff to feel manly."

He shot her a look. "Be honest. If you saw me walking around with a teacup poodle under my arm, what would you think? You'd snicker and wonder if I also ate tofu and manscaped my legs and back."

The silence confirmed his point. "See. I'm right. You can complain about my Cro-Magnon ways all day long, but if I whipped out a ukulele and sang love songs to you while sniveling into an embroidered hanky, you'd never have another hot fantasy about me again."

Darn. He was right. She liked his tattoos and muscles and square jaw. She liked that he ate meat and potatoes and rode a really cool vintage bike. What bothered her was his use of "sniveling" and "embroidered hanky." Was the man a chick flick junky? Lord, she hoped not. "Maybe I'm just shallow."

She didn't realize she said the last part out loud, until he chuckled beside her.

"You aren't shallow, Taryn. Attraction fits all people differently. I have a friend who writes poetry to his wife and she loves it. But that's not me. If you ever need gas in your car or a tire changed, I'm there."

Despite his comment, she suspected there was more to him than tire changing. She'd felt passion in his kisses and seen the way he'd looked at her after the kisses were over. He might not put his feelings to poetry, but she believed that deep down under that bad boy exterior, he might actually enjoy a few minutes of post-sex cuddling, long conversations under the stars, his and hers mani-pedis. The possibilities were endless.

Sure.

"Wait. Hold up." She frowned, remembering his earlier comment. "Who said I have hot fantasies about you?"

"Don't you?"

"Absolutely not." She shook her head a bit too vigorously. Okay, there might have been one or two you-naked-me-naked dreams with her feet up behind her ears and him doing all sorts of naughty things to her body. However, she wasn't responsible for where her nocturnal mind went when she was sleeping. Right?

"I'm not having this conversation."

"Good idea." He sent her a heated look. "It's better to talk fantasies when we're both naked, preferably in bed, when I can show you how a biker makes love with a 'good' girl."

Taryn went hot. Every part of her tingled with raw need that terrified her. She jerked her eyes free of his.

"Just drive." Her voice sounded strangled in her ears.

Rick chuckled as they headed for their first visit of the day.

The Clip and Fluff had a cream colored façade with black paws painted across the wall leading to the front entrance. On the windows were posters of perfectly coiffed dogs and cats in various shapes and sizes.

Inside, a young woman wearing gray hospital scrubs covered in black-and-white cartoon kittens was on the phone taking an appointment. When she saw Rick, she almost dropped the phone. "Mrs. Able, Fluffy is all set. See you Friday."

Once free of business, Kayley, or so her name tag said, smoothed her hand over an ample bosom, somehow flicking open two buttons in the process, and almost dissolved into a puddle on the desk. Her face split into an appreciative smile meant only for Special Agent Rick Silva as she leaned seductively forward over a desktop calendar. The V-neckline of her scrubs struggled to remain in control of her breasts.

"Can I help you?"

"We're here about a dog," he said.

"Is it a little dog or a big dog? I can groom whatever you've got, handsome."

Who ever thought the process of de-matting dogs and clipping their nails could sound so dirty?

A bog barked from a back room and Kayley turned away for no more than two seconds. When she turned back, a black lace bra peaked out from the V.

Seriously? The woman was in heat. She needed a leash and a tranquilizer dart.

Taryn darted a glance at Rick. He looked more amused than intrigued. He was probably used to spontaneous female wardrobe malfunctions.

"We are looking for a fluffy white dog named Brutus," Taryn said, before the girl could dive for his zipper. "His owner is Honey Comstock. When I called earlier, someone said she was a client."

Kayley stared blankly at her like she'd been shaken from a testosterone-filled haze. "I'm sorry, ma'am. Are you here to get your pet groomed?"

Taryn slapped both hands down on the desk. She'd had enough. "We are together," she said slowly, to make sure Kayley could keep up. She pointed a finger at him and back at herself. "Got it? Now tell us about Brutus and Honey."

Two minutes later, they had nothing new for the case file. Brutus hadn't been in for several months and Honey's address was the one they already had. Kayley was nearly in tears that Rick didn't take the bait, and Taryn needed an espresso.

Rick thanked the disappointed girl and they left.

"You know, I've lived on this earth for twenty-five years and not once have my breasts ever spontaneously popped out of my shirt," she said. "In fact, I've never twisted my ankle or lost clothing while running away from machete-wielding killers, either. How does that happen to some women?"

A chuckle followed. "You don't wear button-up shirts? Because when women are around me, shirts pop open and clothes go flying off all the time."

"I'll bet they do." All the more reason to keep her clothes on around him. Rick was clearly not the kind of guy to build a relationship with. He was more the one-night stand sort. And she didn't need that mess in her life. When she finally decided to get serious about finding someone, he'd be stable and safe and drive a minivan.

Sweet'ums stood on his back paws and pushed his face out the open driver's-side window. The morning was cool, and he was bald, so he wasn't in any danger of overheating. Besides, Taryn was an animal lover. She'd never let anything happen to him. She'd become kind of attached to him.

"Do you think Kayley can fix up Sweet'ums? Make him less offensive to the eyes," Rick said and started the SUV. "Maybe put a couple of pink bows in his hair?"

Gack.

Both heads spun around. "Gross," Rick said.

Taryn laugh-gagged. Apparently Sweet'ums didn't like liver and tuna in sauce cat food. Or Rick. Or both. "That's what he thinks about your insults."

Rick drove to a minimart and bought paper towels. Then he proceeded to swear, during the entirety of the three minutes it took to clean up the leather seat. Sweet'ums grinned—at least that's what Taryn suspected—from his place in her arms.

Dropping the last towel into the plastic shopping bag, Rick glared at them, while he tied off the bag. "You should have cleaned it up. You brought him along."

"But you said you wanted to be my sidekick. Sherlock Holmes would never clean up dog barf. He'd leave it to Watson."

The response was a grunt and a mouth twist.

They followed up with the other groomer and the vets. Nothing. Frustration grew. They hit a groomer not on her list and an emergency animal clinic.

Rick tapped the steering wheel with his fingertips. "Brutus must be a healthy dog." He shot Sweet'ums a shaming glance.

They left the clinic.

"Okay, we know Honey existed. You have a fax of their marriage license. She would need ID to get that," she said. "But outside of a few online posts and a dog groomer, we are no closer to Honey or Brinkman."

Rick stopped at a red light. He leaned back against the SUV seat and dropped his chin to his chest. She could see his mind working.

"I think we need to go back to the shooting and the break-in. Despite the contract out on your head, I'm convinced it's no coincidence that both things happened after we started this case. Someone doesn't want us to find Brinkman."

"I think so, too."

"Why don't we get Summer on this? Someone other than Willard is watching you and I think they're not hiding in the bushes."

Rick spent most of his career doing field work and not enough time online. He was as proficient as the next guy, but going deep was not his thing. When he pulled into a fast food joint and called Summer to tell her of his suspicions, he could hear excitement in her voice.

"This will be fun!" she exclaimed, then hung up.

"Do you really think someone can follow us around remotely?" Taryn said, as he shoved his phone in his pocket.

"I do." He made a face at the dog slobbering on the car window glass. Taryn scratched its head and made a kissy face. "How do you think the government finds terrorists?"

"Of course. However, we are looking for a con man, not a terrorist sleeper cell. Brinkman is old school. His Match-Mate post was basic and amateurish. How could a guy like that suddenly become a computer expert?"

He stared down at her mouth. "That remains the question. How is that bastard staying a step ahead of us? Who are the two men who shot at us? He could be working with those men, as part of a bigger conspiracy."

"I have a hard time seeing that option," she said and hugged the dog. "Why cut his take three ways if he can have all his thieving profits to himself?"

He envied that mutt.

"When we find Brinkman, I'll beat the information out of him." Taryn frowned. He grinned. Despite the break-in at the Affordable U-Store, the lock picking, and her many driving infractions, she had a problem with him roughing Brinkman up.

"You'll do no such thing. He's an old man. It won't be a fair fight. Will it, Sweet'ums? No, it won't."

More kissy stuff. Now he was heading toward jealousy of the dog. What was it with women and pets anyway? The ugly dog gacks on his backseat and she still looks at it with unconditional love. And it isn't even her dog!

Shaking it off, Rick pulled back into traffic. "If I'm right about Brinkman and the cyber-stalking," Rick said, "we have a trap to set."

Chapter 21

Rick offered to spring for food, so they headed to a local Asian restaurant for takeout. The parking lot was packed for the lunch buffet and Taryn's stomach rumbled. She loved Asian food. They parked in the shade and cracked the windows and she promised Sweet'ums that as soon as she ordered, she'd come right back to wait with him. They locked the doors and were heading in when a couple exiting the place caught her eye. Her stomach clenched.

Gloria.

Unwelcome images flashed in her head. Tim. Gloria. Naked. Doing the nasty on the fancy green sheets she'd picked out for their wedding registry. Thankfully, she hadn't yet become one of Irving's PIs that night, or she might have shot them both on thousand-thread-count sheets. Okay, probably not, but a Macing was not entirely out of the question.

Going cold, Taryn forced herself to hold it together.

Sometime over the last three years, her former maid had dyed her naturally auburn hair to an unnatural magenta and was wearing skimpy clothing better suited for a hooker. Beside her was a man wearing black spandex bike shorts and a tight blue tank top. He was no more than twenty, with bulging muscles and a missing neck, and his bleached blond mullet was more 1980 than this century.

The guy reached out to grab Gloria's butt and almost dislodged the micro-miniskirt from her rounded rump. Only a quick grab of the hem kept her skirt from becoming a belt and the world from seeing her playground.

Taryn gritted her teeth as they approached. Gloria stumbled on kitten heels when she spotted Taryn. She recovered quickly with a chin lift and jutting jaw.

"Taryn."

"Gloria." Taryn stared at no-neck. "Where's Tim?"

The maid turned to grip her companion's arm as the youngster stared appreciatively at Taryn. Out of spite, Taryn sent him her sweetest smile. Perfectly capped teeth smiled back. Up close, her thirty-six-year-old ex-maid looked like his babysitter. Too much time in bars chugging cocktails had turned her skin sallow.

"Tim's history." Gloria scowled, gripped her boy toy tighter, and cast a sidelong flirty glance at Rick. If she intended payback for her boy toy staring at Taryn, she failed. Rick scowled. Taryn smirked. Gloria blanched and turned away. "He was boring. Serge and I are together now."

If on cue, Serge flexed his pecs back and forth in an odd little dance. "Together," he mimicked, clearly a boy genius.

Well, that explained Tim's calls. He didn't like to be alone. Unfortunately for him, hell had not iced over, and she hadn't gone insane. If he was calling to get back together, he was an idiot.

"I see." What else could she say? A ruined marriage, and the ruiner had moved on to another victim.

Taryn tried to summon up some sympathy for Tim but got nothing. He was in her rearview mirror. She had no interest in being dragged back into his life.

"We should go, babe," Rick said and took Taryn's hand. "We don't want to be late to relieve the babysitter."

Gloria's gasp followed them, as Rick led Taryn around the pair and entered the restaurant. She might have taken satisfaction with Rick taking the smug Gloria down another peg—after all, Taryn had the superior "boyfriend"—but it was enough work to keep her roiling stomach from emptying. When the door closed behind them, Taryn wobbled. He led her to a bench seat in the vestibule.

"You okay?" He sat beside her.

She nodded. "I can't believe I let her rattle me. All I could think of was finding her in my bed with my husband and all the damage she did to my life. We'd only been married a little over a year. I hadn't even used our wedding china."

He took her hand again. "If it makes you feel any better, I think your ex was an idiot. She isn't in your league."

"Thanks for saying that."

"No. I mean it." He turned her face toward him. "You are funny and crazy and a really bad driver. And so sexy that I walk around you all day with a hard-on. She couldn't compare to you even on your worst day. I want to hunt down your ex and pulverize him for hurting you."

Tears welled. She stared into his eyes.

"That's the sweetest thing anyone has ever said to me." The tension in her stomach eased and she fell a little bit in love with him in that moment. He really was a great guy. "I am over him, you know. It was just a shock to see her."

"I know." He skimmed his hand under her chin. "Otherwise you wouldn't be looking at me like that."

She smiled. "And how is that?"

"Like you want me to kiss you." He brushed her bottom lip with his thumb. Her breath caught. Common sense fled and desire filled her senses, along with the scent of fried rice and egg rolls. She really, really wanted to be kissed.

"Then you'd better get to it." Her lips parted.

Grinning, Rick kissed her. The tenderness of the touch, and his warmth, chased off any lingering chill of the encounter outside. She slid her hand up and played with the hair on his nape. The kiss deepened and Taryn was thankful the seat was partially obscured from sight of the hostess desk by a low wall. She didn't want the kiss to end.

When they did break apart, due to the arrival of a large and boisterous family, she looked into his gray eyes. "You are an excellent kisser, Rick Silva."

"I've had lots of practice."

"I bet you have." Laughing, she caressed his chin. The family was led away, leaving them alone again. "I went on a couple of dates after my divorce, but nothing took. I was numb. Tim was supposed to be forever. Then here you come, all tattoos and bossy alpha-ness, and make me laugh. Really laugh again. And I'm not sure what to do with you."

"Do you need a label?"

Shaking her head, she took his hand. "I don't want forever, Rick, I just want honesty. If you plan to sleep with me, then tell me so I can make an informed decision."

He glanced around the vestibule and back. "Taryn, I want you so much I can't think of anything else. Beyond that, I can't commit. Is that enough for you?"

It was hard to speak, but she managed a nod. "I want you, too. Make love to me."

A land-speed record was broken, as well as several traffic laws, when Rick dragged her to his SUV and raced the miles between the restaurant and her house at warp speed.

Taryn laughed as he pulled her from the vehicle and up the stairs into her house, his free arm tucked around Sweet'ums, who growled at Rick but kept his teeth to himself.

The door was kicked closed by a booted foot, the dog placed on the floor, and Taryn was swept into his arms in one bold sweep.

There was no sign of her houseguest. Yay.

"You're going to drop me," she said, clutching his shoulders as he headed for the stairs. He had some strong shoulders, arms, legs.

"Not a chance." He carried her up the staircase easily and into her room. Lowering her to the floor, he pressed her back against the doorframe and kissed her.

Any chance of changing her mind was lost in the kiss. She wanted him so much, she ached with need. As a modern woman, she may have fought against his sometimes overwhelming desire to protect and boss her, but in this moment, she lowered her guard and let herself just . . . feel. The riot of sexual energy between them had her hooked.

Rick teased her with his mouth, while his rough hands found their way under her t-shirt and skimmed her skin. She moaned when his fingertips found the bottom of her bra and his thumbs slipped beneath it. He eased free of the kiss and slid her shirt up and over her head. Her simple, lacy white bra caught his attention and held.

"So much better than red or black . . ." He lowered his mouth to her collarbone and tugged one strap down. He nipped her skin then pressed his tongue to the spot.

Taryn tucked her fingers around his neck and moaned.

"If you have on matching panties, I might not make it to the bed," he said. Hooking his fingers into the waistband of her jeans, he flicked the button open. She looked down as a small patch of white was exposed to his eyes. A slow, wicked grin tugged his mouth. "I just came in my shorts."

She giggled—and she wasn't a giggler. "I suspect that you're lying to me." She reached for him. A second or two later, she had his jeans down around his knees. There was no sign of premature anything. He was still rock-hard beneath a pair of black boxer-briefs. "As I suspected. Lies. All lies."

He didn't give her time to reach for his erection. He pulled her to him. Kissing her again, he slid her jeans down her legs and cupped her butt. His hardness brushed her navel and she was the one who almost came in her panties. The intimacy sent desire flashing through her body.

Moving his mouth to her ear, he nipped her lobe, then moved down her neck. As turnabout is only fair, she reached around and moved her hands over his butt. He had a first-rate butt.

"I want you in bed," he said. She only had time to struggle free of her jeans when he spun her around and moved forward, while nudging her backward toward the bed. The backs of her thighs hit the mattress and she tumbled onto the quilt. She laughed as he kicked his jeans off like he was shaking off a poisonous snake from gnawing his calves. Once freed, he turned back and skimmed his gaze slowly down her body. With bright daylight filling the room, he could see everything.

Humor fled when his eyes went dark and intense. Locking eyes, he climbed on the bed on his hands and knees. She may have whimpered a bit when he positioned himself over her.

Taryn reached up to run her hands over his muscled chest and up to the tip of a wing of some sort of bird tattoo appearing over one shoulder. She slid her hands down to the healing wound on the scorpion and over the hieroglyphics on his other arm.

"I never was a tattoo sort of girl," she said breathlessly. "I may have just changed my mind."

His tongue touched his lower lip and his eyes were heated. "Babe, I'm going change your mind about a lot of things today."

This time she did whimper. He leaned in and kissed her, doing a thorough exploration of her mouth. She teased him back with her tongue, eliciting a groan from him.

"You're killing me," he said, when he pulled back and slid down her body. "You're beautiful."

He closed his mouth over her bra-covered nipple and used his teeth to gently entice first one and then the other to firm peaks, while he pressed his erection between her legs.

Despite only two thin layers of cloth between them, Taryn felt the barrier acutely. "Take them off."

"Hmmm?" There wasn't much else he could say with her nipple in his mouth.

"Take your briefs off." He lifted his head and cocked a brow. Her face flushed at her boldness. "I want to see you."

Rick stood and made quick work of her request. Her heart hitched at the sight of him naked. He was a fantasy she never knew she wanted.

Slowly, she slid her eyes over every line, every muscle, and every inch from his toes to his face. He stood, as if knowing her attention would heat her up, and it did. By the time he reclaimed his position in the bed, she was eager to finish the game.

As promised, Rick didn't disappoint. He kissed her and touched her and would not allow her to reciprocate, taking time to find and kiss the little scars on her skin. He whispered in her ear that this was all for her and she accepted his insistence, at first reluctantly, and then with pleasure. How could she argue when she was laughing, as he pulled her panties down her legs with his teeth? When he finally acquiesced to her pleas and slipped inside her, she was already halfway to an orgasm. He sent her over minutes later and followed her shortly thereafter while she held on tight.

The world exploded into happy dancing sunbeams. Or maybe it was sunlight seeping through the sheers on the windows. Either way, when she tumbled back to reality, satisfied in a way that defied logic, she knew that Rick was one hell of an amazing lover.

He moved off to the bathroom.

With a groan-sigh, she stretched, then curled along his long body when he returned from ditching the condom that he'd managed to slip on without her knowledge. When she was writhing on the bed with her eyes closed, maybe? He lay beside her, and wrapped one arm around her waist.

"That was—" How could she explain what that was? How she felt. There were no words. "Very nice."

Silence fell beside her. Then he said, "Nice? I get nice?"

Mischief came. It was time to give the master teaser a dose of his own medicine. She was so darn happy, she didn't want the moment to turn awkward and serious. "Pleasant? Agreeable?"

A low swear followed. He rolled onto his side and faced her. "Agreeable? Are you serious? That was fantastic!"

"If you say so." A bubble of laughter broke loose. His cheek muscle twitched. She lost it and fell back on the pillows clutching her stomach. "You should see your face! It's priceless!"

Doubling over, she thrashed on the bed. Rick caught on quickly and growled. Before she could see what he was up to, he pressed his fingertips to her ribs and tickled her.

She shrieked.

A tickle-fest followed and dissolved into a butt-naked pillow fight that was super-sexy.

"You don't insult a man's lovemaking," he said and bounced the pillow off her shoulder.

"You totally deserved it!" She dodged and hit him in the side. "You've been messing with me since day one!" She was so turned on, and he was, obviously, too. She backed to the corner of the bed and held up the pillow like a shield. "By the way, you rocked my world. Thanks for that."

He went still, grinning. "You're welcome."

Taryn shucked the pillow and crawled to him. "Roll over."

"What?"

"On your stomach, Special Agent Silva," she demanded. "Now."

"When a naked woman makes demands, how can I refuse?"

He obliged. Across his shoulders, she recognized the image immediately. In black and gray and white with a touch of yellow for its claws and beak was a griffin, wings outstretched from shoulder to shoulder; a perfect mix of eagle and lion. The artist, whoever he or she was, was a genius.

"Wow. It's beautiful." She traced her fingertips over the image. "Why did you choose a griffin?"

"It was a drunken decision I made after boot camp."

"You were in the military?"

He rolled back over. "I was an army ranger for about five minutes. We were sent to Iraq on my first tour. I was riding in a Jeep and the driver lost control to avoid a kid on the road. We rolled, I got pins to fix my shattered leg, and I was out."

"But you don't have a limp."

"It doesn't matter." He rubbed her thigh. "I'm a hard hit away from possibly rebreaking the bone. The army can't take a chance that I could be a liability in the field."

That was understandable. "Do you miss the army?"

"Occasionally. But I'm happy with what I do." He moved his hand to her inner thigh and up her leg. "I'm happy to be here with you."

"I'm happy you're here, too." Seeing his intentions, she straddled his hips. Leaning close, she bushed her breasts over his chest and touched her tongue to his lips.

"Let's do it again, ranger," she said softly.

"Yes, ma'am."

Rick didn't wake up for three hours. When he did, Taryn was sleeping and he was starving. Pulling on his jeans, more for Alvin's benefit than his own, he padded downstairs on bare feet and headed for the kitchen.

Something smelled hinky as he approached.

There he found Alvin, wearing a shirt and slacks and a floral apron, cooking something on the stove. Despite the failure of the air conditioning to bring the temperature of the house down below eighty degrees, the dog shivered at his feet like a coatless kid in a snowstorm.

"That mutt needs a sweater," Rick said and he headed for the fridge. Inside were a four-pack of chocolate pudding cups, wilted lettuce in the crisper, cheese, bottled water, and a handful of condiments. What the other stuff was he couldn't discern from the wrappings. So he claimed a pudding and figured takeout for dinner.

"The mutt needs a dentist," Alvin said in response, looking down. "And a plastic surgeon."

Rick smiled, then searched for and found a spoon. He sat at the table and peeled off the foil lid. Licking the pudding off, he nodded and tossed the lid into the trash can. "Or a paper bag over his head."

"Two, in case one breaks," Alvin said, without missing a beat. He stirred the smelly stuff in the pot.

Sweet'ums growled while Rick smiled at the old joke. He wasn't about to trust the guy by any stretch, but Alvin was pretty quick on his feet for a primate.

"What are you cooking?" Rick asked when he finally acknowl-
edged the odd odor. "It smells like a cross between skunk and pig entrails." Or what he thought pig entrails and skunk would smell like.
Nasty.

"It's cow tongue soup with barley and pork. My gran used to
make it when I was a kid." He took a sip off the spoon. "Want some?"

Rick grimaced. No wonder he hadn't recognized the ingredients in
the fridge. The last time he ate tongue was, well, never. "No thanks."
He pulled his phone from his jeans pocket, scrolled for pizza delivery,
and ordered a large pie with everything.

Leaving Alvin and the dog to their dinner, he went back upstairs
for his wallet. Taryn slept on her side, her hair brushed back from her
face and with only the sheet covering her nakedness from his view.

His heart tugged at him to stay. He wanted to crawl back into bed
and wake her up by nuzzling her neck, but didn't think meeting the
delivery guy naked, with an erection, would endear him to either the
delivery boy or the neighbors across the street.

Instead, he collected his wallet and headed back downstairs.

Taryn awoke to the smell of pepperoni and . . . wet dog? She
lifted her head to find Rick eating pizza at the end of her bed, and put
a finger under her nose. The pepperoni must be rancid.

"What did you order on that? It smells horrible."

Rick snorted and swallowed. "That smell is your houseguest
making dinner. I've opened the kitchen windows and the screened
door out back. It's not helping." He waited for her to push up and
lean against the headboard. "Pizza?"

Her stomach recoiled. She might never be hungry again.

"What is he making? Boiled roadkill?"

"Something like that. He says it's cow tongue but I think it's de-
ceased possum scraped off the interstate."

"Or a week-old raccoon, with a side of flattened squirrel," she
said. Making a face, Taryn went to the window and shoved open the
pane. The evening breeze helped clear out the smell. In a few minutes, her appetite returned. She devoured two slices.

Rick's bare chest proved distracting as he finished the rest of the
pizza. Her hands reached out for exploration of their own volition.
She knew she should have a whole hell of a lot of regrets but couldn't

manage to lock down one. She'd wanted sex and had three really great orgasms. What was there to regret?

And since he was already half naked, getting him out of his pants shouldn't prove that difficult. After all, why waste another moment wearing clothes when you don't know how long this brief sexual relationship might last?

"Are you tired?" she said and let the sheet slip.

He dropped his pizza crust. "Not that tired."

Chapter 22

"What did you do to yourself?" Taryn asked, when she and Rick wandered into Summer's computer room the next morning. Jess was wearing sweat pants with one leg pushed up her thigh and an oversized Detroit Lions jersey, and was seated on a chair with a brace on her leg.

"I twisted my knee chasing a fifty-five-year-old poacher who was carrying a deer over his shoulder and gasping the whole time like he was having a heart attack."

"You're lucky he didn't shoot you," Taryn said.

"Exactly. And he could have," Summer added. "He had a sawed-off rifle shoved down his pants."

"But he didn't get a shot off," Jess said. "When I went down, he dropped the deer and came over to check on me." Jess tried to get a finger under the brace for an itch. Summer handed her a pen. "He was laughing and clutching his giant beer belly."

"You didn't exact revenge?" Rick said.

Smiling, Jess shook her head. "I may have 'accidently' clocked him with my binoculars when he bent over me. My arm may have involuntarily flailed around some, while I was writhing on the ground."

Taryn chuckled. Of the three women, Jess was the one you'd least like to mess with. She was tough.

"Did he call for help?" Taryn said.

"Nope, I did." Jess adjusted her leg. "He laughed, then clutched his chest, then pitched over face first into a patch of poison ivy. The paramedics said he'd had a heart attack." She frowned. "After they took him to the hospital, I felt kind of bad for clocking him."

Taryn and Summer agreed on that point. The former handed her a water cup. "Is there anything Rick and I can do for you?"

"I have that mall theft case I started yesterday and was wondering if you can work the stakeout tonight?" Jess said. "I was told to stay off my leg until Tuesday, and it's delivery day at the stores and a good night for thieves. Summer said you aren't set up for dates tonight."

"Of course I can fill in." Taryn glanced at Rick. Silent and naughty promises filled his eyes. Warmth crept up her neck.

"Thanks." Jess pushed to her feet and collected one of Irving's canes she'd leaned against the desk. Once balanced, she glanced between Taryn and Rick and winked at the former. "Have fun tonight." She hobbled out.

Taryn knew Jess wasn't talking about the stakeout.

The one thing about longtime friends was that they knew all your secrets. Summer lifted a questioning brow, stared intently at her friend, then her mouth dissolved into a knowing smile.

"You two did it."

Rick's mouth twitched. Taryn frowned.

Summer had her confirmation. She ran her eyes appreciatively down Rick. "So much for keeping a professional distance. I must tell Irving. You broke the Brash & Brazen code of ethics. That cannot be tolerated."

"You are so not funny," Taryn said. "Can we get back to the case, please?"

Laughing, Summer spun around. "While you two were off breaking several morals clauses set down by this organization, I was discovering the real identity of one Teddy Brinkman."

"Are you serious?" Taryn hurried over.

"Indeed I am." Summer brought up the screen. "I used that old Social Security number to trace back forty years to a man named Karl Ridley. With further digging, I found records that showed he was actually born a U. S. citizen named Otto Karlheinz Fenstermacher, to German parents who'd come over from Germany shortly after World War II. There were sealed documents on the parents so I suspect they were either former allied spies or war criminals. When Otto was twenty-three, he became Karl Ridley and got a new Social Security number issued. The government does not do that as a common practice. That's why I think there was something odd going on with his parents."

When she finished, she dropped back on her seat.

Taryn scanned the screen. "So Teddy Brinkman was born Otto Karlheinz Fenstermacher."

"No wonder he changed it," Rick piped in. "That's one hell of a long name. Can you imagine having to sign that on your kindergarten school papers?"

Summer turned. "I've seen worse. There once was this terrorist named Jorgeo—" Taryn nudged her, before she got off track. Summer did love to talk terrorists and international criminals. It didn't exactly make her a sought-out conversationalist at cocktail parties. Then again, with her looks, she could discuss icky bowel issues at length and still land at the top of everyone's guest list.

"Sorry." Summer scrunched her nose. "I'll print out all I discovered about Otto, but don't expect much. His parents are both dead, his old high school was torn down in the seventies, and from what I could dredge up, he didn't have many friends. It seems like he reinvented himself after college with his new name and eventually became the con man we now know and love."

Taryn nipped her bottom lip. "We take one step forward and twenty back. We may never catch this guy."

"We'll catch him," Rick said. "He has to make a mistake."

The three fell silent. Taryn felt Rick's frustration. She wanted to close the case and put Brinkman in jail. The con man was a menace.

An idea came. "We know we're dealing with a seasoned criminal. Brinkman has years of bad behavior behind him. I think the only way to flush him out is if we push the Honey angle. She will be the bait to snag the fish."

"But Honey has vanished, too," Rick said.

"Yes, but someone has to know her. Can we set up a 'Where's Honey' Facebook page?" Taryn clasped her hands together. "We'll claim to be a family member who's concerned about her well-being or something like that. We'll ask anyone with information to message us for a meeting. Hopefully, we'll get a hit."

Summer was already typing. "It's worth a try. I'll also hack into her Match-Mate page and put in a connecting link to your Match-Mate page. If Honey's fans can't get to her, they might contact you instead. We could find someone who once dated her."

For the first time in days, Taryn was hopeful. Then worry welled. "Wait. What if we put Honey in danger? What if Brinkman panics and hurts her, or worse?"

The idea of putting Honey in danger was a real concern. "Shit." Rick struggled with his desire to catch Brinkman and the idea of allowing another woman to be hurt by the con man because of them. "Damn."

Summer and Taryn shared a glance. "It's his mental process. Swearing helps clear his mind," Taryn said.

Rick ignored them. "Okay. Summer hasn't found any dead wives or evidence that Brinkman is a murderer, correct?" She nodded. "Then I think we should chance this. At best, Honey is happily Mrs. Brinkman, or whatever name he's using now, and at worst, about to get ripped off for everything she has or murdered. If we can keep that from happening, then we're saving her from financial ruin, or death."

"He's right," Summer said.

"But you also need to factor in the storage unit shooting and the break-in at my house," Taryn said, playing devil's advocate. "It's possible that Brinkman has upped his game."

"I don't think so," he said. "We know that neither of the shooters was Brinkman. Although we didn't get a clear look at their faces, they carried themselves like younger men. The burglar at your house was not Brinkman, either. He was too tall. What we don't know is how it's all connected."

"Then we still aren't sure Honey isn't in danger," Summer said, changing sides.

Taryn played with her ponytail. "We never did connect the storage shooting to our visit."

"You're right." Rick explained their theory. "If the shooters targeted us, there is no other explanation to how they knew we'd be there."

When he finished, Summer was already typing. "Sorry. I forgot I was supposed to check this for you. Irving distracted me with a story about one of his godchildren and polygamy charges, and I lost track. This shouldn't take long to figure out. A hacker can find anything with one hand behind her back."

While Summer dug, Taryn and Rick pulled up Jess's mall case on Taryn's computer. Several high-end stores had reported large thefts of merchandise, despite tight security. Jess had interviewed a few people, but hadn't made much progress. She suspected an inside job but hadn't had time to uncover a solid suspect.

"We'll wait until after the mall closes and see what we can find," Taryn said.

He'd rather be home in her bed.

"Got it!" Summer cried. "You were right. When you searched for Brinkman's name, someone was watching!"

Chapter 23

Summer dragged the mouse around what appeared to be a mish-mash of numbers, letters, and symbols and explained in the most confusing technical geek-speak what she was looking at. Taryn's mind went blank. "In English, please."

Summer grinned. "I forget you don't speak geek."

Taryn imagined what kind of reception her sexy friend would have if she ever dropped into the middle of a nerd convention where everyone spoke her same language. Mixing her brilliance with her pinup looks, Summer would probably give the drooling nerds strokes.

"I'll speak slowly so you can understand," Summer teased. "Rick was right about the cyber-stalker. Someone loaded up a program so that anytime a search was made for Teddy Brinkman, any of his known aliases, or Honey, the author got a ping. Then any searches you made after that initial ping were watched by the hacker."

"Damn. Stalking without hiding in bushes," Taryn said. She'd have to have Summer clear her laptop of malware. "That's how the shooters knew we'd be at the storage unit. It wasn't just a coincidence."

"They were probably waiting for us," Rick said. "The question remains, why? Why would they care if we were searching that unit? Other than the car, there wasn't anything of any worth in there unless you viewed the Pinto as valuable."

"Unless they didn't know there was nothing in there to steal," Taryn said. She paced the room. "Is there any way to link the hacker back to the source?"

Summer shrugged. "I can try, but it won't be easy. Whoever set this up did an elaborate cover-up. I might be able to get something, but it may take weeks. If ever. The hacker is good."

"Then we'll have to narrow down our suspects and find Brinkman and the shooters through deductive reasoning," Taryn continued without missing a beat.

"Where are you going with this, Sherlock?" Rick crossed his arms and waited.

"Let's see. Who do we have in play? Brinkman, Honey, her two sons, the former wives and their friends and family. The two sons could be the shooters and our burglar. That fits. The former wives would have every right to be angry and could have hired someone to find and take Brinkman out. " She shifted her eyes to Rick. "But then they wouldn't get their money or property back."

He frowned. "I've never denied wanting to pound Brinkman, but trust me, my mom doesn't have the means or the contacts to hire a hit man on the side."

Taryn smiled. "We'll count her out." She moved on. "We know Jane Clark wants him to suffer and admitted to having friends ready to shoot him, but I think she just wants her painting back. Can we agree that she's low on the suspect list?"

"I agree," Rick said.

"The other wives could have motive. However, it's unlikely a scorned wife from more than, say, five years ago is involved. They'll cheer if he goes to jail, but probably wouldn't still be actively searching for him."

"Good point," Summer said. "I'll check on the wife from Arizona with the website and see what she's been up to, though I suspect she's not our hacker."

"Then we're back to Honey's sons," he said. "They'd be protective of their mother and young enough to be in the age group of our shooters. Yet why they'd want to chase us away from the storage unit is a mystery."

Agreeing with everything, Taryn's brain seized with the complicated puzzle. Although they'd made progress, there were still a lot of questions remaining.

There was an avenue they hadn't gone down. "What if they weren't protecting the car but looking for it?" As soon as the comment left her mouth, the idea took off. "Could they have used us for a lead? If Brinkman stole from Honey, they may be looking for his cache. We led them to the unit."

"Huh." Rick rubbed his chin. "They might have been worried we would find his secret stash before they did, and warned us off. It's a stretch but could fit."

"Of course it fits. You are a genius, Taryn," Summer said and clapped. "No wonder Irving hired you. It wasn't just because you look good in tight pants."

Taryn's eyes narrowed. "Thanks. I think."

"Before we celebrate, we have to figure in the break-in at your house," Rick said. "What's the point of that?"

This wasn't easy to untangle.

"Unless the sons thought we found a secret treasure in the car," he added without waiting for an answer. "But what would Brinkman have worth stealing?"

"It could be anything," Summer said. "Or nothing."

"I think I need an aspirin." Taryn closed her eyes and rocked in the chair. "I thought having no clues was frustrating. Now we have lots of clues and we're still missing the middle and hardest part of any puzzle."

"Like when a third of a puzzle is blue sky," Summer offered and clicked off the screen. "I'm heading over to see Irving's new plaid golf balls. Anyone else want to come along?"

"Nope."

"No."

Sighing, she left.

Rick took her open seat. "I think we should go home, have sex, and think about this later with clear minds."

Taryn smiled. "Is that line supposed to work with all women, or just me?"

"Just you." He nudged her chair with his boot. "Many a crime has been solved after sex, a beer, and a hoagie. Just ask J. Edgar Hoover. He closed some big cases in a post-coital haze. I'm sure I read that somewhere."

"Wrong. I think he solved crimes while wearing pantyhose," she said and nudged him back. "That's why women are premier problem solvers. Wearing too-tight hose pushes all the blood up to their heads for optimal brain power."

Rick chuckled. "Then no sex?"

"I never said that." She stood. "I'll race you to the car."

* * *

Despite Rick's assurance that sex would solve their case, they were no further ahead than before. "You lied to me. The case is still stagnant in the water." Taryn ran a hand over his bare chest and teased his nipple. "I think you just wanted sex."

Rick kicked the sheet off and dislodged Sweet'ums from the bed. The dog growled from the floor. "It would have been better sex if that dog hadn't spent half of it sniffing my balls."

Taryn laughed. "He was just feeling nostalgic and jealous. He's fixed."

Laughter deepening, she rolled over and lay half on top of him. He cupped her bare butt. "Next time I'll lock him out. I promise. He just looked too sad when we went to the office without him."

Rick lifted his head. "Sad? The dog looks like he was hit in the face with a shovel. How can you tell what he's thinking?"

"Be nice." Despite his outward coolness toward the dog, she was sure she'd seen him rubbing the top of Sweet'ums's head with an index finger when he thought she wasn't looking. That was progress. Soon they'd be sharing a water bowl.

"I let him sniff my balls. I am being nice."

Taryn almost fell off the bed. As the laughter died a moment later, she turned serious. "Do you really think Honey's boys are behind the shooting and break-in?"

"I do."

This was hard to argue against. They fit the general description of the shooters. "What would be their reason?" She had her own ideas and wanted to know his.

"Like we discussed, the attack might boil down to retrieving stolen property for Honey. Or maybe Honey is missing and they're trying to find her. This wouldn't be the first time a corpse was found in a storage locker."

"Nice. Let's not go with that," she said.

"Or Brinkman could have run off with her. If they discovered his con too late, they could be worried for her safety. Or maybe they thought we were stealing the Pinto. At this point, anything goes."

His thoughts were similar to hers. They made a good team. She laid her head on his chest and listened to his heartbeat. Even if the romance was temporary, she'd take what she could. It was better to have loved and lost than to have never had mind-blowing sex at all. Wasn't that saying embroidered on a pillow somewhere?

For the first time since her divorce, she'd let herself cut loose and have fun with risks. Even Dave the race car driver had been all about getting over her hurt and proving she was still attractive. Now, she was with a man who knew her imperfections and liked her anyway. And she liked him back.

"We need to get up." She pushed off him. He groaned in protest. "We have thieves to catch."

Chapter 24

The mall was emptying out at ten o'clock when Taryn and Rick rolled into the parking lot. She drove around the building twice and picked what she thought was the best place for staking out: a space near Macy's and behind a semi-truck trailer reconfigured into a mobile construction company office. The mall was doing work on the façade on the east end of the building and repaving the lots. She got out of the car, pulled her camera from the trunk, and rejoined Rick inside the Olds.

"We are not to engage, but to observe," she said. "If we see anything suspicious, we are to call the mall manager."

The instruction sounded good, but Rick suspected that Taryn seldom followed the directive. "Is that what Irving says?"

"It is." She checked the camera and settled back in the seat. Dressed all in black, with her hair in a twist at the back of her neck, she looked like an international jewel thief. "He said that if I don't start sticking to that motto, he's going to have it tattooed on my forehead."

"Smart man. Even you could make that look sexy." Irving knew Taryn well and obviously tried to rein in his PI. It didn't work.

It wasn't that she was intentionally reckless, she just headed full throttle into everything she did. He admired her for her spunk, as much as it worried him. She could put herself in serious danger someday.

Leaving her at the conclusion of the case meant he wouldn't be around to watch her back. Thinking of leaving her at all left a hard lump in his stomach. Without him around, it meant she'd move on with someone new and no one would steer her clear of the Hunters of the city.

Annoyance welled up in him. He couldn't imagine her with that skirt-chasing cop. She'd already dealt with one cheater in her life. He didn't think she could survive another heartbreak.

Then what was he doing? He'd made her no promises of a future. He couldn't. His job currently had him living in L.A. Her home was here. Even if they tried the whole long-distance thing, odds were against that working out.

At least she wasn't in love with him or him with her. Emotional detachment would work in their favor. Then why did the idea of her with another guy piss him off?

The thought of her naked with another man weighed him down through the next two hours as they sat mostly in silence and waited for something to happen. The idea of her marrying and making kids with someone else really annoyed him.

"How long until we call it a night?" he asked. The car was starting to feel very small.

"I don't know. An hour or two?" Another hour passed. Taryn was twitching on her seat. He knew her well enough to know that patience was not her strong suit. Or his. "I'm going to walk around the mall. Coming?"

She didn't have to ask twice.

The empty parking lot was quiet but for passing vehicles on nearby I-94 and the soft sound of their boots on blacktop. Rick fell into step beside her as they headed right around the building. Though she didn't think the evening would prove successful, she had to cover all avenues of investigation before heading home.

Despite her earlier attempt to keep him out, she liked him living under her roof, and sleeping in her bed. He'd seen her in the morning at her worst and still found her appealing.

Oddly, she also liked having Alvin around, though she'd never admit it publicly. After forbidding him to ever bake, boil, or roast tongue in her house ever again, she realized that her house felt homey with the big menace in it. At least she didn't have to come home to an empty house.

Not that she wanted him there permanently. Just for now.

The lack of cars in and around the mall further confirmed that the mall thieves were probably tucked in their beds.

"We should have brought Sweet'ums," she said softly. "He would like the mall. He'd have lots of bushes to defile."

Rick grunted.

What, no insult about the dog? Rick had been quiet all night. She wondered what he was thinking. What was the point of having a partner, if not to entertain her during a stakeout?

They strolled on. Parking lot lights allowed her to examine his set face, as they neared the building and stopped in front of Macy's. Something had his briefs in a bunch. What?

Soft light spilled out of the tall glass doors. She checked the locks and looked inside. There was no sign of thieves.

She moved on. "Do you realize we've spent most of our time working at night? I'm surprised we haven't run across any vampires. Heck, I'm starting to crave a juicy neck for biting."

He failed to comment. She tried again. "I'll bet you can't wait to get back to the excitement of breaking down doors and arresting drug dealers." She glanced inside a restaurant. Nothing untoward. Then back at Rick. "I bet burning up bales of pot makes one hell of a party."

"Sure."

Her eyes narrowed. Was he even listening? "Well, look at that. I forgot to put on my panties before we left the house. How could I be so forgetful?"

His head swiveled around. Finally.

"I don't know what's up, but you've been a stone for the last two hours," she said. "What gives?"

Frowning, he yanked on a mall entrance door. "I didn't know conversation was a requirement of stakeouts. You should have brought Summer."

Grrr. She should have. Summer would be more fun.

And men thought women were hard to figure out. "Fine. No talking. But if you decide you want to express your feelings, go call one of your beer buddies. Don't come crying to me."

Although she hadn't quoted him exactly from an earlier conversation, she got the desired response. The scowl faded from his face. "That's really cold, Taryn."

She smiled. Rick was back.

"I think we can safely call it a night," she said eight and a half minutes later, when they hadn't seen anything suspicious. They'd didn't have much more area to cover. Macy's was around the next corner.

She reached into her snug jeans for her car keys. Rick's hand over hers pulled her to a stop.

"I'd hold off for a minute." She followed his gaze. The front end of a black panel truck peeked out from behind a wall. An engine rumbled.

"That's strange," she said.

He pulled her into the vestibule of the north entrance of the mall. Muted voices floated over. They couldn't hear what was being said. Rick murmured, "Unless they're part of the cleaning crew, there's no reason for them to be here at this time of night."

"Let's find out." Her excitement kicked up a notch. She loved catching bad guys. Clutching the camera, she edged in the direction of the truck.

The voices became louder as they approached. One man was talking about how smoking pot ten times a day had lessened the consistency of his erections, while another swore that wearing his rent-a-cop uniform got him laid more over the last year than the thirty-seven years previous.

As Taryn got close enough to peer around the wall, she wasn't too surprised by what she saw. Jess had figured the thefts were an inside job and that tonight would be the best night for thievery. She'd been right.

A mall security guard stood in blue slacks worn over his pudgy hips; a white shirt stretched to its limit over a beach-ball belly. Pinned to a polyester breast pocket was a name tag and security badge. Dangling from his chin to his chest was a scrappy brown beard that resembled a dead chipmunk.

She wanted to pipe in and tell the guard that his success with the ladies had less to do with the uniform and more with the insecurity and desperation of his dates, but held her tongue. A third man came out of an open brown door, wheeling a trolley piled high with unopened boxes.

"This can't be that easy," Rick whispered over her shoulder.

"Sometimes, but usually not." She lifted her camera. "It's a happy day for Brash & Brazen, Inc."

Rick reached for his gun. "I'll hold them, while you call the police."

"We can't do that." At his stare, she explained. "The mall management wants to keep this quiet. They're afraid that they'll lose store rental business if it's discovered that a criminal enterprise was allowed to work out of their property. They want evidence, and the stolen property recovered, and they'll handle the rest on their own."

"So I can't shoot anyone?"

"Not tonight, cowboy."

Moving on stealthy feet, she rounded the wall and stepped between the truck and the brick wall. The trolley guy rolled up the ramp into the truck, followed by his two companions. Taryn paused near the back of the truck, pulled off the lens cap, and made sure the camera was on auto mode. The task took less than fifteen seconds.

"Watch a professional at work," she whispered.

Feeling Rick tense behind her, she grinned and stepped around the truck, and spread her feet for optimal camera steadiness. The men were stacking the boxes in neat rows. She went in for the kill.

"Smile, gentlemen." *Click. Click. Click.* The digital camera took a full dozen pics of the wide-eyed men and the license plate of the truck before they realized what was happening.

"Fuck!"

Taryn spun. Rick, quickly getting over his own surprise at her move, was already spinning around. They tore off past the truck and out onto the sidewalk.

"Which way?" he shouted.

"Follow me!"

Taryn's two trips around the mall hadn't been just to check for the best place to park, but also to plot out escape routes. Since the thieves may or may not be armed, she had to be cautious. The car was still some distance away, so she opted to hide instead. They rounded JCPenney with the sound of pursuit behind them. She took heart in not getting shot at.

"Why are we running? We're armed!" he called out.

"I'm not allowed to shoot anyone unless I'm in danger!" she said. "If we fight them, they might hurt my camera and we'll lose the evidence!"

Of course, there was the part about the fun of outsmarting idiot criminals that she left out. Rick would discover that soon enough. And if she failed, they did have guns.

Ahead were half a dozen dumpsters. She headed for them.

Rick, sensing her plan, said, "That's the first place they'll look."

"Just keep up." She chose the farthest right corner of the two rows and they pushed up the heavy lid. Thankfully, the bin was for recyclables and not rotted food trash from one of the restaurants. "Get in."

Rick shoved her up and over and joined her, closing the lid quietly, just in time for their pursuers to catch up.

"Check over there," a man said. "If you find them, I'll filet them like trout."

Fileted? So much for unarmed criminals.

Taryn and Rick quietly burrowed down beneath the flattened boxes. Taryn sent a quick text to Summer to let her know where they were and turned off her phone. Rick did the same. When she slipped a box over her head, she suddenly felt as if the confined space was closing in. She pushed the box down and reached to move his from his face.

"Do you think we can smother in here?" she whispered. "I think I'm losing oxygen."

"You're just having a non-fatal panic attack," he whispered back. "Hold my hand. If you pass out, I'll give you mouth-to-mouth. Or feel you up. That will bring you around."

Holding back a laugh-snort, she reached out. He took her hand and they slid the boxes back in place. Silently, they listened to lids being opened and dumpsters investigated.

"Fuck! This one smells like your ass, Tommy."

"Suck it, dickweed!" the insulted man replied.

Dickweed? Was that a native plant?

The first guy chuckled.

"Shut up, assholes." The guard piped in. "We have to get that camera." A lid slammed shut. Feet shuffled over to where Taryn and Rick were. She held her breath as the lid popped open. Rick's hand tightened on hers.

The height of the dumpsters wouldn't allow for more than a cursory examination of the contents unless the searcher climbed in. She didn't need to see him to know that Rick had his free hand on his gun, as she did on hers.

"Hold the flashlight." A scrape of a foot on metal followed, as one of the men tried to boost himself up the side. Then the thief followed with the sound of boxes being shoved around. Taryn held her breath.

"See anything, Phil?"

"I don't see shit." The box slid backward, almost exposing the top of her head. She tightened her grip on her gun.

Shoes hit concrete. She breathed again. Thankfully, the man had not climbed in.

"They must have gone around the mall." The trio left. Swearing followed their path. Taryn and Rick stayed put for another twenty minutes, in case it was a ruse to get them to expose themselves. Finally, Taryn relaxed and pushed the boxes off. Sometimes she really loved her job!

"Are you laughing?" Rick said.

"Nope." She was laughing—shaking with it, actually. She helped uncover him. "Now that was a fun stakeout!"

With parking lot light through the gaps between the lid and the rest of the dumpster, she could see his disbelieving stare. This deepened her giggles. "Come on. When was the last time you were chased around by the Three Stooges?"

Instead of answering, he reached for her wrist, spun her around, and dropped her on the pile of boxes. Covering her with his body, he grinned. "I don't know about the stakeout or the Stooges, but I'm about to do some dumpster diving of my own."

Chapter 25

It was sometime later when Rick helped Taryn out of the dumpster and helped her straighten her clothes. Her hair had escaped the rubber band thing, falling in clumps around her face, and her shirt was inside out.

They hadn't gone all the way; after all, they were in a dumpster and despite being relatively clean, it was, well, a dumpster, and not the most romantic place for lovemaking.

But it ranked up there as the hottest make-out session since Kelly Gilly in tenth grade. Since he'd been a hormonally overloaded teenage virgin that time, this was better; because Rick knew that when he got Taryn home, he'd get lucky.

"Here, let me." He pulled her shirt off, and may have "accidentally" copped a feel in the process, and turned it right side out. She was wearing a simple cream bra, with an edge of lace and a tiny pink flower between her breasts.

Sexy but understated. Like her. He almost flipped her back into the dumpster to finish what they'd started.

"If all stakeouts end this way, I get why you like your job," he said against her ear and pulled the shirt back down over her head. Skimming his hands over her trim waist, he settled the shirt into place.

She sighed and leaned into him. He held her and lowered his face to breathe in the scent of strawberries from her shampoo. She did like her fruity scents.

"I like you," she said, muffled by her face buried in his shirt. Her hand slipped to his butt.

"I like you, too." He more than liked her. He was falling hard for her. How could a guy not like a woman who made out with him in a dumpster, behind a mall, while being hunted by mall thieves? She was everything he liked and everything he should run away from. He'd always lived a carefree existence, never making women any promises or commitments, while keeping his heart unattached. Taryn was smart and beautiful, but more than that, she was a safe place to land, a home.

She was a forever.

And he wasn't sure he was ready for that. But he knew he wasn't ready to let her go.

She tipped back her head and looked at him. His heart softened as one hazel eye peered through her bangs. Her hand moved from his butt to caress his chest. His breath hitched.

Yep. Forever.

"We should go in case our thieves come back," she said.

Instead, he kissed her. Her mouth was warm and soft. She teased him with her tongue and sent heat through his body. He cupped and kneaded one ass cheek, pressing her against his erection. "You drive me nuts."

She smiled under his mouth.

He broke the kiss. "Let's go before I change my mind and show you what I can really do on a bed of cardboard."

The walk back to the car was uneventful. There was no sign of the thieves. She had photographic proof of the thefts and the men responsible, so tomorrow it would be handed over to the mall manager to use for criminal apprehension. Otherwise, their part of the case was closed.

Oddly, the panel truck was still in place, though the engine had been turned off.

"How odd." Taryn scanned the shadows outside of the streetlamps. Nothing. If the thieves were hiding, they were doing a very good job of it. "I'd have thought our criminals would be halfway to Canada by now."

"I think they were waylaid." Rick pointed toward the Olds when it came into view. Lined up on their stomachs, on the hood of the Olds, with their hands taped behind their backs, were the three thieves unsuccessfully fighting their bindings.

A large man holding a very ugly dog stood watch nearby.

"What in the—" Taryn knew that face, and that dog. She walked over to Alvin. "What are you doing here?"

"Bodyguarding you." Taped mouths kept his prisoners quiet, yet it didn't take words to figure out that their opinion of Alvin was negative. "I did good, huh?"

So much for Irving's rule of observation, not interaction. So much for keeping the thefts quiet. They couldn't release the thieves now. And his criminal apprehension couldn't have come at a worse time. She should be on her way home for some hot sex, not spending the next hour or two making reports.

"I'll call the police," Rick said and stepped away.

Ultimately, she kept her disappointment to herself. "You did fine. But I don't need a bodyguard."

His expression disagreed; then he spent the next two minutes telling her how he nabbed the thieves. It mostly involved head knocking, and whimpering on their part. They'd all but lain down and let him tape them up when he threatened to skin them.

What disturbed her was the not knowing if he was serious about the skinning part.

Pinching the bridge of her nose, she said, "How'd you get here, Alvin?"

"Kitty drove me." He pointed to a small red car at the edge of the lot and waved. Headlights flashed in response.

Great.

Sirens screamed in the distance. A shadow crossed his face. He handed the dog over and headed toward Kitty's car. "I gotta go. I may be wanted in a couple of states."

Taryn spent a lot of time explaining to the Ann Arbor police sergeant how she and Rick had captured the thieves, the reason she would take a dog on a stakeout, and the fact that the three men must all be collectively hallucinating about a large hairy man. Drug abuse was a problem throughout the world, after all.

How she managed to lie to the police without cracking was still a mystery nine hours later, when she pulled into the lot at Brash. She wasn't the best liar anyway and her respect for law enforcement ran deep. But the thieves were caught and what did it matter how three criminals were apprehended? The end game was the same.

"I'm just happy you're using your bullshitting skills for good instead of evil," Rick said, when she expressed her concern, for the hundredth time, about fibbing to the police. "You could have turned Alvin in."

"You know I can't do that." Why remained a mystery. He'd once manhandled her, Jess, and Summer by throwing them off the team bus. He'd been hired to kill her. Yet she still protected him. Again, why? "He helped us bring down a gang of thieves. Doesn't that deserve a little loyalty?"

"The guy is an admitted criminal with warrants and an admitted would-be assassin. As a sworn member of law enforcement, it's my duty to see him locked up."

"I can hear you, you know," Alvin announced from the backseat. Sweet'ums yipped.

"You wouldn't," Taryn said. She glared.

"If not for those damned-good chocolate chip pancakes he made this morning, I might have," Rick said. "I still think he's a danger to you and to society as a whole. Say the word and I'll get him and Brinkman matching prison jumpsuits."

"Again, still listening."

Taryn pushed open her door and climbed out. She caught Rick's eyes over the roof of the car. "This is my call. If you trust me, you'll leave this alone."

While she waited, he shrugged. "Okay, but if I ever suspect he's become a danger to you, I'll see his ass put in jail."

"Once again . . . Oh, never mind," Alvin said and collected the dog off the seat. He climbed out of the car.

The office was quiet when Taryn and Rick walked in with Alvin and the dog in tow. Gretchen gasped at the sight of Alvin and Sweet'ums, but recovered quickly when the dog wagged his pom-pom-tipped tail and snorted a happy doggie snort.

"Aren't you an ugly little monster," she cooed. "With a face only a mother could love. Yes, you are. Yes, you are." She took the dog from Taryn and walked off.

The mutt did have a way with women.

"Oh, hell no." Jess had arrived. "What is he doing here?"

Taryn didn't need to turn around to know who "he" was. But she spun anyway. Jess, in gray sweat pants with one pant leg pulled up over her knee, and Alvin were glaring at each other.

"Alvin has been secretly following me around with my neighbor who he's having sex with. He thinks I need a bodyguard," Taryn said. "He wouldn't take no for an answer." Translation: She forgot the creaking board on the porch and she and Rick were caught by Alvin while trying to sneak out this morning. "The dog just invited himself."

"What about Rick?" Jess pressed. She and Alvin locked glares. "I know he's been guarding your body. You don't need that one, too."

Taryn's cheeks warmed. She pulled Jess aside. "I tried to dissuade him, but he's stubborn. Rather than spend the morning arguing, I let him tag along this one time. If Honey's sons shoot at us, I only have to outrun him, or stand behind him, to survive. It's a win-win."

"I can't believe you're letting him stay with you. What if he suffocates you with a pillow or burns down your house? You don't know what he's capable of. He was supposed to kill you."

"Jess," she warned. "I'm not having this argument again. Let it go."

Scowling, Jess hobbled off. Taryn knew the argument wasn't over. Although her friends cared about her safety, they couldn't rule her life. As far as she was concerned, Alvin was a closed topic, as long as he behaved.

Summer texted her. Taryn turned to Alvin. "Wait here."

Rick followed her back to Summer's office. "What's up?"

Summer pulled off a sticky note and held it out. "You got a hit online. A man wants to meet with you. Carl Evans. He sent a private message to the 'Where's Honey' Facebook site. He says he knows Honey."

"Did he say how?" Rick asked.

"No, he just said that he knew her."

After all the dead-end leads and dates to nowhere, it was the 'Where's Honey' site that got a hit? Knowing more about Honey was a good thing, but Taryn didn't get excited. There were too many ways this could be another flop.

"I guess we should check it out." Taryn took a sip out of Summer's coffee cup. "We don't have anything else."

Taryn set up the meeting at a local café. Rick wired her for sound and sat at the counter. At Taryn's insistence, Alvin waited in the car with the dog. His presence alone would likely scare off Carl—and all of the other patrons.

Ten. Fifteen. Twenty minutes past the meeting time. Taryn wondered if the contact was a hoax. Then at ten twenty-three, a thin man of medium height with lanky black hair brushed back from his face stopped just inside the glass doors and looked around. Spotting Taryn, who'd texted him a description of herself, he headed for her table.

His shuffling gait and lined face put him somewhere in his sixties. She suspected he was younger, though, closer to Honey's age. His worn blue pants and matching shirt pegged him as a working man, and the smell of cigarettes and phlegmy cough left little doubt that he probably wouldn't live to be seventy.

He took the seat across from her. "Carl."

She took his hand. "Taryn. I'm a PI."

Carl coughed into his sleeve. Recovering, he got right to it. "You're looking for Honey for a case?"

"I am. She may be the victim of a scam."

For a long moment, he stared, his pale blue eyes confused. Then he leaned forward and flashed a set of crooked, nicotine-stained teeth, before breaking into rattling laughter, coughed again, then settled back with a low chuckle. "Sweetheart, if Honey is involved in a scam, she's not the victim but the perpetrator."

Chapter 26

"Explain," Taryn ordered. She didn't hide her surprise. "First, why are you looking for her?"

There was no point lying. If this man knew Honey and wanted to help, she might as well tell the truth. "We think she married a con man and may be in danger."

He gave a low whistle. "I need caffeine."

Carl called for the waitress and ordered a large coffee with a shot of espresso. While Taryn waited impatiently for him to be served, she glanced over at Rick. His posture was casual. His eyes were not. He was just as puzzled by this turn of events as she was.

Honey a crook?

After Carl was settled with his coffee, he began, "Now don't get me wrong here, Honey is a good woman. She's made some mistakes in her life. If anything bad has happened to her, it'll partially be my fault."

"How so?"

"Them boys of hers are mine."

What? Taryn tented her fingers in front of her mouth in surprise. "You're their father? Why isn't their last name Evans?"

Carl chuckled. "Well, there weren't no DNA test, but she says so, and I take her word." He began a long-winded tale of teen pregnancy, marriage, and a move to Las Vegas that started Honey's slide into the dark side. "I was an alcoholic and couldn't keep a job. With two kids by then, she turned to stripping to feed us all. Then came the shoplifting and writing bad checks. Now I ain't saying that I'm at fault for all of that, but I wasn't much help to her either. Eventually she kicked me out and took up with a guy who owned a car dealership.

A weary expression followed. "I wasn't a good father. I think that's why they took her maiden name."

Like getting hit in the face by a Mack truck, Taryn hadn't seen any of this coming. However, that was history.

Inasmuch as the life of Honey Comstock was a fascinating tale, she didn't have time to go through about thirty years of needless stuff to get current.

"What can you tell me about Honey over the last couple of years?" she pressed. "We need to find her ASAP."

He chugged down the last of his coffee. "I know she'd given up stripping, became a secretary, and then married some guy and moved back to Michigan. Joey and Ronnie kept in touch, so that's how I know. She was widowed shortly after, when her husband crashed his car. The boys said she received some money from her husband's insurance so she didn't need to work."

A spotty work history and maybe a couple of aliases could explain why Summer couldn't find much about her.

"I'd thought about looking her up when she was still in Vegas. I've been sober for seventeen years now and thought maybe she'd take me back. Then she ran off and married that dead guy."

Taryn thought it unlikely Honey would see Carl as a prize worth revisiting, but who was she to crush his dreams? "The insurance would be enough to tweak Brinkman's interest," she said into the mike in her bra. Rick nodded.

"Who are you talking to?" Carl asked.

"Myself. It helps me think." She tapped her fingers on the tabletop. "Do you know where Honey could be now? Did your boys give you any information about her new husband?"

"Other than that they thought he was an ass, no."

"Are you still in contact with Joey and Ronnie?" This was the best lead so far. If anyone knew her movements, it would be her gun-toting sons.

She might actually crack this case.

"Not for the last four weeks or so." Carl played with his cup. "Ronnie said there was trouble with the marriage and then the three of them fell off the grid."

Shoot. "Okay. Let's start again from another angle. You said Honey is from Michigan. Does she have family she'd go to if she was in trouble?"

He shook his head. "Her mama ran off when she was little and her pa died about five years ago. Her sister lives in Iowa, but they had a big fight and haven't spoken in probably twenty years. Lauraleen is one judgmental woman."

"What about aunts, uncles, cousins?" Taryn continued. He shook his head. "Friends from childhood?"

"Nope. She cut all ties when we ran off to Vegas."

She dropped her head into her hands. "You have to give me something, Carl. Honey couldn't just vanish."

Silence fell. The theme for *Jeopardy* went through her head as Carl racked his atrophied brain for clues, or at least that's what she hoped he was doing. He could be thinking about Honey's sizeable chest. Who knew? He still wanted his wife back.

"Did you check that house she inherited from the dead husband?"

Taryn's head popped up. "What house?"

He pulled a cigarette out of his pocket and put it unlit between his teeth. The waitress walked past and frowned.

"Joey said her husband left her a life insurance policy in his will, a white Mustang, and a house somewhere out in Irish Hills. The rest of his money went to charity. He didn't have no kids."

Before he finished, Taryn was already texting Summer.

"Look, I've gotta get back to work. My lunch break is over." He stood and reached into his breast pocket for a crumpled pack of smokes, realized he already had one, and tucked them back in. "If you find Honey, can you tell her to call me?"

"I will." She meant it. If this tip about the house cracked the case, she'd willingly play matchmaker. "Thanks, Carl."

He nodded and shuffled off. Rick pushed back his tall stool. Before he could get up, a figure blocked him from her sight and dropped into Carl's vacated chair.

"Hello, Taryn."

There had been times over the last few years, usually after a few cocktails with her friends, when Taryn had secretly wished that the sight of Tim in bed with Gloria, and their subsequent divorce, had all been a bad dream from which she'd awaken and be happily married again. He'd been her first love, after all. That was hard to give up. But to see him now, slightly mussed up, with circles under his eyes, and tight lines around his mouth, made her realize that she really was over him after all.

Huh. That wasn't just a lie she'd told herself, and others, to appease her friends. She really, really was over him.

"Tim, what are you doing here?" She glanced at Rick. He didn't look pleased. "How did you find me?"

"I came to see you." He ignored the second question and unleashed his boyish grin. Instead of endearing, it annoyed her. "You wouldn't take my calls."

"You had sex with our maid. Why would I talk to you?"

"Because a love like ours should transcend one little foolish mistake and we should be together?" He ran a hand through his hair. Tim looked a little bit like a young Harrison Ford and he used it to his advantage. He'd been a player in college. A red flag she hadn't wanted to see. He was so loving and attentive in the beginning, and so cute that she'd believed all his bullshit. Not anymore.

"You followed me here. Have you been spying on the house, too?" She lowered her voice and hissed, "What in the hell is wrong with you? Did you break in last week?"

"What? No!" Several customers looked up from their phones. He blinked and lowered his voice. "I may have driven by a couple of times. I had to see you. But your tenant scared me off. He looks like an escapee from a Russian gulag. Is renting to him a good idea?"

They were not getting off track. She crossed her arms, more to keep him from staring at her chest than to show her displeasure. "What do you want, Tim?"

"Um, okay. I'll be blunt." The boyish grin returned. "I miss you and I want you back."

"No."

"Come on, Taryn." He reached for her hand. She pulled it away. "I made a mistake and corrected it. I sent Gloria packing. We can be together forever like we planned."

Now she was really mad. "Funny, when I ran into Gloria and her boy toy a few days ago, she said she left you."

A flush crept into his face. "Does it really matter who left who? Her departure made me realize what a jerk I was. You and I are meant to be to be Dr. and Mrs. Applewhite. Always."

The worst part of this whole thing—other than that she'd once been Mrs. Taryn Applewhite—was that Rick was listening to every word and scowling. How blinded she had been to marry Tim when she was barely out of her teens, against the advice of, well, everyone. How had she expected the marriage to work?

Oh, right. She'd thought her love would save him.

It clearly hadn't worked. He was still trying to play her.

Not this time. "Tim. Listen and pay attention because this is the last conversation we will ever have. I will never, ever, ever, take you back. Not ever. I don't love you anymore. You hurt me and that can never be forgiven." She pushed back her chair and stood. "If I see you again, I will shoot you. Got it?"

Not waiting for his answer, she left the café. By the time she reached the Olds, she was shaking.

Rick joined her. "Are you okay?" He touched her arm. She stepped out of reach. He let her go.

"I'm fine. I'm just feeling foolish. I told you I was a bad judge of men, and I was right. Tim proves that."

"You can't blame yourself for one failure. He screwed you over. "

She knew he was trying to help, but she was too angry to accept the attempt. Somewhere during the last three years, she'd gone through the stages of grieving and realized she'd overlooked the ticked-off stage. Well, she was in it now.

"I chose him. Do you know that my father wanted me to walk away from the wedding? He thought I was too young and Tim too slick. But I held my ground. I didn't want to see that Tim was a jerk beneath his sweet and polished exterior."

Rick went silent while she closed in on herself as he watched. Despite his assurances, she was a bad judge of men. One of her dates after Tim had tried to lift her wallet out of her purse, and another had wanted her to be a baby surrogate for him and his husband. Was she so sure about Rick?

Slowly, he nodded as his jaw muscle pulsed. "And now you are rethinking me," he stated bluntly.

This would be the time to assure him that she wasn't thinking that he'd eventually turn into a cheating jerk. But what did she know about him, really? He could have six wives and ten children scattered across America, be a cootie carrier, or collect drain lint. Who knew?

Somehow the words didn't form. At this moment, she didn't know what to think; only that she didn't know Rick well enough to trust him with her heart.

"Great." He pounded his closed fist on the hood of the car. "Two days as lovers and it's over."

Her heart pounded painfully in her chest. She wanted to step into his arms and feel his warmth. She wanted to tell him that she'd fallen in love with him, despite only knowing him for a few days. However, that would be an unmitigated disaster. He'd probably awkwardly pat her on the back, thank her, then run for his bike and tear off for the California sunset.

Instead, she fought the burn in the back of her eyes and steeled herself. "It's for the best. You live in L.A., I live here. We both know that this won't last. Why don't we cut it off now and avoid an awkward and tearful good-bye later."

"Shit." He scrubbed his hands over his head then lifted his eyes to her. There were so many emotions there. Most of all anger, and then acceptance. He wouldn't fight for her. "Fine. We're done."

Since he'd readily agreed with her to end things before they got in too deep, why did she feel so bad?

Chapter 27

Something was wrong, Rick thought over and over as they walked up to Honey's house. The area was too quiet and the house seemed empty. Gray clouds scattered across the sky, and the occasional kick-up of wind bent the trees and promised rain.

The grim afternoon matched his mood. First, the tension with Taryn weighed on him, and now they might be walking into a trap. It was too coincidental that within hours of their meeting with Carl Evans, Brinkman was back online and trolling for dates.

He should call the police for backup, but he was sure that if Brinkman saw them coming, he'd run. Besides, getting a posse together would take too long, and he'd look foolish if the cops came down on the house only to find Brinkman barbecuing burgers on the back deck.

It was better to check the situation out first. Police could be called if things turned sour.

"That idiot had to have heard the car engine and crunch of tires on gravel. Why isn't he looking out the curtains or coming to the door? Where is he?"

"Good question." Taryn was tense beside him. "When Teddy contacted my Match Mate profile this morning he seemed excited about the date. He should be at the door with flowers."

"Or he saw me and bolted."

Taryn smiled ruefully. "You are kind of scary."

When Taryn called him at dawn with the address of Honey's house from Summer and the request and acceptance of the date with Brinkman, they'd shared their concerns. Why had Brinkman surfaced now? And why was his first date request to Taryn's fake profile?

The only way to answer those questions was to follow up, so here they were.

When they climbed onto the low porch and got to the door, it was cracked a couple of inches. His sense of danger slipped into over-drive.

"Dammit. The bastard is up to something."

"This is the setup for almost every scary movie," Taryn agreed. "We walk in and a demon jumps out and bites off our heads, or a killer sticks a knife between our ribs."

"Thanks for those images."

She brushed a long bang out of her eyes and tucked it behind her ear. "Just sayin'."

Every part of him wanted to demand she wait in the car with her gun. Every instinct told him she wouldn't. Wasting time arguing would be counterproductive. Besides, he knew the two of them watching each other's backs was ideal. Taryn was well trained for dangerous situations.

It was he who wanted to protect her.

He pushed past his hesitation, pulled his Glock, then nudged open the door, peering through the space between jamb and door to see if anyone was hiding behind it.

"It's clear. Brinkman!" he called out. "Teddy Brinkman."

Nothing. He adjusted the gun. "Stay behind me."

For a second, he expected her to protest and give him a lecture about his caveman ways, but for once, she did what he asked. He lifted the Glock. "Is anyone here?"

Stepping over the threshold, he saw no immediate threat. The smell of lemon furniture polish hit him as he scanned the spotless space. The entryway opened into a large living room done up profes-sionally in muted pastel colors familiar in a beach house: pale blue, white, and cream. A hallway led into the rest of the house and from where he stood, he could see down a wide hallway to a set of glass doors at the back of the house, and through them the lake beyond.

"It doesn't look like anyone's here," Taryn said quietly.

"You'd think so." He lowered the gun slightly. "A friend of mine was shot by a twelve-year-old in a closet who was protecting his mother's cocaine stash. Thankfully, Chip was wearing a vest."

He continued forward. Sweeping through the downstairs of the house, they checked a family room off to the right side and the at-

tached enclosed porch. He became resigned to the fact that they'd
been duped. There was no sign of Brinkman. "Someone is playing
games."

"Could it be Evans?" she asked.

"The timing fits." Rick looked in a closet. "Could he be working
with Honey?"

"At this point, we can't rule anyone out." They moved on.

Taryn stayed right behind him, her hand on her gun. When they
stepped into the kitchen, he slowly lowered the Glock. "Damn.
Where in the hell is he?"

Taryn checked the walk-in pantry. "No one in here." She walked
out. "Should we check upstairs?"

"In a minute." He laid the Glock on the counter and texted Summer to see if Brinkman had messaged a change of plans. She texted
back: no. Shit. Taryn walked to the deck doors and pulled them open.
A cool wind swirled in and blew some food flyers off the table. The
fresh smell of a coming storm erased the scent of lemon polish. The
lake appeared empty.

"I don't see a boat at the dock. Maybe they're on the lake." She
stepped out on the deck, paused, made a funny sound, and then
backed into the kitchen.

Before Rick could move, a man of medium height followed her
in, clutching a pistol. He glanced sideways at Rick.

Rick went hot with rage.

"Touch your gun and I'll shoot her." The stranger smirked and
stepped around behind Taryn. He took the gun out of her hand and
tucked it into his waistband. "Now, let's go into the living room
and have a little chat." He waved the pistol at Rick. "You first."

Had Taryn not been there, he would have gone for his weapon.
But he couldn't risk her life. He loved her too much.

The thought startled him. But he didn't have time to focus on the
feeling. He walked past Taryn, looked into her worried eyes, and
headed down the hallway.

"Sit over there." Rick took a seat on the edge of a chair. The gunman pushed Taryn down on the oversize couch and stood behind her.
The pistol was pointed at her neck.

Satisfied his prisoners had complied, he put his face next to her
ear and one hand under her chin. "Comfy?"

"Who are you and what do you want?" Rick said. Given the chance, he'd snap the gunman's neck for touching her.

"You haven't figured that out, dude? I know all about you from my brother. He's been spying on you online." The stranger smirked. The guy was no genius, but he had a gun. That made him dangerous.

He tapped Taryn on the temple with the pistol. "And what about you? Here's a fancy PI who can't catch one old con man."

"We're here, aren't we?" she said, smugly. "I'd say that I'm darn good at my job."

The stranger stiffened. "If you're so smart, then who am I?"

Rick figured he was one of Honey's sons but wasn't in the mood for twenty questions. The hand on the weapon shook. Rick had to force himself to stay calm when what he wanted to do was jump between them. "Why don't you skip the games and enlighten us."

Taryn spoke up. "You're either Joey or Ronnie. Which?"

There was a slight tremor in her voice. Knowing her as he did, he knew she'd never outwardly show fear in the face of danger; rather, she was probably plotting a way to save both of them.

That worried the hell out of him. One misstep and she'd die in front of him. Rick hoped to find a resolution that didn't involve a gun battle and her left dead. He hadn't had the chance to tell her how he felt, to earn her trust, to love her.

The gunman's stupid grin wavered. "Ronnie."

The younger son. "Okay, Ronnie. I assume you know who we are, so let's cut through the crap and you tell us what you want. No one needs to get hurt here."

"You know what I want, Mr. Silva," he said, as if he were addressing a two-year-old. "I want the money that was stolen from my mom."

Huh. He didn't use "Agent" or "DEA" in that sentence. If the two brothers had been spying on the two of them, why did he not know who Rick really was? Obviously they hadn't hacked into his background. They had been too focused on Taryn.

Interesting. This was one plus on their side. His title could up the seriousness of the situation. Criminals sometimes targeted law enforcement. It was safer to keep Ronnie clueless.

"What makes you think we have her money? I'm a PI, not a thief," Taryn said before Rick could ask the question. "We're looking for Brinkman ourselves."

Ronnie shook his head. His dark eyes went hard. "Bullshit. I know you found the Pinto. That's the only thing that piece of crap Brinkman owns. You must have found something when you searched the car. Cash, diamonds, gold?"

"We found nothing." She kept her tone calm. "You and your brother chased us off before we could complete the search. If there's anything there, the cops have the car locked up so none of us have access."

In not denying he was one of the shooters, he confirmed their belief that Joey and Ronnie had been at the storage unit, and that one of them also broke into Taryn's house. They'd been searching for the missing cash.

Releasing Taryn, Ronnie paced behind the couch. The way he twitched made Rick think the gunman was a tweaker. Adding meth addiction to an already unstable mind notched up the seriousness of the situation. His mind raced for a solution.

"I think you're lying," Ronnie said without much conviction. He appeared confused. "Just because you're a PI doesn't make you honest."

Rick glanced at Taryn. To his surprise he saw not a scared hostage but a confident investigator. She'd taken control of Ronnie by using reason and calm and the idiot didn't know it yet.

He wanted to kiss her.

"I swear, we didn't take anything," she said. "If you know Brinkman, then you know that he's a skilled thief. He wouldn't hide valuables in that car. He probably pawns the items and banks the cash, or spends it gambling with hookers. Who knows? I think rather than waving a gun and making threats, we should all work together to take that conning bastard down."

Ronnie stopped and glanced up at the ceiling. "I can do this on my own. I don't need you or Joey to get her money back."

Her? Was this about looking like a hero to his mother? Rick might be able to use that against him.

They didn't have to wait long for the situation to turn around in their favor. The front door opened and, to everyone's surprise, Honey walked in wearing a pair of shorts and a red tank top. She appeared completely at ease, for a second anyway. Glancing around the room, she stared at Rick and Taryn, then focused onto her son.

"Ronnie. What is all this?"

The guy flushed beneath outdated blond Bieber bangs. The twitching got worse. Rick felt the situation take a downturn. He had to get between Taryn and that gun.

"He's kidnapped us." Taryn said matter-of-factly. She introduced herself and rushed through an explanation of their presence in the house. "He thinks we have your stolen money and hopes to retrieve it for you."

Honey paled. She placed a pair of grocery bags on the floor and put her hands on her hips. Despite pushing fifty, Rick could see her appeal to youngsters like Chad the Surfer. She was fit and built, though tanning had aged her face. Brinkman would have thought he won the dating lottery with her.

"That's sweet, baby, but these people don't have my money." She walked to her son and reached out a hand. "Give me the gun before you hurt someone."

Ronnie looked at Rick, then Taryn, then back to his mother.

"But, Mamma." She snapped her fingers. He handed her the gun. Rick exploded up from the chair, jumped over the coffee table, and hit Ronnie, knocking him back and against the wall behind them. Honey screamed. While he pummeled the gunman to the floor, Taryn took her chance, bolted for Honey, and disarmed her before she could use the gun to protect her son.

"Please don't hurt him!" Honey pleaded.

Rick rolled Ronnie onto his stomach and put a knee in his back. A pained grunt followed. "Taryn, get me something to tie him with."

Taryn glanced around the space.

"There are zip ties in the drawer to the right of the stove," Honey said. At Taryn's surprise, she shrugged. "Just trying to be helpful and to keep my son safe."

Honey was sharper than her kid.

Once Ronnie was secured, Taryn collected the guns and called 911, while Rick dumped Ronnie facedown onto the couch. Honey hurried to him and checked for injuries. Other than a banged-up face and some whining, he appeared okay. His mother sat at his head and played with his hair.

"You can't go around kidnapping people, baby," she cooed. "I told you that before. We don't have another spare room for hostages. What did you think we were going to do with them after the kidnapping?"

"Shoot them?"

Honey clucked her tongue. She glanced at Rick. "He doesn't mean that. He's just distraught."

"He kidnapped a federal agent at gunpoint," Taryn said. "Despite his noble reasons, he's in some serious trouble."

Silence filled the room.

Then she said, "Oh, dear." Honey placed a hand to her ample chest and scanned Rick up and down. "Are you with the FBI?"

"DEA." Rick sat on the coffee table and leaned toward their captive. Ronnie blanched. His mother tried to shield him with her outstretched arms should Rick decided to punch him again.

Done with the bullshit, Rick told Ronnie his rights off the top of his head. "Do you understand these rights as I have explained them to you?"

Ronnie nodded.

"Would you like an attorney?"

Ronnie shook his head. Satisfied, Rick pulled out his phone and started the recorder app and began questioning the guy. The dope was quite forthcoming.

Yes, Ronnie had been the shooter at Affordable U-Store. "Joey freaked out when I pulled out the gun that night. Wimp."

He went on. Joey was the nonviolent computer geek who'd cyber-stalked them. That was how the sons found out about the unit and hoped to catch them discovering Brinkman's stash. The break-in at Taryn's house had been all Ronnie. He'd done some time for previous burglaries and thought he could get into her house, search for the missing cash, and get out without detection.

"You should get those stairs fixed," he complained.

Taryn scowled. He looked away.

"Was it Joey who lured us here?" Rick asked. He wanted everything recorded.

"Nope. I did that, too. Joey knows more than me about computers, but I can send a message." He coughed and a little drool slipped out of the corner of his smug mouth. "You fell for it easy."

"I wouldn't get too cocky," Taryn said. "You're the one hogtied and headed for prison."

The smugness vanished. Footsteps coming down the stairs brought all eyes around. A tall guy with dark curly hair, wearing a t-shirt that declared "Cyber this, A-hole" and checked pajama pants, appeared on the landing, and stumbled to a stop. Wide-eyed, he took in the scene and pulled off a pair of oversize earphones. Ear-splitting music pounded from the headset.

"Mom?" He seemed genuinely surprised by the presence of Taryn and Rick, and by his brother lying facedown on the couch. "What's up?"

Honey gave him a thirty-second explanation.

"Hell." He dropped into the chair. "I should have known that 'hotsmmrnites' chick would find us eventually. She's sick."

Rick turned to Taryn. "Summer," she mouthed. He nodded.

"Hey, I lured them here—" Ronnie protested. He wasn't about to let anyone snag his so-called glory.

"Shut up!" the other four said in unison. He grumbled but zipped it. His mother patted his head.

Rick told Joey his rights and Joey confirmed what Ronnie had confessed to, and his own small part in some of the situations. Whether he downplayed his role or not remained in question, and Rick wasn't completely satisfied with his answers. The three of them were hiding something.

One thing a cop or agent or PI learns is that if you keep your mouth mostly shut during an interrogation, it makes suspects nervous and they start to ramble. Rick stared at Joey, while the guy fidgeted in the chair.

Joey finally peered at his mom. She played with a cuticle. "Did you tell them everything?"

"Shut up, Joey," Ronnie said. In his position, the threat carried no weight.

Honey gave a tiny head shake.

Yes. Rick pounced. "You're already in trouble for the shooting and the stalking, Joey. You might as well come clean before I bring the DEA down on your ass." That this wasn't a DEA case, unless they were cooking meth in their basement, but it didn't matter. Feds of any department scared people.

Joey scratched his ear.

"It's okay, sweetheart. I guess this can't get any worse," Honey said and stood. Her tanned shoulders drooped. "Follow me."

Leaving Ronnie on the couch, and motioning Joey to follow his mother lest the two brothers decide to make a run for it, Rick and Taryn followed mother and son up the narrow stairs to the second floor.

Rick had his hand on his Glock when they turned left and headed for a room at the end of the stark white hallway. He kept an eye out for anyone else in the house and saw no one.

Taryn watched their backs.

Honey stopped at the closed door, took a deep breath, and pushed the door open. "This is what you're looking for."

Inside, seated on the bed with a chain around his ankle, was a man with graying hair and matching beard shadow, wearing a pair of men's dark blue shorts and a gray t-shirt. He was reading an issue of *People* magazine and sipping something from a cup. Brutus lay curled up beside him. The guy either hadn't heard the commotion downstairs or didn't care. He casually lowered the magazine.

It was a face Rick knew well.

Stunned, it was Taryn who spoke first. "Teddy Brinkman?"

The man smiled. "The one and only."

Chapter 28

Brinkman let his eyes roam over Taryn and Rick. With years in the game, he read them quickly. They weren't there to read the gas meter. "I guess you caught me," he said matter-of-factly, as if he were welcoming them to a party instead of his arrest. "I see you've met my beloved wife, Honey."

He said beloved like belove-*ed* and stared at her with a dimwitted grin. The man had it bad for this wife. But was it an act? Did he know what real love was? "We celebrate our second month anniversary next week."

Honey sighed and stepped closer to the bed. "See what I'm dealing with," she said. Joey leaned back against the wall and scowled at the prisoner.

Taryn held Rick back when he closed a fist and stepped forward. "You son of a bitch. You scammed my mother."

Honey froze.

The con man went from smiling to puzzled by his comment. He pushed up on the bed and stared. "Which wife was she?"

"Joyce Silva."

"Oh, yes. Dear Joyce. She was a sweet little gal."

"I should kill you," Rick growled.

Brinkman flinched and pulled a pillow to his chest, as if that would keep him safe from an outraged son.

The threat itself worried Taryn more than she worried for Brinkman's safety. She turned so she and Rick were chest to chest. Taking his face in her hands, she got his attention and said quietly, "Killing him won't help find your mother's money or Jane's painting."

"But I'll be happy."

"In prison? For real this time." Her eyes begged him to get control of himself. "If you can't do this for yourself, think of your mom, your niece." She wanted to add herself to the list. After their breakup and the subsequent tension that followed, she didn't know if that would help or make things worse. He was still frustrated and she was emotionally wrecked. Tim had unwittingly erected a wall between them.

A moment passed. He pulled himself together and unclenched his fists. She squeezed his arm. "You're doing the right thing."

His expression showed a contrary opinion. Still, he dragged his attention away from the con man and focused on Honey. They still had a lot to sort out.

"You do realize that kidnapping is a serious charge," Rick said to Honey and Joey. "I believe Brinkman makes three kidnappings, between the three of you."

"Technically, he hasn't been kidnapped," Joey said. "After a couple of days of torture and threats failed to get him to tell us where he'd hidden the money, Mom just wanted to be rid of him. We've tried to dump him off four times near the Ohio border, but he always finds his way back here. And he picks the locks in the middle of the night to get back in."

"It's true," Honey said. "It's like those people who lose their dog in Idaho and somehow it returns home to Maine months later. We've been trying to get rid of him for weeks."

"Ronnie offered to shoot him. Mom said no," Joey added.

"You know I love you, lamb chop, and that will never change," Brinkman said. He rattled his chain and went back to smiling. "I'll be forever chained to you by the bonds of love."

"That doesn't explain him being locked up."

"He brought the leg shackle and chain with him the last time he returned," Honey said. "Every time Joey goes after him with the blow torch to free him, he locks himself in the bathroom and cries."

"You can't cut the bonds of true love," Teddy said and began humming the Elvis song "Love Me Tender."

"Please take him," Honey begged.

"Shut the hell up or I will kill you," Rick commanded. The humming stopped. "Why didn't you call the police and have him arrested? He's wanted in several states."

Honey stuck the tip of a pink polished fingernail between her teeth. "I didn't want the cops snooping around. Ronnie is on probation, and may be operating a chop shop out of my garage."

The scream of sirens sounded from outside. "You might want to call a lawyer," Rick said and excused himself to collect the police. With him gone, the tension left the room and Taryn relaxed a bit.

"How did you ever fall for that guy?" Taryn asked. From what she could see, there was nothing special about Teddy.

"Great sex," Honey replied. Jane had said the same thing.

"Gross," said Joey.

Staring over at Teddy, Honey shrugged. "The man knows how to play women. I thought he was my second true love. He thought I was a mark. By the time I realized his con, he had taken twelve grand from my account. He went missing for two days before showing back up and declaring his undying love."

"Yet he kept the money," Taryn said.

One carefully plucked brow went up. "Yep. I guess karma bit me in the ass with this guy. I used to rip other people off." She glanced at Joey. "I've changed my ways. Sadly, Ronnie is my bad apple from that tainted tree."

"Karma also bit Teddy in the ass," Taryn said. "He's finally fallen in love with a woman who doesn't want him."

Honey smiled. "Twelve grand is a lot to lose to learn a lesson about online dating. I think I'll swear off men and get a lot of cats."

Taryn tried to picture Honey buried in felines. The image didn't fit. She was too . . . over the top for hiding in her house and cleaning up hairballs all day.

"Oh, I almost forgot. Your ex, Carl, wants you back." Taryn threw that out before the vow to become a crazy cat lady was set in stone. A promise was a promise.

"Excellent." Honey shook her head. "My one true love dies in an accident, leaving me with two adult kids who refuse to move out and a new husband and ex-husband who I can't get rid of. I think I'll join a convent instead of cats."

Chuckling, Taryn figured Honey would quickly snap back and be off to her next romantic adventure before the ink dried on her annulment from Brinkman. She looked like a woman who wouldn't let a couple of bad marriages turn her from the male species altogether, despite what she said.

While Rick led the police around the house, Taryn updated Summer with a phone call; Summer found the entire episode both terrifying and amusing.

"This whole time Brinkman was a hostage?" Summer said. "I can't believe this. I thought he'd fled Michigan in search of his next con."

"Truthfully, I wondered if we'd ever find him," Taryn agreed. "Now the wives will get justice, and hopefully some of their money back."

"Don't hold your breath."

"What can I say," Taryn said. "I'm an eternal optimist."

"Right." Summer's laughter sounded as she ended the call.

A light drizzle fell and thunder sounded in the distance as the police hauled off the entire Comstock/Evans clan, the dog, and Brinkman, determined to work out the confusion of who'd committed what felony and charge those who needed charging. Before the last police car pulled away, a young cop rushed over to the sergeant taking Taryn and Rick's statements.

"Sarge, I found something!" His round face was flushed and giddy. "You have to see this!" He hurried off.

Curious, they followed. In the side yard, where the driveway curved around the house to a garage in back, was a pair of all but invisible shoe-covered feet sticking out of the weedy edge of the wooded copse. The body was nearly unseen in the overgrowth.

"I tripped over him," the officer said.

They all closed around. A large figure lay sprawled out on his back with a shivering dog curled up on his massive chest. Taryn recognized that dog and body.

"Oh, no." Her stomach clenched. "Is he dead?"

"You know him?" the sergeant asked.

"He's with us." Rick stepped in the weeds and leaned to press a couple of fingers to Alvin's neck. "He's alive."

Thank goodness. Their relationship may have started out badly all those years ago, but Taryn was kind of attached to the big guy now, sort of like gum stuck on a shoe.

Rick patted Alvin on both cheeks until his eyes fluttered open. The dog growled half-heartedly at Rick.

"Alvin, what happened?" Taryn leaned over and examined him. There were no bullet wounds on his front side. That was a good sign.

The bodyguard shook his head and rubbed an eye. "I followed you here. I thought you'd need protection. Someone tased me." He pushed to his elbows and Sweet'ums jumped off. Rick helped him up with some effort. The giant wall of man and hair was intimidating as he unfolded to full height. The two officers stepped back and palmed their guns. "I heard a crackle and it was lights out."

He rubbed his bearded face, caught sight of the police, and his eyes went wide and panicked. "Gotta go!" He spun and bolted off into the trees, Sweet'ums yipping at his feet.

Like that wasn't suspicious.

"Who was that guy?" Sergeant Smith said, his eyes narrowing at the sight of Alvin fleeing through the underbrush like a giant boar fleeing from hunters.

"Never seen him before," Taryn said.

"I thought you said you knew them?" the sergeant pressed. He crossed his arms and waited. She smiled sheepishly.

"Did I say that?" Taryn looked at Rick and shrugged.

"I don't recall," Rick answered.

"Hmmm." Sergeant Smith scowled and walked away.

When everyone was cleared out but for a couple of officers left behind to guard the house and garage for the crime techs, Taryn and Rick climbed into the Olds. She pulled in a deep breath and leaned back against the headrest.

"We got him. We got Brinkman." She smiled. "The sweetheart con man is finally going to prison."

"All thanks to you and Summer."

She rolled her head to look at him. He was mussed from the fight with Ronnie and had a scratch under one eye, yet both only added to his handsomeness. Her heart melted. She wanted to make everything better, only wasn't sure how, or if, she should.

"And you. It was a collective effort."

Not wanting the happy moment to get awkward, she started the car and pulled out. There were a lot of things to say, but now was all about the successful conclusion of the case, not about her and Rick. Besides, he was heading home to his life in California, a life without her. A clean break might be best.

Too bad her heart didn't agree.

When they returned to her house, Alvin was already there, seated on her still crooked porch swing with Sweet'ums and a woman Taryn didn't know. The woman had on a navy suit with her brown hair twisted up high on the back of her head. The dog lay sprawled on his back on her lap and she rubbed his belly.

"I think Sweet'ums is smiling," Taryn said as they left the car. The dog lifted his head.

"How can you tell?" Rick said. "He always looks to me like his face was hit by a bus."

Taryn choked back laughter. "Stop it!" she scolded under her breath. "They'll hear you."

"And you think, what, that the mutt will feel bad that I called him ugly? It wouldn't be the first time he's heard that."

She met his eyes. "You know that deep, deep, deep down you like him. You'll be sad to see him go." Not waiting for a response, she hurried off.

"This is Karen, Sweet'ums's mom," Alvin said as they walked up. Karen stood, scooping the dog into her arms.

"Thank you so much for retrieving my baby for me," the pretty brunette said. "I missed him so much." The rest of the next few minutes were spent in a happy-unhappy blur. Karen promised they could visit the dog anytime and they all said good-bye to the mutt with hugs and slobbery kisses. Even Rick rubbed Sweet'ums's bald head with some affection, then headed inside the house.

"I'm open for babysitting anytime," Taryn said with tears as she handed Sweet'ums back over. "He's a good dog."

Karen hugged her. "I'll take you up on that."

Dog and owner left. Alvin and Taryn waved them off, as Rick returned with his duffel, wearing a clean t-shirt. He was so serious that she ached with misery.

Alvin excused himself and went inside.

"You're leaving?" Taryn asked and leaned back against a porch pole. Her heart twisted and her eyes misted. She silently begged him to say no, wanted it, but couldn't bring herself to ask him to stay.

"I think it's for the best," Rick said with conviction. "You need to decide what you want. If it's me, I'll be back. You know how to find me. If not, it's been great knowing you, Taryn Hall."

With rough fingertips, he touched her face. She leaned against his hand. "One thing you should know before I leave is that I've fallen

210 • *Cheryl Ann Smith*

hard for you and that isn't going to change even with thousands of miles between us." He leaned to kiss the side of her head. "See ya."

With that, he walked away.

A sob caught in her throat as she watched him collect his helmet, start up the bike, and drive out of her life.

Chapter 29

Two weeks passed after the capture of Brinkman and every one of those days was cold, empty, and miserable. Rick hadn't contacted her, Sweet'ums was home with Karen, and Alvin had gone off to meet with Irving two days ago and never came back.

Feeling abandoned and heartsick, even the ultimate sacrificial offer from her friends—a bar trip to sing karaoke—hadn't cheered her up. Summer and Jess were starting to worry.

Missing Rick had become a pain she couldn't shake. She assumed he was back in L.A., living his life with bikini-clad women and spending his time breaking down doors and arresting dangerous criminals.

Many times she wanted to call or text or email, but couldn't bring herself to do it. If he was so into her like he'd said, wouldn't he have contacted her? The case was closed, even though they still didn't know what Teddy had done with his stolen property. So there really was no reason for him to see her again. She'd have to resign herself to their brief romance being over, and move on, too. Shouldn't she?

She dressed in black jeans and a black tour tee from Journey that she'd found at a thrift store. She'd chosen the tee today partly as an homage to her mood, and also because she felt like she hadn't had a chance to say good-bye to Rick. Maybe this would get him out of her mind, and heart.

Her phone pinged. A text arrived from Summer.

Meet us at Affordable U-Store.

Us? "Who's us?" she texted back and got silence. "Hello?" Still nothing. Curious, she grabbed her stuff and headed out.

A pair of police cars sat in the storage facility parking lot with several other vehicles when she rolled up. What was going on?

Taryn drove through the gates and parked in one of two open

spots. Summer's cotton candy mobile sat off to one side, as well as Jess's SUV, so apparently Jess was included in the "us."

The noise of a lot of voices led her down a familiar walk between the rows of units. The place looked less foreboding during daylight, and without bullets flying.

A crowd of people filled the space in front of Brinkman's storage locker, which upped her curiosity to critical level. The first person she recognized on approach was Irving, standing with Alvin, and both men were wearing pink Polo shirts with matching pink-and-black plaid pants. The sight of all that pink made her brain hurt.

"Irving, what is going on?"

"Alvin is my new bodyguard. All rich old guys should have a bodyguard," he said. Alvin looked down and scowled. "I don't really like pink," Irving muttered out of the corner of his mouth. "I'm just testing Alvin's loyalty."

She blinked. This was a conversation for later.

"No. I meant, what's going on here?" She made a circle with a finger, encompassing the crowd. "Did someone find a corpse under the Pinto?"

"Okay, right. No, no corpse. Summer got a mysterious text from someone while she was in my office, telling her to meet here." He cleared his throat and peered down at his feet. "She wouldn't tell me anything more, so don't ask. We come out of curiosity. Jess, too."

"Why don't you go find out," Alvin said. He and Irving shared a glance. The two of them clearly knew something and weren't telling.

Confused, Taryn pushed into the mass. Strangers came first, then familiar faces began to appear. She passed Gretchen and a woman from accounting; Andrew, Thurston, and soul patch guy, as well as several others who looked like college-age kids. At her frown, Andrew shrugged. "Alvin texted us. He's kept us filled in on your case. This is so sick."

Great. Did she have any privacy?

Oddly, she wasn't surprised to see Honey and Joey, since this was their case, too. "Someone named Summer texted us," Honey explained. "My husband couldn't make it. He's busy making new friends in jail."

Taryn liked Honey and her ability to bounce back from Brinkman. In another life, they might have been friends. "Will you wait for him to be sprung in three to five?" she asked. "You two make a cute couple."

"Not a chance." Honey laughed.

Taryn moved on. At the front of the group were Summer and Jess, huddled together in a girl clutch. "Isn't this exciting," Summer said. "It's a mysterious adventure for all of us."

"She needs to get out more," Jess said, nodding toward Summer. The latter grinned.

"What is this?" Taryn said, quickly losing patience. She'd been invited to a party and didn't know the reason or the host.

"You'll have to ask him." Summer pointed to Rick, whom Taryn hadn't seen. He stood with his back to her, talking to Jane Clark and another woman, while a pair of policemen loitered nearby. One officer held a pair of bolt cutters.

A shiver went through Taryn. Fifteen days and not a word, and now he stood twenty feet away, and her stomach went all knotty. She should be over him, but all she wanted to do was run to him and jump into his arms.

As if sensing her presence, he turned, glanced down at her Journey tee, and a grin split his face. "Nice," he mouthed and pointed to his chest down. He was also wearing a Journey tee from a different tour year.

Fate? Maybe.

Her knees knocked a little. Okay, a lot. Would he always have that effect on her?

Probably. She loved him.

He glanced at the unit. In his hand was a pair of crowbars. She took that as a clue. The unit was another. If she wanted to learn the entire mystery, she had to straighten up her spine and ask him. It took solid control of her emotions to walk to him, calmly, while all hell broke loose inside her.

"Taryn."

"Rick." She inhaled deeply. With limited space, they stood close together. She covertly inhaled his spicy cologne. "I thought you were back in L.A."

"I still have time on my leave and wanted to see more of Michigan. Nice state. Besides, I couldn't leave without finding Brinkman's stash."

"Oh." Of all the things she wanted to hear from him, that wasn't it. Was it wrong to want to be his number one reason for staying? Then again, why would she be? She hadn't left things between them on a good note. "Of course."

He turned slightly and reached for the woman standing patiently with Jane. Both women were listening intently to their conversation. He reached out to the dark haired woman. She stepped close. "Taryn, this is my mother, Joyce Silva. Mom, this is my PI, Taryn Hall."

"It's nice to meet you, Taryn." Joyce took her hand. She had the same gray eyes and dark brown hair as her son. Her expression was warm when she squeezed Taryn's hand. "Thank you so much for catching Teddy, or whatever his name is. He's hurt a lot of women. It's time he spent some time in jail."

"It's nice to meet you, Mrs. Silva, and you're welcome." She glanced at Rick, more puzzled than ever. Obviously, he was the person behind all this. She was tired of waiting for the why. "Can I speak to you privately?"

Rick nodded and pulled Taryn aside. He signaled to the cop with the bolt cutters. The officer cut the lock and stepped aside.

"Explain, please?" she said.

He grinned. "Over the last couple of weeks, while trying to get over my broken heart with booze and casual sex with multiple women, I did some thinking that didn't involve you and your naked body."

Her eyes darted to his mother. "Shhh!"

He chuckled. The man was shameless.

"Anyway, every clue, everything led me back to that piece of shit Pinto," he said and rolled up the door. "It's the only constant in Brinkman's life. I knew we had to search it again."

"But we didn't find anything the first time." The car had been rolled back inside the unit and the flat tire was now half off the rim. Otherwise, nothing had changed, right down to the chalky smell and mummified mouse in the corner.

"The police didn't, either. However, we also didn't pull the car apart. So I finagled a court order—I won't go into details so as not to bore you—but I wanted you to be here for the opening of Al Capone's vault."

Taryn got the reference. Many years earlier, Geraldo Rivera had put on a TV special devoted to opening Al Capone's secret vault; he was convinced he'd find some hidden treasure left behind by the mobster. Her parents had been glued to the TV, as were millions of other viewers. Instead, it was a bust. Ratings gold was the only gold Geraldo found when opening Al's dusty old vault.

"You can't seriously think Brinkman stuffed the gas tank with cash?"

"Probably not. Removing the tank would take more than one person to accomplish. But there is a lot of car left."

His excitement was infectious. Being with him made her feel happy again and she smiled. At this moment, he could ask her to help him to do anything, and she'd say yes.

Taryn reached out a hand. "Let's do this!"

"That's my girl." He handed her a bar. Their fingers touched. Darn, she'd missed those hands.

For the next hour or so, they pulled apart the car from the outside in, laughing the entire time, to the encouragement of the gathered onlookers. The strangers eventually dispersed until only friends, family, and ex-wives remained to see if Rick's theory was right about a secret treasure.

The police stood by in case they found evidence of a crime. Otherwise, the pair was left alone to their destruction.

Once inside the car, they threw out boxes and junk, tore up seats and removed and looked under floor mats until there was nothing left to search.

Taryn didn't hide her disappointment when she faced him over the top of the car. "It's Al Capone's vault all over again."

"Not yet." He motioned for her to get back into the car. She sat on the ripped seat and watched. Rick pried open the pillar on the left driver's side window. A roll of papers fell out. He unrolled them. "Oh, look. Bank statements."

Rick had found them a little too easily. She frowned. "I think you knew you'd find something in there."

"Wait." He lifted a hand to the roof lining. With a hard pull, the fabric came loose and fell down onto the head rests in a whirl of dust, along with something wrapped in cloth. Taryn waved her hand and coughed. "What is that?"

He pulled back. "Not yet."

With a wink, they exited the car. He faced Jane. "Looking for this?"

Slowly, and with great fanfare, he unwrapped the package and dropped the cloth on the cement floor. He turned it over for Jane to see. Both Taryn and Jane gasped.

Joyce took her new friend by the elbow when she wobbled. The hidden treasure was the beautiful Edward Cucuel painting of Jane as a girl. Although the frame was gone, the painting was still in perfect condition.

"That bastard kept it. Thank God." Jane found her footing and walked over, pressed a kiss on Rick's cheek, and took the painting from him. She looked heavenward and tears filled her eyes. "We got it back, my darling William."

The passenger side pillar held more documents that would be sorted later. Once Brinkman's property was seized, the court would dole out what he had left among his wives. Ronnie would go to jail for kidnapping Taryn and Rick, and Joey and Honey would probably get wrist slaps for whatever part they played in the Brinkman mess.

When Rick finally declared the car cleared and the case officially closed for good, Summer took Rick's pointed stare as an unspoken hint to leave, so she ushered everyone out.

"Party at Brash & Brazen, Inc.!" With a smile, she and the group left to excited chatter. There would probably be many social media posts about this day, mostly from Andrew and his bros, no doubt.

Taryn waited a minute to savor the moment before leaning her butt back against the car. "You never did answer my question. Did you know where Brinkman hid the documents and painting before we tore apart the car?"

"No. Not for sure. After I nailed down the car as the only hiding place that made sense, I used experience with drug smugglers to guess the rest."

She pushed a door handle aside with her foot. "Then why make us go through all this? We destroyed the car."

"Because watching you wield a crowbar was hot." He was completely unapologetic. "Besides, I had to take some revenge for my mom. Since I couldn't take my anger out on Brinkman, ripping apart his prized Pinto was second best."

There was no fault in that reasoning. Demoing the junker had been fun. Watching his muscles bunch when he pulled off the bumper or pried free a panel was sexy. Everything about him was sexy. Even Tim, whom she'd once thought of as an attractive man, didn't hold up next to Rick. What she felt for him was deeper than the blind crush-love she'd felt for the charming and shallow Tim. She hoped that one day he would think the same about her.

"I was surprised to see your mom and Jane here." Nervous to be alone with him, she kept to neutral subjects. "Did Summer text them, too?"

"No. I did." Rick moved close and dropped his crowbar on the car roof. "They met online through Brinkman's ex with the website in Arizona. They've been chatting for several weeks now. Jane invited her to visit and they were together when I called."

"Then something else good came of all of this. They both made a new friend."

Rick nodded. He slid his hand to touch the back of her neck. A shiver slid down her spine. "Do you really want to spend this time alone talking about my mother and Jane?"

She bit back a smile. "No, I don't."

"Me neither." He dropped his arm, sidestepped in front of her, and took her hands. He shifted his legs outside of hers. "I want to talk about how much I've missed you, and how sorry I am for walking away and not calling. I wanted you to decide what you wanted, and I also had to do some thinking about us."

Mischief welled. "Is this one of those 'feelings' talks you claim to hate, caveman?"

"Maybe." He pressed a kiss on the side of her neck.

She wriggled. "Then say what you have to say, because football starts in a few minutes and the guys and I don't want to miss the kick-off."

He dropped his hands and took her into his arms. "You think you're funny, do you?"

"I know I'm funny." She slid her arms around his waist and fell into his warmth. "We still have the matter of you living in CA and me living in MI. When will we ever see each other?"

"Changes are in the works, Danica," he teased. "L.A. isn't my permanent home. Remember, I'm from Indiana. Besides, I'm tired of all that sunshine and ocean. What's wrong with a little Michigan snow, a fireplace, and you naked on a bearskin rug?" He nuzzled her neck. "A fake bearskin rug, of course."

"Of course," she said, happier than she'd been in weeks. "Well, that covers the geography concern," she added. But there was another important issue left to cover. "I also want you to know that I love you and I want to be with you. That's forever. So if you don't think you can ever love me, then get on your bike and ride back to L.A., Special Agent Rick."

Chuckling, he leaned down to kiss her and she felt it to her toes. When he lifted his head, his warm gray eyes held hers. "I've known from day one that you were a 'forever' girl and I'd have to be all in if I wanted to be with you. Well, I'm telling you now that I am all in." He kissed her again. "I love you, too, Taryn. All of you. Forever." He lifted his head and stared into her eyes. "Bad driving and all."

A fan of romance fiction since the dark ages, **Cheryl Ann Smith** loves to throw her heroines into danger, just to see what they'll do. She's currently working on an exciting new contemporary romance series that mixes her crazy sense of humor with the adventures of a trio of female PIs who are the kick-ass heroines Cheryl has always wanted to be.

Cheryl lives in Michigan with her family, and when she isn't writing, she dreams of living in a grass hut on her own tropical island. Since that's unlikely to happen, she looks forward to any vacation that gets her near an ocean. If you'd like to learn more about Cheryl or her books, you can visit her website at www.cherylannsmith.com, or on Facebook at https://www.facebook.com/cherylannsmithauthor

Please turn the page for an exciting sneak peek at
Cheryl Ann Smith's next book in the Brash & Brazen series,
THE SWEETHEART GAME
Coming to you from Lyrical Press
in January 2017!

Chapter 1

Summer O'Keefe, former kiddie pageant star and Miss Precious Universe, fired pro football cheerleader and private investigator, saw movement from her third-floor window, in the backyard garden of the Nealy house next door, and immediately jumped to an ominous conclusion.

A shadowy shape stood near the seven-foot-tall bean cage shaped like a Christmas tree and her imagination overrode common sense, convincing her that a slobbering pervert was waiting for her lights to go out so he could press his icky face against her bedroom window and watch her sleep.

All this without a speck of evidence to back it up.

Unfortunately, the wood and metal frame kept her from getting a clear view to solidify her suspicion, and the shadow was too far away to confirm that he was indeed a creepy peeper and not a trick of moonlight and oak tree branches. But she was sure someone was there. She felt it in her bones.

Snick. Thump.

Snick. Thump.

Pause.

"What the heck?" The shadow was making too much noise for someone trying to lurk around a winter-ravaged pumpkin patch for a chance to peep at her in skivvies. Still, she wasn't about to let go of the creeper theory altogether.

Snick. Thump.

"Who else would be out at this hour other than a troublemaker?" It was almost midnight on a Monday night. Only raccoons and college students wandered around this late. Most of her neighbors would be asleep in preparation for work tomorrow. Or having sex.

Sigh. She missed sex. She was probably the only person on the block with cobwebs down there. Maybe that was why her mind shot right in the direction of the gutter?

Snick. Thump.

"Okay, this is getting weird."

Could it be a thief, someone out to steal garden tools, or Mrs. Johnson's garden gnomes from her yard directly behind Summer's? She did have quite a collection of the creepy little figurines. She wouldn't put it past drunken college students to make off with an armful of the plaster and plastic eyesores, as a prank gleefully hatched in their alcohol-soaked brains.

It wouldn't be the first time. Mrs. Johnson had wept and wailed to Summer over their shared fence about the time she'd come home from the International Gnome and Pink Flamingo Yard Art Convention to find herself five gnomes short.

The police had been called and everything.

Snick. Thump.

Squinting, she leaned forward and peered out. From what she could see, Mrs. Johnson's yard appeared quiet. A second flash of movement caught the corner of her eye near the Nealy toolshed and then nothing. In an instant, the shadow had vanished.

"Drat."

Feeling like a woman who spent too much time looking for criminals under every rock and behind every bush, she clearly needed a new hobby. Something light like collecting ceramic bunnies or garden gnomes.

"You're seeing things," the rational, if often misused, part of her brain, told her. Taking one last look, she reclaimed her seat at her computer. If someone was out for gnomes, Summer wouldn't be sad to see them go. If he was looking for a place to relieve himself from too much drinking, she was happy that it wasn't her bushes he'd chosen to target.

Ugh.

"Summer, let it go." Her computer chimed with a new message. The gnome thieves were forgotten as she jumped back into the game. The Hunters were waiting.

JBeam: HSN, are you still there?

Hotsummernites: I'm still here. Okay, I'm two terrorists and one assassin down this month. Anyone else?

in her shorty pink PJs

e anyway? She'd seen
ing beer cans and col-
as top notch, and she
ccessfully accomplish

loudly that he had to
as she crept across the
outspread for balance.

e hole, tuck the shovel
aused and looked up at
e roof, half onto a patch
the other half on slip-

at and the dying street-
ot. But she waited for a
o peer over the edge of

ree-story house with an
d see for several blocks
problem. Being a floor
to the garden.
, or to climb out a win-
l people.
cept for the whole hunt-
sonal space. Most of the
east some minor investi-

out now. Perched on the
here was nothing to see.
alfway blocked the view

ot slipped on the leaves.
slime on her top. Yuck.

JBeam: I have one kidnapper and a terrorist.

Sexyvixn: You both have me beat. I got nada.

Poefan7: I've got one Ponzi scammer and a foreign dictator.

Summer, aka Hotsummernites, aka HSN, clapped her hands and did a funky geek dance in her chair with a lot of arm waving and feet stomping. She'd won again for the fourth month in a row! Of course, it would be rude to be publicly smug. These were her friends. But a little chair spin was not out of order, she thought, as she whirled into a three-sixty. After all, no one could see her do it.

Hotsummernites: Well done, everyone!

JBeam: You are smokin', HSN!

Hotsummernites: Thanks, JBeam. I'll add our captures to the board and send the info on to the appropriate agencies. See you all on Sunday!

Poefan7: Night, HSN.

Her stomach did a little hitch. Although she'd never met Poefan7, or seen a picture of him, there was something about the way he messaged that was oddly sexy. She grinned. Yes, she was indeed a dork.

Hotsummernites: Night, Poe.

A chilly breeze slid through the crack under the open window and she rubbed her goose-bump-covered arms. Logging over to the leader board, she wrote out all the captures and sent off emails to her contacts at the FBI, CIA, and Interpol, as well as a couple of others. She belonged to an anonymous group that hunted international and domestic criminals on the run, for fun. They called themselves the unoriginal "The Hunters." The club was made up by a dozen fellow geeks who dug through crimes and rooted out criminals through extreme deep web investigations. They only knew each other by their code names for safety.

Her day job was as the cyber PI for Brash & Brazen, Inc., a female PI investigative firm. Summer loved working with her friends, and adored her boss, Irving. Life was good, albeit a bit lonely. The only man in her life was a cyber crush online. Poe.

Sad.

Really sad.

Twenty minutes later, she finished up, glanced at the clock, and logged out. It was after one. She'd be drained tomorrow if she didn't get to bed.

Walking to the window, she looked out toward the Johnson

house. All was quiet in Gnomeville. She shrugged, sligh
pointed that all the gnomes were safely tucked in.

The figure was probably just a shadow and the *snick, t*
sound of the garden shed door blowing open and closing
hinges. Over the last year, poor health had kept Mr. Nealy
thing but basic gardening, so the property and shed had f
disrepair.

She'd tried to help revive the weed patch, but he brushe
thanked her sweetly, and decided to let the garden grow
more garden goodies in the fall for his neighbors.

The bright moon caught her attention and drew her e
was beautiful in the night sky. She stood and enjoyed the
several minutes before a yawn reminded her to get to bed. M
below stopped her.

A hooded human shape carrying what looked like a stuf
garbage bag crossed the Nealys' yard and circled around b
bean cage. This time she wasn't overtired.

Her senses zipped into overdrive. She hadn't been seei
of moonlight earlier. Someone had been out there. Was (
Her heart skipped.

The person dropped the bag and reached for a shovel.

Snick. Thump.

Snick. Thump.

The strange sound had been him, or her, digging a hole i
mant garden. And she had a feeling he wasn't getting an e
tilling the soil for rutabagas.

With dark clouds passing over like harbingers of doom
the moon and add to the creepy factor of the situation, sh
shoved up the pane and leaned out for a better look. Darn
cage.

She tried to make out the grim reaper's face beneath t
hoodie to confirm whether it was either Satan's minion or tl
arrived grandson from Mr. Nealy's old framed photo, but it
dark and too far away to make a match. She'd rather the vi:
the latter, but if he was in fact the former, that would be coo

Lord, she was losing her mind.

Snick. Thump.

Fearing he'd look up and catch her spying, she reached an
off the light on her desk. It wouldn't be respectable to be cau

for courage, she slowly went out the w
and fuzzy bunny slippers.

How hard could walking around on a
college boys do it all the time, and while
lapsible camp chairs. Her fitness train
loved James Bond movies. If anyone cc
some rooftop recon, it was Summer.

The sound of her heartbeat whoosh
hear. But he kicked more dirt into the
narrow and slanted second-floor roof, :
He seemed unware of her presence.

See. Easy. Now to find a place to sit.

Turning back, she saw the man fill
into the garden shed, and close the door.
her window. She flopped belly down on
of damp leaves from a huge oak nearb}
pery, mildewed shingles.

Had he seen her? The office light w
lamp was a few houses down, so probab
full minute before pushing up to her kn
the roof. There was no sign of him.

The advantage of living in a very ta]
attic turret for office space was that she
either way. Spying on her neighbors wa
down gave her an advantage of being clo

Until now she hadn't had a reason to
dow. Most of her neighbors were just no

Still, she wasn't a snoop at heart, well
ing criminals thing. And she believed in
time. This strange occurrence warranted
gating.

Right?

"Wrong." Still, it was too late to bac
roof, she was kind of committed. Sadly
The man was gone and the bean cage stil
of the hole.

"Drat." She moved slightly and her
She looked down her body to see gree
She'd have to pitch the PJs.

"Maybe this wasn't a good idea." She moved her foot to a dry shingle to brace herself. The effort proved futile and caused her body to shift slightly downward, the slimy leaves turning into a slippery ski ramp.

"Oh, no." She dug her fingernails into the roof but the shingles didn't give an inch. The effort produced the same success as a de-clawed cat on a scratching post.

The feel of shifting plant refuse beneath her sprawled body caused a squeak of panic. She was two stories up!

That was her last clear thought as gravity propelled her down, down, down and over the edge of the roof into a cataclysmic vortex of darkness!